NEW HAVEN
NEW HAVEN PUBLIC
3 5000 09373 7640
P9-CFH-259
EN, CONN.

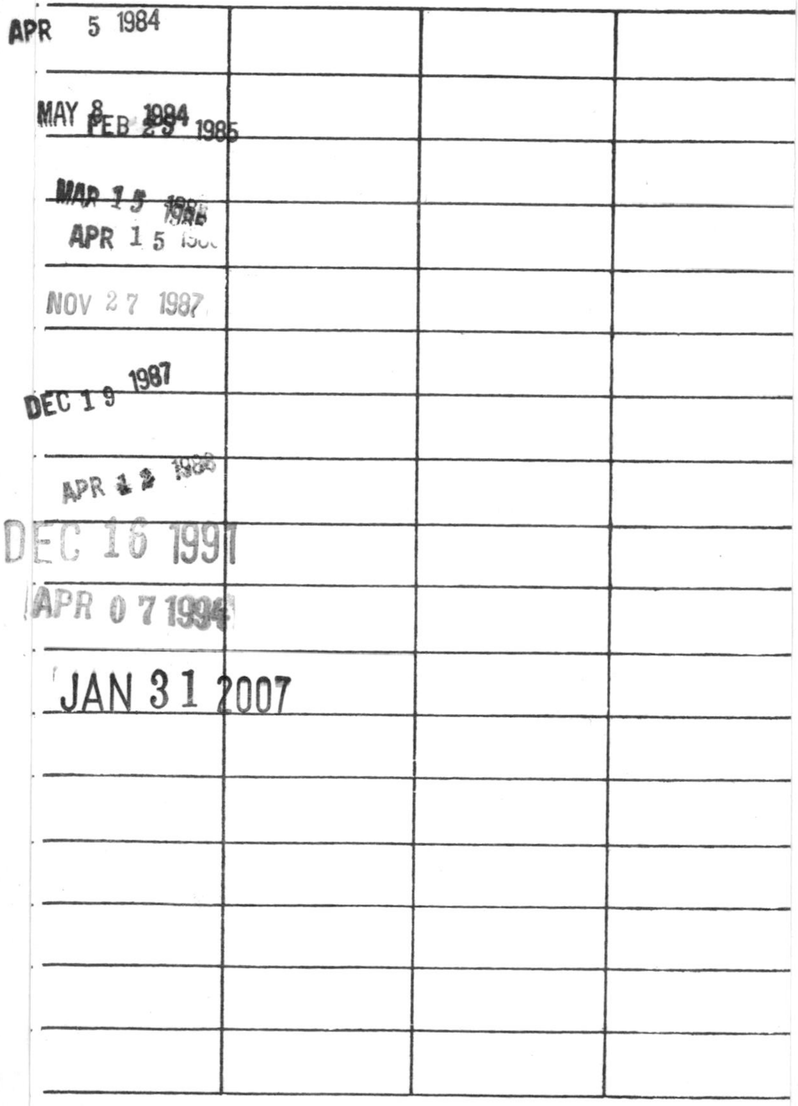
APR 5 1984
MAY 8 1984
FEB 29 1985
MAR 15 1986
APR 15
NOV 27 1987
DEC 19 1987
APR 12
DEC 16 1991
APR 07
JAN 31 2007

GIDEON'S BADGE

Books by J. J. Marric

GIDEON'S BADGE
GIDEON'S LOT
GIDEON'S VOTE
GIDEON'S RIDE
GIDEON'S MARCH
GIDEON'S FIRE
GIDEON'S RISK
GIDEON'S STAFF
GIDEON'S MONTH
GIDEON'S NIGHT
GIDEON'S WEEK
GIDEON'S DAY

GIDEON'S BADGE: By J. J. Marric

HARPER & ROW, PUBLISHERS NEW YORK

FIRST EDITION

LIBRARY OF CONGRESS CATALOG CARD NUMBER: 65-21382

I-P

GIDEON'S BADGE

1:

Preparations for a Voyage

KATE GIDEON saw her husband's car draw up outside their house, saw his driver jump out and open the rear door, and saw George bending very low to get out; obviously he was in a hurry. She stood at their bedroom window, conscious of the surface reflections passing through her mind, less aware of those she registered subconsciously. Consciously, she noted the certainty of his haste; subconsciously, the fact that George had not been sitting next to his driver, which meant that he had a lot on his mind. Consciously, that as he had pulled up outside the house, and had been driven, he was going out again; subconsciously, that he had been working harder in the past few weeks than she could recall for a long time.

And yet London's crime had been quiet this hot summer, with few sensations and little to keep the Commander of London's Criminal Investigation Department at his desk night after night.

Now it was nearly eight o'clock, past the time he should be home. She felt an echo of resentment because of the demands of his job, but it was neither bitter nor strong, for they were both over the age when long hours of separation caused any emotional upset; rather, Kate was anxious in case he was working too hard, and it would affect his health.

She smiled at the thought and at herself, as George came striding up the path, shoulders and head thrust forward in a characteristic "nothing must get in my way" attitude. He looked so fit and full of energy that it was laughable to think he was overworking.

As if sensing she was looking down on him, he stopped short of the porch and glanced up and saw her. He backed a pace and waved. He looked to Kate as if he was excited, and the years of responsibility as well as of stern self-control made that a rare, almost an alarming fact.

Kate waved back; then Gideon stepped onto the porch, and Kate hurried across the bedroom, rounding the foot of the big double bed, and headed down the stairs. The front door was open and Gideon was in the hall by the time she was halfway down; there was still no doubt of his excitement, but suddenly her sense of alarm vanished; obviously his news was good.

"Hallo, Kate."

"George, what is it?"

"What's what?"

"Don't stand there and pretend there's nothing. What is it?"

Gideon did not answer at once, but quite unexpectedly he held out his arms toward her, almost remarkable in so undemonstrative a man. At the same time he smiled, and his dark-blue eyes glowed. He was not handsome, but strong-looking, with his broad forehead, the iron-gray hair sweeping right back from it, his big chin, his full mouth and rather broad nose. Weekend work in the garden had given him a healthy-looking tan and made him look much younger than his fifty-two years.

He gripped her hands.

"Ready for a surprise?"

"Not if it's bad."

"Oh, it's not bad." Gideon chuckled. "Not bad at all." When Kate did not speak, but simply stared into his face, her eyes demanding an end to this suspense, he went on: "We're going on a journey."

"Where to?"

"Care to guess?"

"I'd like it better if you'd stop behaving like a little boy."

"That's just about what I feel like," Gideon said, and the laughter echoing in his voice told her he felt very happy, and was sure she would be, too. "A boy going on holiday to New York."

At first Kate didn't really understand, perhaps because "to New York" seemed like saying: "To the moon."

"What did you say?"

"I said I am going to take you to New York."

Her heart leaped. "George!"

"Next week."

"*When?*"

"Next Tuesday. We're to sail on the S.S. *Fifty States* from Southampton, at twelve noon. I'm told the big ships always sail on the dot, so you'd better get moving." Before Kate could comment, while she was still trying to absorb the news and beginning to realize that she had only six days—six *days,* less a Sunday, for shopping—he drew forward, gave her a great, bearlike hug, then let her go and backed away. "Like the idea?"

"It—it's wonderful. But . . ."

"You wish you'd had more notice. I know. But I dared not say a word before in case it fell through. There's the International Office Conference in Washington in a couple of weeks, and I thought I might have to fly over just for that. Now I'm going to consult with Nielsen in New York about a job that's been worrying us on both sides, then go on to Washington."

"How long *have* we got?" Kate asked in sudden wonder.

"A month at least. Official business will take two weeks, and I'll have a fortnight's leave," Gideon told her. "I'll tell you all about it later. I've got to get back to the office for half an hour, there's a bad man I want to put the fear of death into." He moved back and Kate stepped into the passage. "Care to come back with me? We can go somewhere for dinner."

The suggestion was tempting, and twenty minutes earlier Kate would have jumped at it, just as she would have asked: "Which bad man?" Now, she was preoccupied. There would be a hundred things to do in preparation for the trip. Quite suddenly she was in a hurry, at a time when haste seemed to have become part of the past.

"You are sure we're going, aren't you?" she asked with belated caution.

"Positive. Scott-Marle's secretary made the reservations while I was in his office. I can even give you our cabin number—A16. The trip's been in the air for weeks, because of the Conference, with the FBI acting as hosts. Drugs and currency problems, mostly. The Assistant Commissioner would go normally, and as that job's still vacant, I'm to go. Nielsen of New York telephoned an official request for me to send someone for consultations over one or two specific cases. It was only a matter of getting the accommodation. We're provisionally booked on the *Queen Elizabeth* for the return journey, too." Gideon, blocking the hallway, still had the boyish, eager look in his eyes. "I wanted to tell you face to face, and I was just coming home when I heard that a man we want badly has been picked up. I came home anyway," he added. "How about dinner?"

"No," said Kate, quite positively. "I'll have to write and tell the children, and there'll hardly be a minute to spare. We'll have supper here when you get back, and you can tell me more about it then."

"Right," Gideon said. "Now I'm off."

He touched her hands for a moment, and turned away. The front door was still partly open and Kate could see a wheel and part of the black Humber car. As George opened the door wider, it passed through her mind that she had hardly said a word, she must have put a damper on his buoyant mood. He stepped onto the porch as she cried:

"George!"

He half-turned.

"Hallo?"

"George," she repeated, hurrying toward him, "it's absolutely wonderful. I'm so surprised I hardly realize it's true, but—*New York*. It's—" she searched for a word which would give him some idea of her sudden surge of heady excitement, but he was waiting and the car was waiting, and all she could do was repeat "Wonderful!"

She saw his face light up, and knew that her eyes must have told him all she wanted to say.

Late though it was, there was a bustle of activity at the Yard, a sense of urgency, even of excitement, which was not often apparent. It touched the eyes and faces of the men at the gates, the hall duty sergeants, several detectives whom Gideon passed on the way to his office. A woman police constable was coming out of the sergeants' room, an attractive young woman who looked fresh and unsullied by the squalor and the filth, the wickedness and the perversion which her job made familiar. Smiling when she saw Gideon, she sprang sharply to attention.

"Good evening, sir."

"Evening," Gideon grunted. He wondered what she was doing here, was tempted to ask, resisted the temptation, and went along to his office. It was getting dark inside the building, and a light showed beneath his door. Who was there? He opened the door and saw Lemaitre, his deputy, sitting at one of the two desks, writing very fast. Lemaitre looked up, startled.

"Strike a light! They said you'd gone home."

"Didn't they tell you I was coming back again?"

"I thought this was one night you wouldn't be able to prize yourself away from Kate." Lemaitre looked spruce and fresh and bright, with thin dark hair brushed neatly over the front of his head, lean, bronzed features, bony nose and aggressive chin, red and white spotted tie splashing color across a detergent-white shirt. "I'll bet that news shook her, George."

"She won't shake for long," Gideon said. He took off his coat, for it was very warm in this office overlooking the Thames, on which gaily colored boats carried tourists and London's day trippers west to Teddington Weir and east to Greenwich Ferry. A loudspeaker on one of these boats was blaring: *"On your right, the London County Hall, seat of the Council, comprising representatives from 48 London boroughs. On your left, the red brick building, the famous Scotland Yard, home of London police for many years, soon to be moved to a fine new building. We are about to pass the Festival Hall, all that remains of . . .*"

The metallic voice faded.

"Fadiman's still here, isn't he?" Gideon asked sharply. If the Yard hadn't expected him back, the prisoner he wanted to see might have been sent to a remand prison.

"Cannon Row," Lemaitre said.

"That's all right." Cannon Row Police Station was only a hundred yards away, virtually part of the Yard. "Who searched him?"

"Doc Hughes, with Cooky and me there to make sure he wasn't hiding anything in any orifice. Doc even took away his dentures and had 'em checked to make sure he hadn't got a hollow false tooth." Lemaitre leaned back, very pleased with himself. "He's for the Old Bailey on a couple of charges, and then for topping. If there's a squawk about the death penalty for him if he's found guilty, I'll blow my top."

"Capital punishment may be a thing of the past by the time he's sentenced," Gideon said. "What did he say?"

"Nothing."

"Is he represented?"

"A solicitor was here for ten minutes. He saw a TV flash saying we'd caught him. Fadiman didn't ask for him, didn't say a word."

"What's the solicitor like?"

"Everybody's uncle."

"Lem," said Gideon, "I want that case sewn up so tight that there isn't a hope that Fadiman will be freed on a technicality. If he is guilty—" he broke off, and grunted. "Forget it. I'll go and see him."

"Shall I warn Cooky you're on the way?"

"Don't you always?" demanded Gideon.

Whenever he was going to any part of the Yard or to Divisional Headquarters anywhere in London, word sped on wings to warn those whom he was about to visit. He knew exactly what happened: a brief, brusque "Gee-Gee's coming," and dramatic transformations of behavior, appearance and attitudes took place. There had been a time when Gideon had been annoyed by this, but nowadays he looked on it in a more benign light; anything that kept people on their toes was a good thing, whether he was regarded as a kind of bogeyman or not. Now he sensed Lemaitre wondering how serious he was, whether he—Lemaitre—had spoken out of turn. There wasn't a more loyal man in London. Gideon winked at him, and Lemaitre responded with a relieved smile.

"Don't you worry," he said. "The case will be all sewn up ready for you when you get back from the States."

Gideon went out of the office, a little disgruntled with himself. When he had talked about having the Fadiman case sewn up, and added: "I wish . . ." he had betrayed an anxiety which in the first place he shouldn't have shown, and in the second, most certainly shouldn't have voiced. Lemaitre had, of course, noted the implication at once. "I wish I could have seen the case through before leaving for New York," he had started to say. Taken a stage further, that could be understood to mean: "I don't trust anyone here to handle the job properly," which was nonsense. The dispensability of the individual was the first thing to accept, especially when that individual was oneself. Difficult to acknowledge, all the same. How would they get on here?

By the time he was at the foot of the steps leading from the main entrance he felt a little happier. They would get on exactly the same as when he was on holiday, or on the Continent for a few days at an *Interpol* meeting, or at some conference. He strode across the courtyard. As he did so, two detective sergeants, three constables, and a chief inspector watched him, while two officers in a Flying Squad car grinned before scorching out onto the embankment.

"Gee-Gee's in a good mood tonight."

"So he should be. It's taken a year to catch that bloody poisoner."

The first man said: "God! What a devil."

Gideon reached the street gates and turned left along Cannon Row, almost oblivious of the beautiful evening, the soft air and the pale-blue sky, and thinking on exactly the same lines as the driver of the squad car: "What a devil."

Gideon had been in the Metropolitan Police Force for over thirty years. He had been in the Criminal Investigation Department for twenty-five of these, and had rubbed shoulders with every imaginable form of vice and crime. Like all successful policemen he had come to accept much of it as inevitable, unnatural practices as natural, evil as normal. But Fadiman—

There had been one case similar to it in history—of a man who first gave prostitutes strychnine, and then lay with them, to find some hideous, awful ecstasy in their dying convulsions. The difference was that Fadiman had sought and found his victims, not from the ranks of prostitutes but from the suburban homes of contentedly married women; nine of them in all.

At intervals over a year, the crimes had shocked not only London but the nation; nevertheless, the Yard had failed to find the killer. A painstaking door-to-door canvass of London's residential suburbs, instigated by Gideon, had eventually yielded a description from which an *Identikit* picture had been fashioned of a man seen in the immediate neighborhood of each murder some time before the crime had been committed. Only after the eighth murder had there been reason to believe the murderer was a door-to-door salesman. The picture had been circulated through the letter boxes of a quarter of a million houses, but not yet by newspapers or television.

Today, the murderer had found, and claimed, yet another victim—a little woman with fading eyesight who had not read or heard much about the killer. She had allowed a cake-mix demonstrator to come in and had eaten his "sample" . . .

Neighbors had noticed Fadiman, and in that strangely simple way, which sometimes ends a long and difficult man hunt, he had been arrested in a tobacconist's during the rush hour: no fuss, no struggle, not even an attempt to run away.

A policeman on duty outside Cannon Row Police Station saluted. As Gideon reached the front hall, Superintendent A. C. Cooke, the officer in charge, came in. He was a man whose weary gray head and flabby body masked a keen mind. They shook hands.

"Thought you wouldn't miss this, George."

"Been waiting for it too long," said Gideon. "Anything new?"

"His solicitor's still with him—a Joseph Todhunter."

"Any special angle?" asked Gideon.

"I think I know what's coming."

"Mistaken identity?"

"Yes."

Gideon thought: If he's guilty, mistaken identity is Fadiman's one chance, of course. We mustn't run the slightest risk of having the wrong man. Again the wish that he could see this case through himself entered his mind, but he crushed it. Policemen, sergeants, the policewoman who had been at the Yard, a cleaner and a drunk in one of the cells, all took the chance to look at Gideon as he passed through the station.

Two men were in Fadiman's cell, the door of which was being unlocked by the sergeant in charge.

One man had his back to Gideon, a rounded back in a dark coat, with a few loose hairs and some specks of dandruff on the shoulders. He had lank white hair and small pink ears. The other man stood by the side of a bed, staring at the bars, the sergeant, and then at Gideon.

The first thing Gideon noticed, with a sense of shock, was the likeness of the face to that of the *Identikit* picture; the similarity was almost uncanny. The second was the look of fear, of dread, of horror, on the faded face. There were actually tears in Fadiman's eyes.

"Who's this?" he gasped, and as the white-haired man turned, Fadiman went on in a choking voice: "I didn't do it, I don't know anything about it. It's a mistake, it's all a mistake."

He spoke with such conviction and such emotion that Gideon felt a sudden, swift twinge of doubt: *could* this man be such a hideous murderer? As the question passed through his mind, Gideon looked into the calm and untroubled eyes of white-haired Joseph Todhunter. "Everybody's uncle," Lemaitre had said, and no description could have been more apt.

2:

Misgivings

FADIMAN'S VERY heart seemed to be in his voice, as he repeated: "It's a mistake, I swear it's a mistake." Gideon, watching both the accused and Todhunter, admitted to himself that few men could have made a better first impression than the solicitor. He waited for him to speak, while Fadiman moved to one side, clasping his hands as if in prayer. He wore no tie and no stud, his shirt cuffs hung loose, his shoes gaped at the instep because his shoelaces had been removed.

"Commander Gideon, I believe," Todhunter said.

"That's right."

"Mr. Gideon, I want to make it quite clear that Mr. Fadiman is not guilty of these dreadful charges. A grievous mistake has been made, and I am sure that you will be the first to wish to verify that."

"Yes, I want the truth," Gideon said. Now he looked into Fadiman's pale and watery eyes. Just as he liked Todhunter, so he took an immediate dislike to the prisoner. Gideon did not trust either reaction, but could not ignore them. "There will be a hearing at the Central London Police Court tomorrow morning, when I shall proffer evidence of arrest and ask for eight days' remand in custody." He felt the sting of frustration at the words, because he would not be present when Fadiman came up for the second hearing.

"Commander," Todhunter said, "you know as well as I do that once Mr. Fadiman has been charged every newspaper in the land will carry the story, and he will be judged in advance. Later, when a jury has had the opportunity of considering a just verdict and has found him not guilty, he will nevertheless have been destroyed. His wife, his children, his relatives, his friends, all these will have their lives blighted to a greater or lesser degree by the awful consequences of this impetuous arrest. I would like to ask you—"

Gideon broke in: "If you want to talk to me in my office, I'll be glad to see you there tomorrow morning. Is there anything else you need here?"

"Can you imagine the effect that a night in a police cell under the shadow of such a charge will have on an innocent man?"

Gideon looked steadily into the sky-blue eyes of "everybody's uncle," then glanced at Cooke.

"What time did Mr. Todhunter get here, Mr. Cooke?"

"Just after six-thirty, sir."

"If you want to see your client again before the hearing, that can be arranged at the court," Gideon said pointedly.

He expected Todhunter to make some kind of protest or attempt to gain time, but the solicitor obviously decided that it would serve no purpose. Instead he turned to Fadiman.

"Cedric," he said, "there is nothing I will not do to help you. And of course I will look after Joanna and the children." He gripped Fadiman's hands, and again Gideon had an impression of men praying. At last he moved away abruptly. Cooke had signaled to the sergeant in charge of cells, and his keys were already jangling as he unlocked the door. Todhunter did not look around. Gideon waited until the man had walked along the passage, then turned and looked Fadiman up and down. The man's lips were moving as if in supplication.

"You're in good hands," Gideon said gruffly. "And Mr. Todhunter couldn't be more right. All we want is to find out the truth. Good night." He turned away and joined Cooke in the passage. As he did so he heard a movement behind him, and glanced around. Fadiman, a sob in his throat, was throwing himself down on his knees by the side of the narrow bed. He buried his face in his hands, and the last glimpse Gideon caught was of his hunched shoulders and his quaking body. The steel door clicked, and the key turned with sharp finality. The sergeant, hardened though he was, coughed as if to cover some kind of emotion. Gideon passed the station superintendent, who spoke as they turned the corner and were out of Fadiman's hearing.

"What's Fadiman up to, George? A kind of act?"

"Could be."

"I've seen some Holy Joes, but this one seems to mean it."

"I'd like to see what you took from his pockets," Gideon interrupted.

"It's all in my office."

A minute later, when they turned into Cooke's small, old-fashioned office, overlooking Cannon Row, Gideon gestured toward a telephone.

"Go ahead," said Cooke.

Gideon lifted the receiver of the instrument, which had a direct line to the Yard, and said: "Give me Lemaitre." He waited while Cooke went to a long table beneath the window. On this were the contents of Fadiman's pockets, as well as his tie, cuff links and collar studs, shoelaces and braces. All were labeled so that there could not be the slightest mistake. Lemaitre answered almost at once. "Lem," said Gideon abruptly, "I'll be over in about twenty minutes. I want the files on Fadiman, from the moment he was picked up back to the moment those neighbors of the murdered woman said they identified him. Every statement, everything—if I have to sit up all night I want to read the lot."

"Now what's got into you?" demanded Lemaitre.

Gideon rang off. Cooke, standing with a photograph in one hand and a photo-copy of the *Identikit* picture in the other, was watching him curiously.

"Fadiman's not selling you his innocence, is he?"

"He's sold me the idea that we don't want to make the slightest slip," Gideon said dryly. "It would be easy to take this one for granted."

"If you ask me, he's as slimy as a snake," Cooke said. "Todhunter's one thing; Fadiman—but you don't want to know what I think. Here's the lot we found on him. He was searched for everything—even hidden poison capsules, couldn't be sure he wouldn't swallow a dose of strychnine himself once he realized the game was up. We didn't find anything hidden away even in the cake-mix samples in his case." The small sample case stood open next to the articles taken from Fadiman's pockets, and was filled with Bake-Quik Cake Mix in packets about the size of a pocketbook. No one who watched television regularly or read the newspapers could be in doubt about the qualities claimed for Bake-Quik. Quite apart from Fadiman, Gideon was aware that the mix was sold not only through supermarkets and grocery stores, but also by door-to-door salesmen; Fadiman was one of hundreds of these. There was literature in the case, too, gaudy leaflets offering "great free samples" and special offers, trading stamps, and money-back guarantees.

"If he did what we think he did, he persuaded the woman to let him in, got her to try the mix and bake a cake, and slipped strychnine into some of the mix," Gideon said. "He's tried it with several different mixes, with sweets, chocolates, soft drinks– Can you tell me why any woman would let a man into her house when she's alone, and swallow whatever he gave her?"

"Not a man like Fadiman," Cooke said.

Gideon stared at him, lips pursed, and Cooke's gray eyes changed their expression as he went on:

"That what you're driving at?"

"That's exactly it," said Gideon. "You'd expect him to put any woman off. Instead, she asked him in."

He looked through the contents of Fadiman's pockets. There was nothing remarkable or unusual–a wallet, seven pounds ten shillings in notes, a few shillings in silver, some coppers, a penknife, some pieces of string, ballpoint pens, two handkerchiefs, a wristwatch, some keys, some visiting cards printed with the address of his home in Hackney. These were carefully listed, and there were several written copies of the list alongside the items.

"Has Lem got one of these?" Gideon asked.

"Yes."

"Spare me another," Gideon said. "When are they going to be collected?"

"A man's due over here to pick 'em up any time."

Gideon nodded, relaxed for a few minutes as if he were able to put the case out of his mind. He sensed that Cooke had something he wanted to say.

"All right, what is it?" Gideon asked.

"Is it true you're going to America?"

"Yes. Next week."

"Lucky devil," Cooke said, and after a pause he asked: "Who'll see this one through for you?"

"I'll be back long before it reaches the Old Bailey," Gideon said.

That wasn't the real answer, he knew, and Cooke was equally aware of this. So was Lemaitre, when Gideon got back to his office. Lemaitre had prepared the files, the statements from housewives who thought that they had seen a man answering Fadiman's description, and all the evidence. This was spread out on Gideon's desk in the way that Lemaitre knew he liked, but Gideon wasn't looking very pleased with life.

"What's got into you?" Lemaitre wanted to know.

"Caution, Lem."

"Goddammit, you can't doubt *that* lot."

"I hope not," said Gideon. "I wouldn't like to charge a man with those particular crimes, have him committed, and then find out that there was reasonable doubt." When Lemaitre didn't comment but simply looked skeptical, Gideon went on: "What's Miller doing at the moment?" He took off his coat and hung it on a clothes stand, dropped into his chair, and contemplated the documents spread out on the desk, including the photograph and the *Identikit* picture.

"Miller's on the Gordon bank job," Lemaitre answered.

"Not in the building, by any chance, is he?"

Lemaitre grinned.

"No one's in the building who hasn't got to be, and if I know Miller he's swimming or playing tennis out at Imber Court. Just the man for this job, if you think there's more in it than meets the eye. Mind you, I think you're crazy; it's an open-and-shut case. But if you want to make trouble—"

"Call Imber Court," interrupted Gideon. "If Miller's there, leave a message asking him to look in here as soon as he can."

He began to go through the papers. One of the first was a physical description of Fadiman and it tallied perfectly with the physical descriptions given by neighbors of various strychnine victims. The similarity was quite remarkable, like that of the photograph and the *Identikit* picture. On the next sheet of paper was a hastily assembled dossier on Fadiman, not yet put on any official form.

Married: Wife's name Joanna.
Children: Three; married son named David of 23 years, unmarried daughter of 18, named Elsa, schoolboy son aged 13, named Leslie.

What would they be feeling now?

It was none of his business to wonder what they were feeling, but there was nothing Gideon could do to prevent himself from wondering. These children were roughly the age of his own, he could think with them and think for them.

Occupation: No regular employment. Has inherited capital earning an income said to be about £1,000 a year. Represents several firms as door-to-door salesman, including *Bake-Quik, New Age World Encyclopaedia,* and *Home Confectionery* . . .

There was a ting as Lem replaced his receiver.

"Miller will be here in about an hour. He was at the bar."

"Good," said Gideon. "Why don't you get off, Lem?"

By the time Miller arrived, Lemaitre had gone and this part of the Yard was quiet, as it usually was at night, all the activity of the police taking place in the divisions and downstairs where the Flying Squad was on call. On the ground floor, Information Room was full of activity, with messages coming in from all parts of London and from many parts of the world, yet upstairs in the passages and the offices there was an all-pervading stillness, with only here and there a lighted office.

Miller tapped on Gideon's door, and entered on Gideon's call. He was surprisingly thickset and heavy for an athlete, and at forty-nine took much pride in his physical fitness as well as in his prowess at swimming and most games. He looked glowing with health, and there was a spring in his step and in his body movements which was partly natural, partly assumed—but he had walked that way for so long now that the real and the assumed were inextricably united. In a large egg-shaped face his small, almost delicate features gave his appearance a touch of the unusual. As a detective, however, no one could have been more matter-of-fact or down-to-earth. He worked as he played, giving the job everything he had, determined to be as good as he possibly could be.

"Sit down, Dusty," Gideon said, his casual address an indication that at this time in the evening formality could be ignored. "Heard about Fadiman's arrest?"

"Fadiman the supposed murderer of the nine strychnine-stricken housewives," said Miller. "Only the blind and the deaf could have missed it. It's on every placard and every television news, and half London seems to be talking it over." He sat down, frowning at Gideon's expression. "Shouldn't they be?"

"Fadiman's lawyer takes the view that his client will be prejudged guilty by tomorrow morning," said Gideon. "That makes me anxious to be sure we don't make any mistakes. We've had three different men in charge of the investigation. One is on holiday, one's gone over to a division, and the third is on another job. So I want you to take over." He put a loosely clenched fist on some of the papers on his desk. "I can't see much that's wrong. I've drawn up a kind of summary of all the evidence we've collected about what happened today. The woman who was murdered this morning lived in Gale Street, Camberwell, on the ground floor of a house converted into three flats. She's a Mrs. Corbett, forty-one, childless, husband a shipping clerk. A man answering Fadiman's description called on her and was seen by a neighbor from an upstairs window, by a woman living across the street, and by a gas fitter working three doors along. All of these agree on what he was wearing and what he looked like. All of them have picked his photograph out of six which were shown to them. In the house was a screwed-up packet of Bake-Quik Cake Mix, of the kind Fadiman takes round with him. We haven't yet found his fingerprints at the flat—the division is still working on it, but there weren't many prints anywhere. Fadiman, or someone remarkably like him, was seen walking away about an hour after he'd arrived. The husband found Mrs. Corbett dead when he came home for lunch, an hour after the man was seen leaving. No doubt at all the poison was strychnine, no doubt what the devil did during her spasms, either. Immediately the alarm was raised there was a divisional call for the man, and Fadiman was picked up in a tobacconist's shop in Camberwell High Street. He still had his box of cake mix. He had several of Mrs. Corbett's hairs on his clothes. After his arrest he was examined by a doctor, and there's no doubt he'd had an orgasm within the preceding hour or so, and his semen type was identical with that found on Mrs. Corbett's body. He swears that he left Mrs. Corbett alive and perfectly unharmed; he says he didn't touch her. We're waiting on the autopsy, and when we have the report, we need to make sure what she had eaten just before death."

Gideon paused, and Miller could easily have said: "It looks cut and dried to me." Instead, he remarked half musingly: "Be a hell of a thing if he was telling the truth and someone slipped in after he'd left, wouldn't it?"

Gideon drew a deep breath which was nearly a yawn, and leaned back in his chair.

"I want you to check everything you can between now and ten o'clock in the morning. If there's the slightest reason to doubt whether it was Fadiman, I want to know before ten, so that we can postpone the hearing until the afternoon, which will give us more time to check. Worry the life out of Whittaker, who's doing the p.m. Worry the life out of any one you think could help. Go yourself if you think you should and take some of our chaps. What we need to clinch the case are some fingerprints on or around the bed or bedroom. Fadiman in his first statement said that he didn't go anywhere other than the front hall and the back kitchen. If you can find a print of his anywhere else, that will prove him a liar. And—" Gideon broke off, giving Miller an oblique glance. "You know what to do as well as I do."

"I know what you want," Miller said. "I think I know what's worrying you, too."

"What's worrying me?"

"It might have been wiser if Division had questioned him and detained him overnight, if necessary, but not charged him as soon as they did. Someone was overeager, and that could get us into a lot of trouble. I'll keep at it, don't worry."

"If you need to talk to me during the night, call me," Gideon said. "If you think it would be a good thing if I came and looked over the place myself, call me. If we've got the right man, fine. If we haven't, we could be making a lot of unnecessary trouble for him—and worse, we could be letting the real murderer run around laughing to himself, if he's running around loose, and it doesn't help to know that sooner or later he'll get up to his tricks again. All clear, then?"

"Don't you worry about it," Miller smiled. "You go and get your bags packed for the big ship."

Everybody knew about the forthcoming visit to the States, reflected Gideon, and it wasn't surprising that everybody envied him. He wished only one thing: that there was no edge of doubt about the Fadiman case. He knew exactly what he would feel like if he had a radio message while on the *Fifty States* to say that the charge wouldn't stick.

Could that weak-looking, broken-down man who had dropped to his knees as soon as Gideon's back was turned, really be such a monster?

Joanna, Mrs. Fadiman, sat in the living room of the small house in Hackney, looking anxiously into the eyes of her daughter, Elsa. Elsa's face was expressionless. She had been utterly shocked when she had first heard the news and had hardly spoken since. All she seemed able to say, and that only between long periods of silence, was: "It's awful, awful." Her actions were mechanical: making tea, helping with supper, washing up, opening the door to callers, all without a word. Joseph Todhunter and Emily, his wife, had been with them much of the evening, but there was a limit to how long they could stay. Police were outside, Joanna knew, to make sure that no more newspapermen called, so there was nothing to worry about over that. Cedric's room was sealed off; Joanna's room, those of the children, in fact the whole house, had been searched exhaustively by the police; there was nothing that hadn't been examined. At one time Joanna had thought that the police would ask her to move out, with Elsa and Leslie, but they hadn't, so at least they could sleep in their own beds.

Sleep.

Elsa's eyes were haunted; that was the only word. She sat quite still, her hands in her lap, staring at nothing. She looked so much younger than her years, she always had, despite the fact that physically she was as mature as her mother, full-breasted, possessed of a kind of innocent voluptuousness. In a way, that made her more pathetic at this moment.

"Elsa dear," her mother said, "you must go to bed. You'll feel better when you've had a good night's rest. And by tomorrow your father will be home again, the police will know that it has all been a terrible mistake. Go to bed, dear. I'll bring you up a glass of warm milk."

Elsa stared at her blankly.

"It's awful," she said in a bewildered pain-racked voice. "Why isn't he here?"

Joanna Fadiman stood up, and crossed to the girl.

"Who do you mean, Elsa? Why isn't *who* here?"

Elsa raised her hands from her lap and placed them in front of her eyes, as if to shut out some evil vision; then she sprang to her feet and pushed past her mother and ran to the stairs, raced up them, stumbled, fled into her own tiny room at the front of the house, gasping, choking back sobs, talking a kind of gibberish. When Mrs. Fadiman reached the door of the room, she heard her daughter crying:

"It's awful, it's awful!"

And after a moment, in a tone of anguish: "*Why isn't he here?*"

Did she mean her brother David? Didn't she know that David was on his way from Birmingham, where he worked, that he would soon arrive? Why, he had promised to take a few days off, so as to be with them—until Cedric was freed. Cedric must be freed soon. Oh, God, he couldn't have done those awful things, it was impossible, it had to be someone else; it had to be.

She was tapping at the door, trying to make Elsa unlock it, when she heard the thud of the knocker. She made herself go down the narrow flight of stairs, holding tightly onto the banister rail. She opened the front door, praying that it was David, but instead it was a big man with a large egg-shaped face. Just behind him was a younger, almost cherubic man, wearing a clerical collar.

"Mrs. Fadiman," the big man said, "I'm sorry to worry you so late. I'm Superintendent Miller, and I would like to look through your husband's room again." He had a rather hard voice, which seemed to add: "I'm going to, whether you like it or not." Meanwhile, the younger man, so far almost dwarfed by the detective, spoke in a surprisingly firm voice:

"You must say if it isn't convenient, Mrs. Fadiman."

Vaguely, she echoed: "Convenient." She gasped painfully. "Oh, it's Mr. Pell. I didn't recognize you. It—it's all right." She stood aside, and a third man joined the couple on the porch and then went on with the superintendent, leaving the Rev. Jonathan Pell on the doorstep, looking at her pale cheeks and her gray hair, and all the sorrow that weighed her down. "It's nice of you to come, Mr. Pell. I thought it was my son David. Won't you—won't you come in?" She turned and went ahead of him, reflecting that things could hardly be worse, that only three months ago when Mr. Price had been their minister, before his retirement, she would have rushed to him for help and guidance. How could one expect guidance from a boy? Why, *this* minister couldn't be much older than David!

She led the way into the living room.

"I'm sorry everything is in such a mess," she said, "but I've hardly known whether I've been on my head or my heels. Leslie's gone to Mrs. Todhunter's for the night, they've been very good, and I'm expecting David—that's my other son, you know—any minute." She gave a vague, hurt kind of smile, and suddenly sat down as if her legs would not support her any longer. "It's very good of you to come," she went on, "but I don't think you can do anything. My husband didn't do it, of course. He couldn't possibly have done it."

She said that with piteous entreaty in her voice. Opposite, looking at her with great compassion yet with a terrible sense of his own inadequacy, was a young minister of the gospel (as he described himself) who had never as yet, in these first few months of his ministry, faced such a human tragedy.

He knew, and accepted the fact, that it was a challenge and that success or failure would be judged by his ability to help this woman and her family. Sitting there, he simply did not know what to say.

3:

London's Night

WHILE THE Rev. Jonathan Pell tried to call some words of solace from his heart and sought desperately to think of something useful to do, as well as to say, Gideon was telling Kate as much as he felt she should know about the cases which were taking them to New York ahead of the Conference. There were two: one concerning some watches which were being smuggled into England and Europe in huge quantities—the Rite-Time watches, made in a small city in New York State; the other concerning a different kind of crime, that was worrying politicians as well as the police. This was a case of sabotage, in England and en route to the United States, of certain goods manufactured in Great Britain and sold to firms in America. Gideon doubted whether the watch affair would have been enough in itself to take him to New York, but it was the ostensible reason for his early departure. The sabotage was something of which very few people knew, and he certainly did not intend to say much about it to Kate.

Since Gideon had first told her she was to go with him, Kate had written letters to the family and had been through her wardrobe and checked with a friend who had visited New York about this time of year, to find out what the weather was likely to be; very hot, apparently. Now all her summer dresses were spread out on the bed in young Malcolm's room. Malcolm had become an enthusiastic youth-club camper, and was at present in Switzerland, where he would stay for the next two weeks. So far, Kate had not allowed herself to think much about the fact that she would not be here to welcome his return. Of their six children, only Penelope was at home all this summer, and she would be here throughout the month that Kate was away; it was simply an emotional, not a practical, problem, for which the excitement and exhilaration at the prospect of the holiday more than compensated. Penelope, now eighteen, was out at a concert, and would probably be in late, unless she came home with half a dozen friends who were as devoted to classical music as Penelope herself. She dreamed of becoming a professional pianist but so far there was no real evidence that she would be anything more than a good party player.

In his home in Hackney, only ten minutes walk away from the Fadimans, Joseph Todhunter was alone in the tiny room where he worked when not at his office. Tucked in the old-fashioned pigeonhole desk were the papers that had to do with his many voluntary and charitable activities, including his work for the Bond Street Methodist Church, of which the

Fadimans were members. Todhunter was secretary of the church. Now he had Fadiman's statement in front of him, as well as information which the police had given him and which he had picked up from a shopkeeper and some neighbors and also from newspaper reporters. The more he considered the situation the colder and heavier his heart became. It was, of course, unthinkable that Cedric Fadiman could be guilty of such crimes as these, in fact of any crimes, and yet—Todhunter would close his eyes every now and again and lean back in his old-fashioned swivel chair, trying to shut out an evil vision, much as Fadiman's wife had done. For in Cedric Fadiman's past life there was a history of sexual aberration. At one time it had been necessary to watch him very closely where little girls were concerned. Todhunter and the Rev. Mr. Price had once been compelled to bring this out into the open with Fadiman, who had been almost prostrate with fear and guilt and confession and distress, swearing that he would never transgress again, that he had never really *interfered* with a child, he had restrained himself, putting temptation behind him.

And what would happen to Cedric if the police or the press learned about the little girls, Todhunter wondered.

Could it—could it possibly mean that Cedric had repressed his desires in one way, only to find them uncontrollable in another? Once, thinking this over, Todhunter clenched his fists and banged them on the desk, and the word "No!" shot from his lips in an agonized cry.

Above the small shabby room, Fadiman's younger son was sleeping peacefully, untroubled by dreams, the only one of the family not deeply distressed and shocked.

Over London, on this hot still night, a crescent moon shone on the homes of the innocent and the law-abiding, on those who slept together in wedlock, and on those who slept together without thought of marriage; on the old and the young, most of them of good intent, most of them guilty only of trifling crimes which few believed to be crimes at all, yet by such tolerance creating the very atmosphere in which graver crimes were nourished. It shone on the homes of the few people who were really good, like Jonathan Pell, who strove only to attain goodness, and it shone on the homes of those, even fewer, who were really bad, who regarded what they did as natural and normal—their law the jungle law. It shone on those who were drinking at the fountains of vice in the ugly, sleazy night clubs of the East and West Ends; it shone on those husbands who were beating their wives, on those wives who lay submissive, yet hating their husbands.

That moon shone upon the criminals as well as on the police. Superintendent Miller looked up at it when he stepped out of his car at Scotland Yard in the early hours of the morning. It shone on a rusty-hulled cargo ship, the *Maruna*, which had just arrived from East African coast ports. Among her cargo were ten thousand watches which had been shipped out of New York over five months ago—stolen watches, although the bills of lading and other documents had appeared to be in order. The load had been officially consigned to Dar es Salaam, but had never been taken out of the hold. Instead, false papers had been prepared, consigning them to London. The watches were in heavy wooden crates and would be unloaded tomorrow and the day after. Once the *Maruna* was rid of them, she would begin to take on fresh cargo for the eastern seaboard of the United States, including New York itself. She would sail on the very day that the S.S. *Fifty States* was to set off from Southampton.

Partly because of the heat, it was a quieter night than usual for London. Less evil was about. Fewer young people were delving into the excesses of erotic experiences. Fewer thieves were at work, because when one's hands were sticky with sweat it was more trying to wear gloves, more tempting to take them off, and so more easy to leave fingerprints. In any case, it was too hot to work, too hot to worry about the possibility of a sprint to safety. And so the policemen who were moving quietly about London, trying the doors of shops, watching for usually dark but now lighted windows, taking special notice of shadowy figures walking where few walked by night, had less to do. They were glad of the lull.

The Flying Squad was quieter, too, although from time to time a car screeched out of the courtyard at Scotland Yard and along the Embankment, summoned by one of the divisions needing help. One bank, three jewelers' stores, a hundred shops, and several hundred houses were raided that night, and all over London men were being charged, many swearing they were innocent even though they had been caught red-handed. It was all part of the routine conflict between the good and the bad, between those who upheld the law and those who defied it.

Gideon, in spite of the warmth, slept solidly and well. Kate's sleep was more fitful, and when she woke it was with excitement, tempered by the thought of Malcolm and the problem of clothes.

A great many other women thought, that night or early the next morning, about the voyage they were to make the next week on the S.S. *Fifty States,* and what they would wear. Many of them, like Kate, were going to New York for the first time.

One of these was pretty, empty-headed little Marjorie Webb, now sleeping as soundly as a child, hopefully naked on the double bed next to her husband, John, who was no longer her lover.

Profoundly unaware of how much he hated her, she could not know why he had agreed to take her with him to New York.

Another of the women looking forward to seeing New York for the first time was the wife of Dirk Orlick, one of the two partners in the Orlova Watch Company. She was beautiful, her large brown eyes held charm and attraction. She had no idea that her husband was going to America on criminal business—to arrange for the shipment of and the payment for some of the Rite-Time watches, other watches, crates of costume jewelry, which preoccupied not only Gideon and the Yard, but Police Headquarters in New York and in New Jersey, across the Hudson.

Her name, like Kate Gideon's, was Kathleen, but no one ever called her anything but Kitty.

Dirk Orlick was as unscrupulous, and whenever he thought it necessary as ruthless, as any criminal in London. There was, though, one good thing to be said on his behalf: he still loved his wife of three years as intensely and passionately as he had loved her during and immediately after a whirlwind courtship.

And he was still as jealous of her.

Another of the wives who was to sail on the S.S. *Fifty States* was Lady Allingham, wife of the chairman of the Faculty of British Industries, but she had little sense of anticipation and exhilaration, since it would be her twenty-first crossing of the Atlantic. Nevertheless, she was quite looking forward to it. Her chief preoccupation as she lay awake, listening to the rumbling snores from the other bed, was a pleasurable but cautious expectation of the voyage itself. The odds were that the ocean would be fairly smooth since it was summer, but that they could count on at least one roughish day. Also she had no idea who else was to be on board, and fellow passengers could make or mar the voyage. At least one thing she thought was certain: she would be at the captain's table.

She wondered who else would be at that table, and whether Captain Ruthven was still in command; Ruthven was a tall, distinguished, rather noncommittal Bostonian. Whenever they had danced together, he had always managed to give her the impression that he wished he could carry her off to bed.

She smiled to herself.

Her husband went on snoring.

Cedric Fadiman did not snore.

In fact, he did not sleep.

Gideon was at the office just after half past eight the next morning and found Lemaitre ahead of him, with all the daily newspapers placed out on the desk, so that all Gideon had to do was to run his eye down the headlines.

ARREST IN SEX KILLER CRIMES
VICTIM NO. 9—MAN CHARGED
HORROR CRIMES OVER?

Gideon glanced at these and read the beginning of most of the reports; saw that, although they had been written skillfully so as to make sure they did not commit contempt of court, the implications were all too clear. The fact that Fadiman had been charged had given the press plenty of scope. More than ever, Gideon wondered whether it had been wise for the division to charge him so quickly.

"Miller in yet?" asked Gideon.

"There's a memo on your desk timed at 4:45–when he left. Give him a chance."

"Anything else in?" asked Gideon.

Lemaitre, coat off, looking spruce and alert, leaned back in his chair and grinned broadly at his chief.

"Give yourself a chance, too, George," he said.

"Now what's on your mind?" Gideon rounded his desk and sat down. There were fewer files than usual. That could be a reflection of the night's crimes or of the fact that the Yard hadn't yet geared itself for the start of the day. Then he saw that there were more files than usual on Lemaitre's desk, and understanding began to dawn.

"It's Friday," Lemaitre said. "You've got three clear days before you leave. Do you know what you would say to me if the positions were reversed?"

"What would I say?" inquired Gideon.

"You would say that if I had any sense I would concentrate on the two jobs I was going to New York about. That I should pass everything else over to my deputy. Also," went on Lemaitre, with a touch of diffidence, as if even before he uttered what was in his mind he feared that he might be going too far, "you would say that all the great leaders of men know how to delegate authority. George, I don't mean–"

Gideon smiled grimly.

"So you can't wait to take over."

"You know I don't mean that!"

"I know you do, but I can't say I blame you." Gideon was opening a file. "I'd better go through all the outstanding jobs today, and run over them with you tomorrow. You handle all the new ones as they come in. That what you've already got in mind?"

"More or less," Lemaitre agreed. He sounded humble. "I don't pretend I won't enjoy standing in for you. With a bit of luck—" He broke off. "Oh, forget it."

Gideon knew exactly what he meant, and wondered why he himself had been so obtuse. Even before Fadiman's arrest he had been so preoccupied with the American problems, as well as with his eagerness to go to New York with Kate, that he hadn't looked at it from Lemaitre's point of view. This was Lemaitre's great opportunity—or at least, so Lemaitre would see it. At the moment he was Chief Detective Superintendent Lemaitre, Gideon's aide and right-hand man. A new rank, deputy commander, had been instituted, and he was obviously first in the running for it. If he did this job well in Gideon's absence, he would almost automatically be chosen. He wanted that promotion above everything else—and he saw this as the great chance.

Gideon said: "I won't forget it, Lem."

He sat studying the reports, including Miller's, but without really taking them in. He did not realize it but he felt much as Kate did about young Malcolm: how would he get on without her? How would Lemaitre get on? Only last night Gideon had reflected that there wasn't a more loyal man in the Force, but was he the right man to serve as deputy? As an assistant, yes, but deputy meant rather more than that, it meant the acceptance of a great deal of responsibility. There was a needle of doubt in Gideon's mind: how would Lemaitre stand up to that kind of responsibility? There was another, deeper, more subtle and more worrying thought: he could brief Lemaitre so thoroughly that it would be almost impossible for Lem to go wrong on the cases that were already in hand, but—should he? Wasn't his proper course to let Lemaitre take over completely so that he could really prove what he was made of?

There were two sides to that question. If he let Lemaitre have his head, and Lemaitre went in the wrong direction, it would ruin any chance of his getting the new appointment. If, on the other hand, he guided him too closely, how was it possible to be sure that, when he was on his own, Lemaitre could handle the situation properly?

Gideon tried to put the problem out of his mind, realizing that by so doing he was behaving exactly as Kate had done over young Malcolm: pretending that the problem didn't exist. It did exist, and he had only twenty-four hours in which to decide the best way to cope where Lemaitre was concerned.

Gideon began to read Miller's report again, and had hardly started when there was a tap at the door. He looked up to see Miller.

The most noticeable thing about Miller at that moment was his eyes; by some trick of light they appeared huge and very shiny and made the rest of his features seem ridiculously small and insignificant.

"Hallo, Miller," Gideon said. "I didn't expect you." He waved to a chair.

"Morning, sir," said Miller. "Morning, Lem." He sat down. "I can't say I like the Fadiman job at all—at all." He relaxed physically and Gideon felt that mentally too he was letting go, and that he was very tired. "The daughter is in a state of shock—I advised them to get a doctor, quick, but why the hell I should worry myself about that I don't know. The wife's pathetic. The married son was supposed to be down from Birmingham last night but didn't arrive. Todhunter is a family and church friend, as well as legal adviser. All right, I'm coming to it," he went on hurriedly as Gideon looked about to interrupt. "No prints of Fadiman's in the bedroom where the woman was found dead—nothing more than we got yesterday, but at least there's nothing less. Do you want me in court this morning or are you going yourself?"

Slowly, Gideon said: "I think you'd better go. We'll have formal evidence of arrest and a formal request for an eight-day remand. Not another word, no statement to the press, nothing at all."

"Right," said Miller.

4:

Remand—Sentence of Death

In one way it was a pity that the night had been so quiet, that all the crimes committed could be handled by the divisions, and that such help as was required from the Yard did not need Gideon's personal attention. With nothing to absorb this attention he could look through the pending cases with half an eye, and he kept thinking about the coming court hearing. Just after nine o'clock his telephone bell rang for the first time that morning, and he lifted the receiver almost with a sense of relief. He was alone; Lemaitre had gone down to the canteen for some breakfast.

"Gideon," said Gideon.

"Oh, Mr. Gideon." It was a new girl on the Yard's telephone

exchange, who always started to speak as if she had a sensation to announce. "There's a Mr. Todhunter on the line for you."

"Put him through."

"Yes, Mr. Gideon."

Gideon reached for the Fadiman file, which was now underneath that of the Rite-Time watches. As he moved the Rite-Time file, a photograph of an attractive girl slipped out: Mrs. Kitty Orlick. Even in the photograph the beauty of her eyes could be seen. Gideon was quite sure that Orlick and his partner, a man named Cordova, were guilty; fleetingly, he wondered if this wife knew what her husband was doing.

"Mr. Gideon?" asked Todhunter.

"Yes."

"I am at Cannon Row, Mr. Gideon, and would appreciate it if you would spare me a few minutes, as you promised."

"Come straight here," Gideon said.

"Thank you, indeed."

Gideon replaced the receiver. Almost at once it rang again, and the same girl operator said: "Oh, Mr. Gideon, Sir I-didn't-quite-get-his-first-name Fielding on the line for you."

She meant Sir Arthur Fielding, the secretary of the Faculty of British Industries.

"Take the trouble to get names correctly," he told the girl sharply. "Put Sir Arthur through." He stared at the dislodged photograph until Fielding came on the line, brisk-voiced, a very able man in a key position in British industry.

For many years there had been no real coordination in industry; even the Federation of British Industries had been a loose association of large and small groups with individual businesses. The Faculty had been created partly by the government, partly by the Federation and partly by some of the big foundations—Nuffield's, Gideon believed, and Ford's, among others. The purpose of the Faculty was research into the problems of manufacturing the same goods for export and for home consumption, and the problems of overlapping manufacture in the same industries; in fact it was a scientific approach to problems that in the past had been regarded almost exclusively as industrial, commercial and financial. Partly because Lord Allingham had been made its first chairman, it had got off to a very good start. No one scoffed at it, and industry and commerce had already benefited. The Faculty worked closely with the government of the day and with the Federation of British Industries, yet was autonomous and wholly independent.

"Commander."

"Sir Arthur."

"A small matter of procedure has cropped up," Fielding said. Something in his voice told Gideon that this matter was not very serious. "I thought I'd better have a word with you before doing anything."

He was enjoying his little mystery.

"I'll help if I can," Gideon said cautiously.

"It's about the dining room on board the *Fifty States*," Fielding said. "Lord Allingham usually sits at the captain's table. Would you like to be there too, or would you prefer to keep away from business at mealtime?"

The question was completely unexpected, and Gideon felt a moment's impatient uncertainty. Almost before Fielding had finished he was asking himself what Kate would like. The captain's table had a certain prestige, she would probably like that, but Lady Allingham had a reputation of being one of the best-dressed women in England and Kate might feel that she was out of her class. The moment that thought entered his head, Gideon said:

"If you can fix it, yes, I'd like that."

"As a matter of fact the P.R.O. of the line asked me to find out if you would accept a top table invitation," said Fielding. "I didn't want to land you with it if you would have preferred to keep out of the limelight."

"Don't think I should, from the sabotage job point of view, do you?"

"Lord, no!" exclaimed Fielding. "I'll arrange it all, then."

"Thanks." Gideon rang off, and made a note on a pad: "Kate: c. table," and as he did so, the internal telephone on his desk rang. He felt sure who this was, lifted it, listened and said: "Send Mr. Todhunter along." He put down the receiver and stood up, stepping to the window. Now that the solicitor had come, he wondered whether he had been wise to agree to see him, whether the invitation of the previous night had not sprung out of misplaced sentiment. The door opened, and an elderly messenger said:

"Mr. Todhunter, sir."

The solicitor was the second man that morning whose eyes seemed overlarge; almost certainly because he hadn't slept well. As the door closed behind him he looked up at Gideon, who was a head taller and looked twice his size. The two men eyed each other warily as Todhunter moved toward the center of the room, and Gideon left the window. They didn't shake hands.

"Sit down, Mr. Todhunter."

"Thank you, Commander."

It was evident that the little solicitor had slept in his clothes; there was something quite unmistakable about the creases, and he wore the suit that he had worn at Cannon Row last night. He sat down, and Gideon waited, deliberately throwing the burden onto him: after all, he had wanted the interview. Yet Gideon had an elusive, uneasy feeling that he was being hard if not harsh. "Have you seen the morning newspapers?" Todhunter asked.

"All of them."

"I hope you see the force of what I said last night." When Gideon didn't answer, Todhunter went on with a quiet kind of dignity which could not fail to have an effect. "If Fadiman is remanded in custody, it will amount to a sentence of death."

Gideon could have said: "You're exaggerating," or "That's nonsense," or "So what?" Instead, he stared into the overbright, overtired eyes, and said:

"I know what you mean."

"You simply haven't enough evidence to give the Public Prosecutor, Commander."

"Either you haven't seen it all, or you've assessed it wrongly," Gideon retorted.

"You could have the Public Prosecutor withdraw the charge. There is nothing to prevent you from doing that, and it would be a humane thing to do. You could watch my client very closely, and during the next few days you could check your evidence, and then if you were satisfied you could make a charge without any need for a remand for further inquiries. In a case of this kind, with an accused man who has no record, and who most certainly won't attempt to run away, I think that is the course you should take."

Gideon shook his head.

"So far as I'm concerned the evidence is more than strong enough."

"And you won't recommend that the charge be withdrawn?"

"No."

"Mr. Gideon," said Todhunter, "I believe that the divisional officer who made the arrest acted without sufficient consideration. I think he acted as a result of a kind of emotional reaction—the search for the murderer has been going on for so long that this policeman acted before he, or you, or anyone else could possibly have assessed the situation fully. As a result it was necessary for you to have a man at Mrs. Fadiman's most of the night, and to work all night at the home of the murdered woman. Work under such pressures cannot possibly yield the best results. I ask you again to request that the charge be withdrawn."

Gideon said flatly: "No, sir. I think that would be most ill-advised."

"And that is your last word?" asked Todhunter, as if it hurt him.

"It's my final decision," Gideon said. "It isn't the last word. You know as well as I do what could happen if the charge were to be withdrawn and Fadiman allowed to go free." When Todhunter made no comment, he went on: "He might well kill himself."

"You've no right to say that," protested Todhunter. He tried to put a sharpness of reproof into his voice, but did not quite succeed.

"I've every right to an opinion, and I don't think any harm can come from discussing it with you," said Gideon. He wondered if there was any chance that the solicitor shared the same opinion, if this was a desperate throw on his part to give Fadiman the opportunity to kill himself, and so let his family escape the far-reaching consequences of ordeal by trial. "Mr. Todhunter," Gideon went on, "partly as a result of your obviously heartfelt appeal yesterday evening, I put an officer fresh to the investigation onto the problem, and he worked all night. Nothing was discovered to change my view that the arrest was fully justified."

Todhunter's eyes looked very, very tired, and the lids drooped as if he longed to close them.

"I can imagine how the family feels, and I'm sorry that the daughter has been so badly affected, but"—Gideon managed to shrug his shoulders as if this really was nothing at all to do with him—"I've never found a way of making sure that only the criminal suffers. Can you suggest one?"

Todhunter sat looking at him for what seemed a long time. Then he placed his hands on the arms of the chair and stood up, slowly, as if it was a considerable effort. He stood very close to the desk.

"Mr. Gideon, I was told that I would find you an understanding man. I know now that is indeed true. Thank you for sparing me so much time." He held out his hand.

Gideon took it, and their grip was very firm.

Fadiman stood in the dock as if he did not know where he was, staring straight ahead, above the magistrate's bench. Todhunter pleaded "not guilty" for him in a firm, clear voice. A divisional detective-inspector named Carliss, who had made the arrest, gave formal evidence of this on behalf of the police and as formally asked for a remand in custody. Miller watched. The magistrate, a youthful man, took only about ten seconds deliberating. Fadiman turned out of the dock, like an automaton, with Todhunter hurrying round to the cells to greet him on the other side. There was only one thing in the court to show how sensational a case this was. Every seat in the public gallery was crowded, two people squeezing into normal space for one. The tiny press box was filled to overflowing so that there seemed hardly room for reporters to breathe. Outside, on a steamy morning when there was still some overhead haze, herald of a day of extreme heat, a crowd of at least eight hundred, mostly women, blocked the way out of the court. Police were lined up across both sides of the road to make room for traffic to pass; television, movie and flashlight cameras were trained on the back and front entrances. When eventually Fadiman appeared, there was a concentrated scream from at least three hundred women, mostly of youthful middle age; the age of the victims.

Gideon and Kate stole half an hour away from packing and getting ready that evening, to watch the BBC news. They saw the scenes outside the court after the Fadiman hearing. One cameraman with a touch of genius had turned his camera away from the door and toward the crowd, as if he had sensed what was going to happen. He had taken pictures in close-up, as if the scene had been that of the welcomed homecoming of a pop-singer idol rather than the hustling away of an accused man.

The screaming filled the living room in the house in Hurlingham. The picture showed the hatred on the faces and in the eyes of hundreds of women. It showed fists clenched and shaken, teeth bared, eyes glaring, bodies quivering. It was the most horrifying scene of mass malevolence that Gideon had seen for a long, long time.

"George," Kate said in a stifled voice. "That's frightening." Gideon continued to watch pictures of a fatal car crash on a motorway, his face like stone. Kate went on: "I hope it isn't going to spoil the voyage."

It was as if she knew that, in fact, the Fadiman case could cast a shadow over the whole of the time they would be away.

5:

Lemaitre

FRIDAY NIGHT was quieter even than Thursday had been, and the late August heat wave seemed to strangle London. Gideon, a big man, felt the heat more intensely than he had done for some time. It made everything more of an effort, and he had to keep a watch on his temper. Now and again the irony of the fact that he should be so nearly bad-tempered on the eve of a visit to New York made him smile ruefully, but there wasn't much time to think about anything but the work in hand; if crime had flourished he would have had none at all. Tonight and tomorrow there were three conferences with the divisions, assistant commissioners and commanders of the other departments, and it was difficult to make himself realize that all the other problems of the Force and the C.I.D. would be dealt with without his knowing what was going on.

He was in his office, with Lemaitre, ready to go through the various pending cases when his telephone bell rang. Automatically, he lifted the receiver.

"Gideon."

"Good morning," a man said, and there was no mistaking who it was—Sir Reginald Scott-Marle, the Police Commissioner, the man who had really made the trip to New York possible. "How busy are you this morning?"

So busy, Gideon thought, he hadn't time to breathe. Lemaitre, perky and polished, saw the change of his expression and listened.

"There's enough to do," Gideon said cautiously. "What have you got in mind, sir?"

Lemaitre mouthed: "Scott-Marle?" Gideon nodded.

"I find that I have to go to Scotland tomorrow and am not likely to be back until the middle of next week," said the Commissioner. "Can you spare an hour to come and see me at my home this morning? There are several things I would like to get quite clear."

This was framed as an invitation, but it was tantamount to a command. To be invited to the Commissioner's house was in itself a rarity, and a mark of distinction, and Gideon was keenly aware of it.

"What time would suit you?" he asked.

"Shall we say eleven o'clock?"

It was now nearly ten, which meant that Gideon would have to leave in half an hour or so. Without a change of expression he said, "I'll see you at eleven, then, thank you," and replaced the receiver, knowing that Scott-Marle would not waste a moment on the line. Lemaitre was grinning across in a slightly irritating fashion.

"Comes to something when *he* works on Saturday," Lemaitre scoffed. "But don't worry, George, there isn't much I need to be told about these jobs." There was a note of buoyancy in Lemaitre, but to Gideon it was also a warning of overconfidence. Lemaitre looked pleased with himself, almost smug. His face was shining, but he was one of the thin and very wiry men who thrived on hot weather and disliked the cold. "I went through them last night, took 'em all home. You've got enough on your plate as it is."

That was true.

"Lem," said Gideon, "I want to go through every case with you before I go. What about this afternoon?"

Lemaitre's face fell.

"I was going to take Chloe to the Lido in Hyde Park. It isn't once in a blue moon we get weather we can really swim in."

"Tomorrow morning, then, whatever the weather," Gideon said. "I'll be in at ten o'clock." He had not intended to come in on Sunday, for he really ought to make time to help Kate at home and to get certain things settled about the house, but this was inevitable. He would have to get some homework done during the afternoon. He didn't give Lemaitre a chance to protest, but went on: "Made any notes of the cases you looked through?"

"Mental notes."

There were times when Gideon gave up any hope that Lemaitre would ever learn anything new; what he didn't know already he would never find out.

"Just pencil a note or two," he advised. "I can't read your mind."

"Slipping, George?" asked Lemaitre.

Before Gideon could reply, and when a retort was hot on his lips, the internal telephone bell rang. He was glad to pick it up and so avoid glaring at Lemaitre. Was Lemaitre really at fault? Or was his own mood insufferable?

"Gideon."

"It's Peters here, of Fingerprints," a man said; he was a newly promoted chief inspector, a little diffident, especially with the top brass. "I had a request from Superintendent Miller to get in touch direct with you if he wasn't in—and I can't get any reply from his office."

"What's the trouble?" asked Gideon.

"There were some fingerprint fragments found in the bedroom at the Camberwell house," Peters said. As he began to talk about his job all hint of diffidence vanished. "I've checked them closely, sir. Tented arch pattern, without a doubt, and as you know Fadiman's pattern is loop and whorl. I think the prints in the bedroom are her husband's—I can't be sure because we haven't yet had any actual prints, we've only had a verbal description of them, but they tally as far as I can judge."

Gideon's hopes fell.

"All right," he said. "Send a note through to Mr. Miller, won't you?"

"Yes, Commander."

Gideon rang off. No matter what, he seemed condemned to leave the country with doubt about Fadiman's guilt in his mind. Lemaitre was busy penciling notes on the outside of folders which contained the progress reports on the cases pending. He was doing this with an air of "I really don't think it's worth the trouble," and didn't look up to ask what this call had been about. Gideon put the Rite-Time file and the Faculty of British Industries file in his briefcase. He was in no mood to discuss anything more with Lemaitre, and decided on the spur of the moment to walk to Scott-Marle's house, in Radlett Square, at the back of Oxford Street. It would take him less than half an hour, and there was some quality in London's streets which always soothed and strengthened him. This was his London, hot or cold, rain or fine, and he would not have a chance to walk through any part of it for over a month. He clicked the lock of his briefcase, and stood up.

"You off?" Lemaitre said.

"Yes. See you in the morning."

"Right." There was little doubt that Lemaitre had taken umbrage, but Gideon shrugged that off. The corridors of the Yard were very hot, and when he stepped into the bright sunlight of the courtyard, heat struck at him from the asphalt surface and from the red brick walls of the old building. He went across Cannon Row and into Parliament Street. Whitehall itself was comparatively empty, as it always was on Saturdays, but Parliament Square was thronged with sightseers, and whole families were tagging along toward the river, the piers, and the sightseeing boats. It seemed only a year or two ago since Kate, too, had brought their brood along and he had met them at the head of Westminster Pier. The youngsters had been thrilled to stand in the boat and see the very street they lived in. Today the land between this street and the river had been built on, and tall blocks of flats hid the Thames from view. There was so much to remember from and to be said for yesterday.

By the time he reached Trafalgar Square Gideon was feeling very much more himself, heat or no heat. For him there was magic in London. He wondered what he would feel about New York, and also whether there might be time to nip across Leicester Square and through Soho, his old "manor," the real heart of his London. If he went that way he would probably be late at Scott-Marle's place, but there was no reason why he shouldn't get a cab from Oxford Street.

Soho drew him like a magnet.

Leicester Square was there with its plane trees and its park benches, and on Shakespeare's statue a plaque to the benefactor who had presented it to London's people. The square was a seething mass of human beings. Every inch of grass was covered. Piccadilly was comparatively empty. The narrow streets of Soho were not only hot but tawdry. The garish night clubs were dead, the touts were missing, even the photographs of nudes and near-nudes posturing behind huge fans had a lifeless, dreary look. The shops were busy. One narrow doorway was wide open, and a black-haired, sallow-faced little man suggested insinuatingly:

"First show in an hour, sir. How about a little drink beforehand?"

Gideon walked past him. By nightfall hundreds would be in there, sweating together, drinking together, getting their vicarious thrills together, pawing those girls who would let them paw. It hadn't changed much; it had kept pace with the time, that was all—there couldn't be a more honky-tonk place in the world, and yet he loved it.

A young girl stepped out of nowhere in his path, and looked up at him. She couldn't have been more than fourteen or fifteen. She had a nice little figure, and showed it off by wearing a tight-fitting black dress; Gideon doubted if she wore anything at all underneath, he could not see the line of bra or slip, of pantie or garter. She had a beautiful peachlike complexion, reminding him of his own Penelope, and lovely, silky, spun-gold hair. She wore no makeup, as far as he could see, and needed none. It was strange, but the girl made a sudden, fierce tug at Gideon's heart in a way so unexpected and so unfamiliar that he did not recognize it at first.

"Hallo," she said.

He was surprised into responding: "Hallo."

She smiled; it was like the smile of an angel, and her teeth were in keeping with all the rest of her, even and white and full of beauty.

"I can give you the most wonderful time you've ever had in your life," she said. "That's a promise." Her voice was soft and husky, the smile only for him. She appeared not to understand the meaning of his bleak expression, the traplike way his mouth closed. God knew what kind of reception she was used to, how often she was rebuffed even with such an ingenuous approach as this. He was aware of movement on the other side of the street, and of people behind him. The girl stretched out a tiny hand, rested it on his arm, and moved toward the doorway from which she had come. "I tell you it's a promise," she repeated. "You'll never forget me."

A man squeezing between two parked cars said:

"Good morning, sir."

The girl glanced toward him, and her face blanched, something like terror leaped into her pale-gray eyes. The man was a policeman, young, thin, looking very hot although he was not wearing his tunic, and his air force blue shirt was damp at the shoulders.

"Was she accosting you, sir?"

The child looked into the cavernous depths of the passage from which she had come and bit her lips.

"I—I was just asking the time," she muttered. "I was just asking the time."

Gideon said: "It's twenty minutes to eleven." He pushed past the girl, and the policeman dodged back, knocked against one of the cars, his expression skeptical. There was a flutter of footsteps as the girl disappeared. Gideon passed the constable, and then waited for him. "How long has she been about?"

"As a matter of fact, sir, I haven't seen her before."

"She's young enough to be pulled out of this business before she gets in too deep," Gideon said. "Find out her name and where she's from, and when you put in a report tell your superior that I asked you to find out if the probation officer could try to help her."

"Right, sir."

Gideon nodded, and went on. Until this moment he had not felt particularly hot, but now the heat seemed to ooze out of him, as if quite suddenly he had stepped into an oven. He knew now that the child—child?—had appealed to some latent fire in him, that it had been a curious kind of appeal, child-like and yet not so childlike. Hardened, cynical, unshockable, it was a long time since he had been so shaken as he was by the encounter.

A taxi slowed down at a corner, its hire sign alight.

A butler opened the door to Gideon, stood aside, smiled and said: "Good morning, Mr. Gideon, nice to see you again." He took Gideon's hat. "Sir Reginald is expecting you." As they walked along the beautifully appointed hall, a clock on a bracket close to the circular staircase chimed eleven. They went into a room alongside the stairs, a small, narrow room. This was a narrow house, one of a terrace built in a crescent by Nash in his most gracious and expansive mood. The room was a combination of study and library, with bookcases, curved desk, armchairs, all in dark oak polished by a century of effort. A tall, narrow window overlooked a garden which was ablaze with roses. The French window was open, and a pleasant breeze fluttered in.

Scott-Marle wore a lightweight, light-colored suit which sat on him perfectly. He was tall and gray-haired, an ex-soldier of the old type, who could be aloof and to some people frightening. The light-colored suit, the cream-colored open-neck silk shirt, the blazing color of the roses behind him took away all sense of austerity and formality. He shook hands.

"Good morning, George."

"Good morning, sir."

"Sit down," said Scott-Marle, and waited for Gideon to settle in a chair which looked uncomfortable with its high back, but was in fact more comfortable than most. "I saw Lord Allingham and Sir Arthur Fielding last night, and I gathered that they're fully satisfied about the approach that is to be made in America over the sabotage. Allingham will go over and discuss the problem with the industrialists, and you'll do whatever you think necessary. Obviously this may be a very long-term job, and Allingham may have to do much more checking before we or the American police can move in. I made it clear to him that you have a free hand and that we will do anything and everything we can to help."

Gideon was feeling much happier, and thoughts of the girl, of Lemaitre, of his own ill-temper, were fading.

"I know you will."

"I'm not so closely in touch with the Rite-Time watch situation," said Scott-Marle.

Gideon spread his hands.

"A total of fifty thousand wristwatches, men and women's evenly split, as well as tens of thousands of pounds' worth of costume jewelry, cigarette lighters, and other things which can be sold in the same kind of shop, have been stolen from the manufacturers near Buffalo, in the United States. Whole consignments have been hijacked, and we know that a lot have eventually reached here. 'Eventually' often means months later. We aren't certain but we think the shipments come in on forged bills of lading at very low manufacturing prices, which rates them low for purchase tax and customs duty."

"So they come in legally," Scott-Marle interpolated.

"Some undoubtedly. Others are smuggled in, but the legal consignments help to conceal the smuggling. Some retailers are blackmailed into buying, others buy at very low prices. As far as we can estimate, there are fifty thousand of the watches in the retail shops, but duty has been paid on only about five thousand. Two or three men each side of the Atlantic and a corrupt ship's officer would be enough." Gideon was completely at home with his job, everything he knew about this case was at his fingertips. "We've inquiries going on in all the countries concerned. There isn't any doubt that the Orlova Company is involved, but I've agreed with Nielsen of New York not to take action yet. He hopes to find out who is involved on his side. If we were to find a consignment of the stolen goods in London, say, or Bristol or Liverpool, and to make arrests, key people all round the world would be warned, giving the American organizers time to get out."

Scott-Marle was frowning.

"Sure this is the right course?" he asked. "I never was happy about the principle of allowing these gentry to get away with anything for too long."

Gideon leaned forward, spreading his hands again; the contrast between the two men was quite remarkable. Cart horse to race horse, some would say. Gideon was very earnest, very sure of himself.

"It's less than two months since we first discovered large numbers of Rite-Time watches in this country. We know approximately how many have been distributed to retail outlets through Orlova. We've traced a definite business association between Orlova—or one of their directors, a man named Orlick

—with several wholesalers and manufacturers in New York. The American police are checking that closely. We've started inquiries about Orlova agencies in the Commonwealth. There's known to be a Swiss agent distributing Rite-Times all over Europe, too, a firm with an association with the Orlova Company. If we can find the head and cut it off . . ." Gideon hesitated, sat back, and clasped his hands together. "See the picture, sir?"

"Cut off the head and the branches will wither, cut off a branch and it could heal very quickly. All right, handle it your own way, but . . ." Scott-Marle hesitated in turn.

"Black marks for me if we let any of them slip through our fingers," Gideon said dryly. "I know, sir." He almost added, "Is that the lot?" but stopped himself, because he could see that there was something else on Scott-Marle's mind. As he waited, the door opened and the butler came in with coffee and with long drinks, ice chinking, cider, and a fruit cup glistening. He put the tray down on a table at Scott-Marle's side without a word and went out.

"Coffee or something long and cool?" asked Scott-Marle. "I always have coffee, whatever the weather—my wife insists that this proves I am the most cold-blooded person of her acquaintance."

Gideon grinned. "Coffee, please."

Scott-Marle laughed, poured out, and asked: "How is Kate? Looking forward to the voyage?"

"Very much indeed," Gideon said.

"I don't really envy you New York if it's going to be hot," Scott-Marle said. "But my wife does—whatever the weather, New York is right for her." He sat back, and sipped his coffee. "There's just one thing I'm not sure of," he went on in the same even tone, but Gideon sensed that a major issue was about to be sprung on him. "How do you think Lemaitre will get on?" When Gideon didn't answer, but allowed the question to settle in his mind, the Commissioner went on: "Let me be absolutely frank, George. I don't question Lemaitre's ability in the job he's doing, but I'm a long way from convinced that he's the right man to be your deputy. You need someone younger. Also I think you need someone who could take over at short notice if you were to go away for a longer period than a month. Are you sure in such circumstances that Lemaitre could cope?"

6:

Dilemma for Gideon

Now that the question had been put, Gideon realized that it had been inevitable, that he should have known in advance that Scott-Marle would raise it. He had done so with tact and understanding. This was an unofficial meeting, in his home, and lacked all the trappings of formality. But the question was as pointed as it could be, and there was no way of evading it without making evasion obvious. Scott-Marle, sipping his coffee, was looking at Gideon over the top of his cup, through a misty haze of steam. Gideon's coffee, hardly touched, stood on the desk in front of him.

Scott-Marle put his cup down.

"You'd like time to answer that question, no doubt."

Gideon, on the edge of a sharp dilemma, picked up his cup. Scott-Marle knew quite well that he was stalling; at moments like these he felt almost as if the Commissioner could read his thoughts. The period of hesitation seemed to grow longer and longer, until it became almost uncomfortable. Desperately Gideon was trying to think of an answer that would be honest and yet would not express his own doubts of Lemaitre.

Scott-Marle said: "George, you can't really divide loyalty on an issue of this kind. Let me put the question even more bluntly. If you weren't coming back, would you leave feeling quite confident that Lemaitre would do the job as well as you do?"

Gideon gave a wry smile.

"If I weren't coming back and you were going to step into my shoes, I would have my doubts about you, too." He felt a risk in talking to Scott-Marle much as he knew Lemaitre sometimes felt a risk in talking to him; he might have said the wrong thing, and consequently lost Scott-Marle's good will. But the way the other man's lips curved, and the gleam lurking in his eyes, told him that he had nothing to fear.

"And I wouldn't blame you," Scott-Marle said.

Gideon felt as if he now knew exactly how to answer, knew exactly how to be loyal both to Lemaitre and to the Yard. It was a good feeling, and it relieved him of a lot of tension.

"The fact is, I don't know of anybody I think can step right into the job. Lemaitre hasn't really had a chance to show what he can do, because I've always been breathing down his neck." Suddenly Gideon grinned. "In fact I was doing just that when you telephoned! Lem was beginning to wish I'd gone to New York last week. *He's* sure he can cope." Scott-Marle didn't answer, so Gideon went on: "In fact it isn't really up to me, sir, is it? In my opinion Lemaitre is the best man available for the post of deputy, but I couldn't honestly say that he's got everything I think the post needs." He felt a stab of conscience as these words came out, but there was no point in failing to convince Scott-Marle that he was being honest.

"Is he as impetuous as ever?" asked Scott-Marle.

"I've no reason to believe that he would be if he were in charge," Gideon said. "As things are today, he can always refer to me, and he knows that if he should slip up I will probably spot it. The only way to find out how Lemaitre will manage on his own is to leave the job in his hands. That's what we're going to have to do for four or five weeks."

"In which time I should have a clearer idea, and so will you," Scott-Marle remarked dryly.

"Yes."

"How long have you known Lemaitre?"

"Nearly thirty years."

Scott-Marle finished his coffee, put the cup back on the tray, straightened up, and said: "What do you think of Hobbs?"

Gideon didn't answer, but thought immediately of Chief Superintendent Alec Hobbs, the youngest of the senior men at the Yard, ex-public school and Oxford, a first-class detective and a first-class administrator, a man who probably knew more about the scientific approach to detection than any other individual at the Yard. Gideon's silence lasted even longer than when he had been deliberating about Lemaitre, but this time Scott-Marle didn't break it. A wasp came in at the window, buzzing about the brown sugar and the cream jug, but neither man waved it away. Beyond the Commissioner the color in the roses seemed to have faded because the sun had risen higher and was shining directly upon them, but Gideon had no eyes for distractions.

At last, he said: "Hobbs has one inescapable weakness, sir—

although weakness is not really the right word." Still Scott-Marle did not help him out. "One handicap, I should say."

"You mean, his social background?" Now there seemed to be a hint of disapproval in Scott-Marle's voice, and his lips hardly moved.

"Partly. His academic background, too."

"Do you seriously think it a handicap to have taken two honors degrees at Oxford?"

It could be that this had caught Scott-Marle on a sore spot; it could also be that the Commissioner was trying to sting him into absolute bluntness, possibly into a betrayal of prejudice. Gideon had a mental image of Hobbs, a compact, capable-looking man, with something of the aloofness that characterized Scott-Marle at this very moment. Gideon was going over alternative words in his mind, rejecting first one and then another, until at last he said with great precision:

"It doesn't greatly matter if you scare the wits out of some of the men. I know I do, at times. It would matter a great deal if Hobbs or anyone else gave the impression that he knew better than they because of his background and his education. It remains a fact that you can't be a good copper unless you can see crime and the background of crime as if you *were* a copper. Lemaitre can. Hobbs can't."

"Are you sure Hobbs can't?"

Gideon hesitated, and then relaxed. "Well, no, I'm not positive. I don't think he can, but obviously I could be wrong. In every other way he's much better qualified than Lemaitre, but Lemaitre would be able to keep his finger on the pulse of the Yard much better than Hobbs." Gideon moistened his lips, feeling suddenly very dry, wondering if he had been so intent on being fair to Lemaitre that he had overdone the case against Hobbs. "I hope you won't misunderstand me, sir. I like Alec Hobbs very much indeed. I think he's probably the best man we've got in straight detection and deduction from available evidence. If I had to have Lemaitre or Hobbs with me on this trip to New York, I'd much rather have Hobbs." He hesitated. "But I think if you were to put Hobbs in my chair for the next month, I'd come back to a department at sixes and sevens." When Scott-Marle didn't respond, only stared fixedly, Gideon went on: "Mind if I make a suggestion?"

"No. Go on."

"Give Hobbs a division. I don't want to lose him, but if he's going to get rid of that handicap, and he's got it whether we like saying so or not, it will have to be that way. Anyone who can get through a tough division will come to the Yard with a lot to recommend him."

"Hmm." Scott-Marle hardly opened his lips as he made that sound. "That isn't what I expected you to suggest."

"Isn't it, sir?"

"I expected you to advise me to groom Hobbs as a future assistant commissioner," Scott-Marle said. "That way he would skip through the problems you've been talking about, and certain issues would remain undecided." The thin, well-shaped lips twisted in a wry smile. "I should have known better. Another thing I want to tell you before you leave is that we've had a new assistant commissioner wished upon us." It was difficult to say whether he approved the choice or not. "We are to have Air Vice-Marshal Sir Wymondham Kell, who will devote most of his time to the administrative side of the office, leaving the executive work to your and our deputy. That will make the deputy commander's task even more important and the selection of the right man even more essential. It rules out Hobbs as an assistant commissioner for an indefinite period, and I'm not sure that I want him to spend too long at one of the divisions, no matter how good it might be for his soul and the morale of the department." After another pause Scott-Marle went on: "You leave us with a lot of problems, George. I hope you won't allow them to worry you or preoccupy you too much. You'll be able to let them soak in your subconscious for a while, and by the time we get back, Lemaitre may have proved that he's exactly the right man for the job." He pushed his chair back. "Let's forget it now, shall we?"

Gideon said, slowly, thoughtfully: "It's not a thing one can just put out of one's mind, but I know what you mean." He gave a stifled sigh. "What with this and the Fadiman job—" He broke off again. "Thank you for being so frank."

"Habit I catch from you," said Scott-Marle. "Not worried about Fadiman, are you?"

"I'll be damned glad when we've got just one more piece of unassailable evidence," said Gideon. "Circumstantial evidence always has its weaknesses."

"As do candidates for the deputy commander's post," Scott-Marle said dryly. "Well, try to take it easy in New York, and have as much time off as possible."

"A change is as good as a rest, they say," said Gideon. "I'll do what has to be done as quickly as I can."

"Of course you will. Come and have a look at my roses." A note of enthusiasm crept into Scott-Marle's voice as he went on: "I've a new bloom, a blue-black beauty which I'll guarantee you've never seen before. It's from Holland, and one of the first in this country."

Gideon saw the roses and heard Scott-Marle talk of them as if there were nothing else of interest in the world. That was the kind of detachment which probably made a good leader; Gideon doubted if he himself were capable of it, and was not sure that he wanted to be.

When he got back to the office Lemaitre had gone. There was no further message from Miller, but there was a handwritten report from MacPherson, the detective superintendent who was in charge of the Rite-Time watches inquiry in Great Britain. MacPherson was a dedicated man, one of the most thorough officers at the Yard, not exactly a likable person but wholly admirable as a detective.

His note read:

Among the first-class passengers on the *Fifty States* will be Dirk Orlick and his wife Kitty. Stateroom B21. Won't O. get a shock when he knows you're on board?

Gideon found himself chuckling. He made a note to write to Nielsen of New York Police Headquarters telling him of this report, so as to make sure that Orlick was watched when he left the ship and during his stay in New York; it was obviously possible that the partner in the Orlova Watch Company would lead to the American end of the racket. Gideon glanced through the other notes which had been put on his desk, then through the reports on Lemaitre's. In his copperplate handwriting, obviously written with great deliberation, were Lem's notes and assessments of the pending cases. There was one trouble with them, which was a characteristic weakness in Lemaitre. They were slick and superficial. Gideon studied, deliberated, then put the reports away. He could think about the problem between now and tomorrow morning, and decide how best to talk to Lem when they started to go through the files.

It was nearly half past one when he had finished, and he put in a call to Fulham. He waited for several minutes, looking out the window. The surface of the Thames was more ruffled than he had seen it for several days, and a breeze with a nip in it was coming through the window; that probably meant that the weather was really on the change. But the crowds still surged on the gay decks of boats and barges, and Gideon heard the sound of music floating across the water.

The telephone bell rang.

"Hallo, Kate," he said, not doubting who it was.

"I'm sorry, sir," a girl said. "There is no reply from your home."

"Oh," said Gideon. "All right, don't worry." It wasn't really surprising, he reflected as he strode through the passages, that both Kate and Penelope were out; they would probably be back by the time he arrived. As he reached the courtyard two squad cars raced out, tires squealing, with all the promise of urgency which might or might not be justified.

A police constable was at the door of his car, with the driving door open.

"Driving yourself, sir?"

"Yes."

"Looks as if the weather might be breaking up," the constable ventured. "Pity if it does for the weekend."

Gideon grunted.

Two minutes later he passed the crowds thronging the little churchyard of St. Margaret's, and even caught a glimpse of the mass of sightseers inside Westminster Abbey. He did not give them much thought as he drove along Victoria Street, where old and new office blocks ranged on either side, some of the old ones demolished so that their sites looked like the huge gum sockets of a giant's jaw; it wasn't like him to be fanciful. Traffic was fairly thin, and he drove between thirty-five and forty miles an hour most of the way, with the rather guilty feeling that he should be right down to thirty. He tried to pass a bus, but a cyclist blocked him; tried again, and the bus pulled out to pass a fruit barrow. He was forced to trail behind the bus for a quarter of a mile or so, finally passing as it slowed down just beyond Wandsworth Bridge Road. Alongside, he noticed movement at the window of the bus. It looked as if a girl was banging at the glass with her fist. He passed, carrying the image of her in his mind, adding to it a flourish of packages and parcels. Suddenly the truth dawned on him —that had been Penelope! He pulled in just in front of the next bus stop, opposite Parson's Green, his window down, looked out and saw Kate, also laden, bending down to smile at him. It was a confused few minutes as he jumped out of the car and helped Penelope and Kate down, then took some of their parcels; they were so heavily laden that he actually burst out laughing.

"Been buying up Oxford Street?"

"Well, Mum can't go to New York first class without a rag to her back, can she?" Penelope, gay, impetuous, warmhearted and generous, scrambled into the seat beside him after Kate had got into the back of the car, parcels all about her. She looked hot and rather more tired than Penelope; certainly she was more silent. Yet there was a feeling of satisfaction and contentment as Gideon drove off, Penelope chattering and Kate gradually taking a part in the conversation. They were only five minutes' drive from home, and Gideon pulled up outside the house in Harrington Street, watched by neighbors and by two men who were not far away. He thought he recognized them, noted that one had a camera, and felt little doubt who they were and what they wanted.

They drew up as Gideon climbed out of the car, Penelope's long, slim legs following him.

"Good afternoon, Mr. Gideon," one of the men said. "We've

heard that you and Mrs. Gideon are going to New York next week, and we'd like one or two pictures to send to our agents over there."

"Make it later in the afternoon, will you?" Gideon asked.

"We won't take two minutes, sir."

"I would prefer—" began Gideon. But it was no use, they were snapping away already, having no need for flashlights. One man was at the other side of the car, taking pictures of Kate as she got out, holding a pile of parcels, looking tired and disheveled and obviously in no mood for being photographed. Penelope, on the other hand, not sensing, or not wishing to sense, the disapproval, had decided to enjoy the occasion. The spokesman of the two kept up a flow of chatter designed to keep Gideon from lodging too strong a protest.

"That's exactly right . . . Very attractive young lady your daughter, Mrs. Gideon . . . Is this shopping all for the trip? . . . Have you ever been with your husband before on his official journeys? . . . Mr. Gideon, would you mind standing by your wife's side? . . . If you would just hold one or two of the parcels . . . No, I understand . . . Miss Gideon, Penelope, isn't it, I wonder if you could tell us what your mother's bought?"

Penelope struck a pose, and exclaimed:

"Well, there were two dustpans, some furniture polish, some bargains in detergents . . ."

Quite suddenly Gideon chuckled, Kate's eyes brightened, and they went into the house, leaving Penelope both attracting and annoying the newspapermen at the same time.

Gideon managed to open the door without dropping a parcel.

"Where do you want the dustpans to go?" he asked.

Kate said: "Most of them are to go upstairs. Shall we take

them up now and get it done with?" They went into Malcolm's room, and Gideon discovered how Kate had taken this over as a pre-voyage storeroom, saw the dresses, the shoes, the hats, the open suitcases, all the paraphernalia of the coming voyage. He put the packages down one by one, and stood back, hands in his pockets.

"It ought to be a nice year's holiday," he remarked.

"I shall need all those things and more," Kate said. She looked into the mirror, frowningly, brushed some of her dark and graying hair out of her eyes, and went on ruefully: "I shall look terrible in those photographs."

"Now you know what it feels like to want to smash a newspaperman's camera," Gideon remarked. "Nothing could make you look terrible, dear, but—you do look tired."

"It was so hot in the shops," Kate said. "And when we got out it was rush hour and there wasn't a chance of getting a taxi. We waited twenty minutes for a bus, and then Penelope recognized the car, and nearly broke the window attracting your attention. We weren't very popular."

"The truth is you ought to get a little car of your own," Gideon said. "Like a drink before lunch?"

"I'd love a cup of tea."

"I'll get it," Penelope called from the hall. "I've got rid of those newshounds and now I can't wait to see what they put in the paper about your shopping, Mummy. Why don't you go in your room and put your feet up?"

Very soon she came upstairs with tea, pork pie, salad, and bread and butter, and they picnicked in the bedroom. It was nearly three o'clock before they finished.

"The afternoon's almost gone," Kate said. "George, I don't think we'll be ready in time."

"You'll be ready even if I have to wave you off over my

dead body," Penelope declared. "Dad, you've got to put out everything you're going to take yourself, half of it's bound to want washing or cleaning, and there isn't much time."

"She'll make someone a good wife yet," scoffed Gideon. "I wonder—"

The telephone bell rang. He saw Kate's expression change, and realized she was hoping that the afternoon would be free from official calls. As he went across to the instrument at the side of the bed, Penelope said under her breath:

"I think we'll cut the wire."

He lifted the receiver, and said:

"Gideon."

"Hi, Dad!" This was Malcolm, in Switzerland, a thousand miles away. "I'm in Zurich. Just had Mum's letter. We're going off on a hike for the weekend, just had to telephone and say jolly-good. How's Mum? Is she . . ."

The only calls that day were from the family, each of whom was delighted that Kate was going to New York with Gideon.

7:

Sunday

SUNDAY MORNING was chilly and blustery. It was almost impossible to believe that it was the same season of the year as it had been last week. Gideon turned into the Yard just before ten o'clock, didn't see Lemaitre's car, and wondered why the other man was late. He should have known better. Lemaitre was at his desk, intent on some papers in front of him; he looked up as Gideon came in, and raised a hand in greeting.

Gideon went to his own desk and found several memos, none of them relevant to Rite-Time or the sabotage problem, all to do with crimes which had been committed during the night. There was a particularly nasty knife murder in North Wales, with all the hallmarks of a case in which the Yard would soon be involved, but the local decision to call the Yard in probably wouldn't be taken until the middle of the next week. "As soon as it was too late," Lemaitre would say sardonically. Lemaitre made a few notes and then looked up: "Seen the *SunPic?*"

"No. What do they want—our necks?"

Lemaitre got up from the desk and brought a folded tabloid across to him, placed it on the desk, and stood back. Gideon glanced down at a large picture of Penelope getting out of his car, skirt halfway up her thighs, parcels actually falling from her hands, but laughing and delightful. Beneath this was a smaller picture of Kate. He had never seen a better one—she looked truly handsome, and the slight dishevelment only added an informality. He was relegated to a small head and shoulders picture in a corner, parcels piled up to his chin.

YARD CHIEF ON BUYING SPREE

ran the headline, and immediately beneath it:

FIRST HOLIDAY ABROAD TOGETHER
IN FIFTEEN YEARS

Gideon was chuckling.

"Penelope must have laid it on thick," he remarked. "Kate shouldn't hate it too much. Is this a spare copy?"

"Keep it," said Lemaitre handsomely. As he moved back to his desk, Gideon had a feeling that there was something on Lemaitre's mind, something he was loath to talk about. "George—a big one's come in."

Gideon thought: Oh. He didn't utter a sound, but waited.

"Over at Lambeth. Post Office raid."

"How big?"

"They're counting now. The estimates are—" Lemaitre paused for effect—"over half a million."

"My God!"

"You're telling me. A nightwatchman was killed–stabbed in the back."

Gideon thought almost in anguish, Why, why, why? He meant Why had it to happen, why did such things happen, why had this happened today, of all days?

"He died instantaneously," Lemaitre stated jerkily. "It wasn't discovered until half past eight. Everything's slow on Sunday morning. I got in just after nine. The division was after you, of course. Told them they would have to make do with me."

Now it was out. Lemaitre believed, in fact he probably felt sure, that Gideon would want to be in this case from the beginning, and Lemaitre saw it as one he could himself perfectly well handle from start to finish.

All the things which Gideon had planned to say to him faded from his mind.

"I've got all the details here." Lemaitre put a hand on the file on his desk. "Haven't had time to go through any of the other jobs for second thoughts. Only just got my breath back on this one."

"Hmm," grunted Gideon. "Bit early to get your breath back." How the hell could he say: "Lem, this is your one chance, it can make or break you"? Watching Lemaitre, he began to realize that Lemaitre knew all about that, and needed no telling. For the first time he wondered if the man who had become his friend realized his own shortcomings more vividly than he, Gideon, had suspected. And he thought how much better it would be if the situation was tacitly understood, rather than having to be hammered home. "Don't you think you ought to be over at Lambeth?"

Lemaitre's eyes glinted.

"Okay with you?"

"No point in my getting my teeth into a job I can't finish," Gideon grumbled. He had never dreamed how much it would cost him to say such a thing. "Better leave the other stuff, I'll make a few notes on your notes, and we'll try and fit in an hour tomorrow."

Lemaitre was already reaching out for his narrow-brimmed hat, a pale-green one with a feather in the red cord band; it went with his greeny-red sports jacket and his sage-green trousers.

"Do something for me, George."

"What is it?"

"Let Chloe know I don't know when I'll be back." Lemaitre was opening the door as he spoke and Gideon felt quite sure that he was already in Lambeth, projecting himself into an inquiry which covered murder and a robbery of staggering proportions. Gideon heard the door snap to, and rubbed his chin, lifted the telephone and asked for Lemaitre's home number; he had recently moved to a small ultra-modern flat in Camberwell. As he held on, the operator said:

"There's a call for you, sir—will you take that first?"

"Who is it?"

"Lord Allingham."

"Oh," said Gideon, and thought: Better take Allingham first. Before he could answer, the girl's tone changed.

"Your Camberwell call is through now, sir," she announced.

"Don't tell me," a woman said. She spoke with a slightly Cockney accent. "You're not going to be in to lunch, because Gee-Gee can't manage the job on his own, and you've got to stay and hold his hand."

"As a matter of fact he won't be back until midnight if I

know Lem," said Gideon mildly. "Good thing you had a few hours off at the Lido yesterday."

There was a long pause; then:

"Why the heck can't I keep my big mouth shut?" There was laughter in Chloe Lemaitre's voice. "I know one thing, George, once you've gone to the U.S.A. I won't see my nearest and dearest for breakfast, lunch, tea, dinner or supper, I'll be lucky if I get him into bed now and again. The eyes and ears of the Yard, that's what he thinks he is."

"So he will be," Gideon said. "And he's off to a good start with a big case. Chloe, I've someone on another line. If we don't see you before we go–"

"Let Kate have a big shopping spree in New York, too," said Chloe, the laughter still in her voice. She was good for Lemaitre, and Gideon wondered again whether she would be good enough to help Lem to take his chance. He rang off, and that thought fled his mind as all the detail of the sabotage affair dropped into it. The simple truth was that this investigation was a challenge to Gideon in much the same way as the Post Office affair challenged Lemaitre. The bell rang, and a moment later a girl's voice said:

"Lord Allingham, sir."

"Good morning, sir," Gideon said.

"Sorry to worry you on Sunday morning," Allingham started briskly. "As a matter of fact I called your home and they told me I would find you here. We've now finished the main report from our side." This was a report on the sabotage of machinery used in the manufacture of goods for export to the United States. "Have you any objection to discussing this matter on the ship? I'm going to have a full day of conferences tomorrow. Think your wife will object too much?"

"This is an official trip, sir—I don't take my holiday until I've done all that can be done in New York."

"Tuesday afternoon or Wednesday morning, then. Shall I send a copy of the report over to you?"

"Two copies, please—one for me to look through, one to leave here for Hobbs and Ormeroyd."

"I'll see to that. Oh—one other thing. I wondered whether it would be possible for you and your wife to come and have a drink with us tonight. You and I know each other but our wives have never met. Always a big help to know someone before you go on board ship, I think—saves breaking the ice. If it's all right, about seven o'clock, but don't worry if you can't make it. Just drop in."

"You're very good," said Gideon.

"Of course I want to go," Kate said. "It will make me stop thinking about packing, anyhow. Why on earth should you doubt whether I'd want to?"

"Didn't know how many of your dresses you'd decided to save for the ship," Gideon said. "I—er—I forgot to tell you that we're at the captain's table, and that will mean dressing up each night, I suppose." He actually felt guilty.

Kate drew back and stared at him; and he was delighted that all sign of the weariness she had shown the previous afternoon had gone.

"I took that for granted," she announced. "I would have wanted to know the reason why if you *hadn't* been invited. And I really don't mind wearing the same dress twice. I'm not going to try to compete with the wives of millionaires, but I won't do so badly for the wife of a copper."

When she was dressed that evening, in a simple cocktail dress of a slightly subdued gold, her hair drawn back loosely from her forehead, she carried Gideon back ten years. She was completely sure of herself, and it did not occur to him that this was due to her very great pride in him and in his position.

He wondered how she would get on with Lady Allingham.

An hour later he knew.

"But, my dear, it's a perfectly lovely picture, I hope they put it in all the New York papers so that everyone will recognize you. . . . And I was saying to Ally, the picture of your daughter is almost *identical* with one of our Fifi falling off a motor scooter—it's my favorite, all legs and eyes. . . . The one thing I think we must insist on is that no matter how much business they talk between meals there must be no shop at mealtimes, unless of course your husband would care to hold us enthralled by some of his criminal stories, but perhaps they wouldn't be quite suitable. A little gruesome perhaps. What do you think, Mr. Gideon? And that reminds me, we'll be on an American ship and we really mustn't allow the Americans to think of us as those dowdy old-fashioned English, must we? Shall we start getting used to calling each other by our first names now, Kate? I'm Justine, which Ally always says savors of the ridiculous, but it isn't really much more silly than Oliphant Allingham, is it, Ally? . . . The one thing that will frighten me, though, is the thought of calling a VIP policeman George . . . or is it Gee-Gee, George?"

Long before she finished all of them were laughing.

The Gideons did not leave until after a light sandwich meal. ". . . Be sure we'll all eat far too much on the ship, I always make Ally go into training at least a week before we sail . . ." And they were not back at the house until nearly eleven o'clock.

Penelope was sitting at the piano, playing a very gentle piece by Liszt. But almost as soon as the front door closed she was up from the stool, demanding to know all about the evening, showing how much packing she had already done, and how little there was left to do. When Kate told her about a photograph of a girl named Fifi, Penelope snatched up the *SunPic* and studied it with her head on one side.

"Well, if Fifi came out in her photograph as well as I did in mine, it flattered her, too. Dad, do you think I could get some copies? Shiny ones, I mean. I'd like to send one to every boy who let me down on a blind date because he thought that classical music devotees must necessarily be dowdy."

Penelope was not alone in studying the back page of the *SunPic* that night.

Dirk Orlick saw it, after his wife had gone to bed. It passed through his mind that it might be wise if he canceled the booking on the liner, and flew to New York instead; but it would disappoint Kitty, and that was the last thing he wanted to do. There couldn't be any connection between Gideon's consultations with the New York police and the Federal Bureau of Investigation and the Rite-Time business; that was going much too smoothly.

But it was a hell of a coincidence.

Diminutive Marjorie Webb, pretty as a pink-lace doll, held the paper in front of her as she sat up in bed waiting for her husband to bring her a glass of warm milk. Soon she would see what a real top man at Scotland Yard looked like. . . .

When Marjorie had settled down, John Webb stared at the picture of Gideon, and wondered whether it could possibly affect his future course of action, which was very simple. He proposed to push his wife out of a porthole during the night. He had chosen a cabin on D deck because it was very close to the waterline. He had his plans carefully laid, and could see no reason why they should not work without a hitch; the only thing that worried him was the danger of some chance interference, and it seemed to him that Gideon's presence on board might mean that he was tempting fate. As he studied the back page, his hands clenched and unclenched. Gradually the face of Gideon's wife and the face of Gideon faded, and in their place in Webb's mind was a picture of Marjorie.

He wished that his fingers were round her neck, pressing her life away.

Captain Ruthven of the S.S. *Fifty States* also saw the photographs, and reflected in passing what a handsome woman Gideon's wife was. *Very* bedworthy, he imagined.

A great number of other people, including at least half the passengers who were to sail on the liner, saw the photographs, and many made lighthearted comments about them. "Better mind our p's and q's this trip, Daisy," or "Keep your hands in your own pockets or you'll be for it."

Many who were not traveling took notice of them, too, including Fadiman's wife. She looked through the paper mechanically, and wondered how much longer Elsa was to walk about the house like a machine, without saying a word. The child was suffering so severely from shock that the doctor seemed unable to help her, and even Joseph Todhunter had virtually given up. Leslie was fortunately still with the Todhunters. David had come down for the weekend, talking a lot, and emphasizing time and time again that he simply couldn't afford to take any more time off work. He would take a day for the next hearing so as to be with his mother, he said, but he couldn't take a whole week, he simply couldn't afford it, he might even lose his job. All these protestations and overearnest explanations were the result of his wife's influence, Mrs. Fadiman thought bleakly; her daughter-in-law had never liked Cedric.

If it weren't for Joseph Todhunter, she felt that she would be entirely on her own.

Every man and woman who worked in the Metropolitan Police and most of those in the other police forces throughout the country saw the Gideon pictures, and Gideon would have been pleased and possibly even flattered had he been able to know how few were the cynical or jealous remarks because of them.

Practically every criminal who was familiar with the C.I.D. force saw the photographs. The *SunPic* was passed round from house to house during that Sunday afternoon, for all the newspaper shops were sold out. Ex-thieves, old lags, men planning some crime or other, all saw it. Some gloated, a few boasted that when Gee-Gee was away wild horses would certainly play. A number of the more thoughtful and clever criminals looked on Gideon's visit to America as a rare opportunity, and when the news of the Great Post Office Robbery broke on Monday morning, several felt sure that the Yard would have its hands so full, without Gideon, that the next week or so would be exactly the right time for them to do a job.

More crimes were planned in the minds of London criminals between that Sunday morning and the following Monday afternoon than had taken place throughout the summer. The quiet spell was about to break, as abruptly as the heat wave had broken. At any other time Gideon might have sensed this, but he was too preoccupied with Rite-Time and the sabotage, with his disquiet about Fadiman and now his disquiet about Lemaitre and the Great Post Office Robbery.

Strangely enough, Lemaitre did sense it.

"Take it from me, Chloe," he said when he got home late on the Sunday evening, "we're going to have a basinful these next few weeks."

"You've been telling me for years what you would do if you had the job on your own," Chloe said. "Don't tell me now that you wish Gee-Gee wasn't going."

Lemaitre looked at her, frowned, and slowly shook his head.

"I don't know," he said. "That's the simple truth. I just don't know."

8:

Tuesday, Noon

"I CAN HARDLY believe it," Kate said.

"It's hard to believe," agreed Gideon.

They stood on the sun deck of the S.S. *Fifty States* and watched the small crowd of people on the viewing deck of the Ocean Terminal at Southampton, the dozen or so men who were performing their individual tasks in the formidable maneuvering to get the fastest ship afloat away from the quayside. No one down there seemed to be in the slightest hurry. Now and again a man would call out, or give a signal, and another rope would be twisted off a stanchion and would flop lazily into the water. The last of the gangways from shore to the ship was hoisted away with funereal slowness and lowered to a spot where it would be out of the way of the rail tracks of the giant cranes.

Alongside the Gideons were hundreds of people, every spot on the rails was occupied, both here and on the deck below. The air was more muggy and sticky than hot, the sky brighter toward the west, as if the sun would soon be shining. The ship's hooter let out a tremendous blast, and two others answered on a muted note, probably from the tugs on the farther side.

The gap between the ship and the quayside gradually widened, and the widening seemed to be quicker and greater at the stern. One foot, two, three, one yard, two, three. Little pieces of flotsam, orange peel, paper, wood, a clutch of feathers, floated on the oily water which swirled between the ship and the wooden quayside with its rope protection. Then the ship seemed to edge onward more swiftly, as if someone on the bridge had decided that there had been enough of this crawling, that it was time they really moved.

"Like to walk round?" asked Gideon.

"Love to."

An elderly American woman next to Kate smiled at her, apparently a little diffident. "Good morning," Kate said. "Why, hello." That was all, but ice of a kind was broken. The Gideons began to walk slowly toward the bow, staring out of the massive steel-framed windows toward a gray-and-white painted ship on which the sailors were still busy battening and fastening ropes and hawsers. Over by the anchor four men were painting, two of them Negroes, two of them white. They were laughing together. Gideon moved away, and Kate followed. Suddenly Gideon started, for a young woman walked from the far deck with a man in tow, and he recognized Orlick's wife from her photograph. She didn't appear to notice either him or Kate, but Orlick did; a glance at Gideon, and he stared straight ahead with glassy emphasis. As Gideon passed, Kitty Orlick said: "I want to see if the Isle of Wight's still there." She was laughing, gaiety in her voice.

A moment later, Kate said: "Did you see her eyes?"

"Whose eyes?"

"That girl's. They were the most beautiful brown eyes I've ever seen—the color of liquid amber."

Gideon grinned.

"Waxing poetical at sea, are you?" He did not tell Kate who the girl was, but wondered whether they would see much of the Orlicks on the voyage. The irony of the fact that they were sailing together amused him; he was tempted to go out of his way to speak to the man, but knew this to be only a passing impulse. The Gideons walked round the deck twice, then down to the promenade deck, which was protected all round by big windows, half of them now open. Deck chairs were lined up in two rows on the side that would get most of the sun during the east-west crossing, and a steward was taking orders for them. To both the Gideons, everything had a freshness which carried them back down the years to their Continental honeymoon. They arranged for their chairs, walked round, sauntered down to their cabin. It wasn't the most expensive but it was large and pleasantly decorated in dove gray and maroon red.

"Flowers!" exclaimed Kate.

There were three vases, one of tall carnations nodding slightly with the movement of the ship, the others of roses. The carnations were from the family, the roses from Scott-

Marle and the Lemaitres. Kate was excited and delighted. Gideon saw three telegrams on the dressing table and hesitated, for any one of them might be about business, in which case he didn't particularly want to let Kate open it. Still, they might all be from well-wishers, so he unlocked the suitcase as she picked them up, glanced at him as if she shared his fears, and then opened one.

"From the Pickards." These were neighbors.

"Nice of them," Gideon remarked.

Kate was opening a Cable & Wireless envelope, and her eyes lit up and then half-filled with tears. She said in a gentle voice:

"Bless him."

"*Have the best time ever,*" Malcolm had cabled from Lucerne.

Gideon saw that the other was a Western Union envelope, watched her open it, saw her frown, then saw her expression clear.

"It's for you," she said, and handed it to him.

Have a wonderful trip and have a wonderful time—Nielsen.

That was the nearest there was to a business telegram, and Gideon found himself wondering how he would get on once he was at Police Headquarters in New York.

At luncheon there was a message from Captain Ruthven. "Hope to see you at dinner." The Gideons reached the table first, vaguely conscious of its prominent position in the big room, of its pale blues and golds, the comfortable chairs, the sparkling silver and napery, the crystal murals, each of them representing a different state.

A quiet-voiced, well-dressed American named Comali was

across the table from them, a man in his sixties. When they were halfway through a meal sumptuous enough to remind Kate of Lady Allingham and her pre-trip training, the Allinghams arrived, Lady Allingham hurrying and breathlessly apologetic. She was a rather short woman, trim, beautifully dressed, giving the impression of trying to catch up with something she couldn't quite remember.

"Kate, my dear, how nice to see you. George, I didn't really believe that you would ever get away from your desk. Oh, isn't the first day tiresome, what with the unpacking and . . ."

On that first day Gideon saw the Orlicks at a side table for four. Without the slightest reason to suspect what was in the man's mind, he noticed the fluffy little Mrs. Webb clinging to her tall husband's arm, met Ruthven, finding him rather reserved and even a little disappointing, went to the pictures, "movies, my dear," danced until half past twelve, and then sat unobtrusively watching a small group of people still moving about the floor. Fluffy Mrs. Webb giggled in the arms of a fat man, and Gideon noticed that her husband was dancing rather aloofly with a young girl who looked more Southern French than English.

"They all begin to emerge as people, rather than mere members of a crowd, don't they?" Kate said. "Let's go to bed, dear."

Marjorie Webb giggled again as she walked down the stairs with her husband, giggled as she waited for him to open the door of the cabin, giggled as she began to pull off her dress, and giggled even more as it caught on her hair, and her husband had to disentangle it. Doing so, he gave her hair a sharp tug, and she gasped: "Oh! That hurt."

"Sorry," said John Webb perfunctorily.

She struggled out of her dress, and turned round to stare at him, bleary-eyed and yet indignant.

"I don't believe you are sorry."

"I said I was sorry."

"I don't believe—"

"Get into bed, you silly little bitch." He buried his fingers in her hair and twisted and pulled, until she gasped with pain. Dragging her across the room, he actually lifted her from the floor and threw her onto the bed, then freed his hand. In doing so he pulled her hair again, this time more savagely. She lay on her side, holding her breath for what seemed a long time, her tiny body quivering. He stared at it and at the porthole, cold-bloodedly comparing the width of her hips with the actual opening space. She would go through all right.

He heard her say in a thin voice:

"You've never deliberately hurt me before, never."

"If you get drunk and dance with another man like that again, I'll do a damned sight worse," he said savagely. "If you want the bathroom go and use it, and then stop sniveling."

The strange thing, in a way the awful thing, was that when they were both in bed, with a chair in the space between the beds, he heard her tossing and turning, then heard her get out of bed. He opened his eyes, and in the reflected light from the bathroom, which had been left on because Marjorie didn't like the darkness, he could see the gossamer cloud of her hair, and the outline of her figure. Suddenly she was pushing back the clothes next to him, and he knew that she was naked, and knew also that she was stone-cold sober.

"Jack, I won't get drunk again, I promise, I love you so much, I can't help loving you. Hold me. Hold me tight." She wriggled down in the bed beside him, warm and seductive, and he knew what he had always known and what he most hated: that she believed she had only to press her body close to him to arouse his passion.

He thought, Why not now?

He was still thinking that, half consciously, when Marjorie fell asleep; and soon afterwards he slept, too.

9: Tactics

"Now we've got to make up our minds what approach to take," said Allingham. He sat with Gideon in the sitting room attached to his bedroom. The reports which had been drawn up for the Faculty of British Industries were on a central table, his copy and Gideon's. There was whisky, a siphon, and some iced water. The portholes were closed because of air conditioning but outside the bright sun reflected on the smooth water, making the ceiling of the room shimmer. "What's your feeling, George?"

Gideon said: "Absolute frankness is essential, sir."

"With the American police, you mean?"

"With the police and with the overseas trades people in

Washington." He tapped his copy of the report, which was thumbed and wrinkled. "Here you have a hundred and seven different British companies, each of them quite small, each of them with a useful export trade. None of this is big by the standards of Big Business, but take them all together and you've got ten million pounds' worth of exports to the United States endangered. That's true, isn't it?"

Allingham sniffed. He was a shorter man than Gideon but nonetheless quite big, his face and mouth rounded, his paunch neat and high. He wore a cream-colored short-sleeved silk shirt and pale check trousers which fitted him a little too tightly. He had a pinkish complexion and mild blue eyes—most people, meeting him for the first time, were not impressed.

"Figures can't lie, eh?"

"These don't."

"Because we prepared 'em? George—" Allingham moved away from the table, and took cigarettes from a small writing desk. He proffered these, then drew the box back. "Of course, you don't. Wise man. They are the correct figures for the situation as we know it, but there are thousands, not hundreds of firms making goods which are exported to the United States. I would say that the total amount which could be involved is nearer twenty-five million than ten. And although I think we know every firm which has had any reason to suspect sabotage in the past, we certainly can't be sure that other firms won't be affected. The pattern is always the same: damage by fire or acid to machines working on special orders for the United States, or on raw materials or stocks of consumer goods for the United States. In other words, it really is big business, and a lot of people are involved."

Gideon said: "I don't think we've ever questioned that."

"I question whether we can go to any of the importers in the U.S.A. and Canada with the figures we have so far and impress them sufficiently for our purpose."

Gideon frowned.

"I thought you were quite sure this was the right approach, sir."

"Ally." Allingham lit a cigarette and let smoke trickle from the corner of his lips, while he watched Gideon without appearing to do so. "I am skeptical of absolute frankness. I prefer always to have something up my sleeve. I'm sure you do, too."

"I should have thought that we had enough up our sleeves," Gideon said. "We have discovered these one hundred and seven manufacturers whose machinery or stocks have been damaged and whose U.S. exports inevitably suffer in consequence. We know that there are a lot of complaints from importers in the U.S.A. that goods they buy are not up to standard because of these saboteurs, and we know that there is considerable pilfering in England, as well as thefts after the goods have been shipped from English ports. We know that a lot of goods which reach New York are shipped from there by rail and road, and fail to reach their destination. On the strength of this, we must ask the Federal Bureau of Investigation if they will help us to find the thieves."

"Cut and dried, eh?" Allingham said.

Gideon was beginning to feel slightly irritated.

"I don't understand you. Surely such blunt facts are of themselves cut and dried?"

"What I'd like you to think about is this," Allingham said, sitting down across the table from Gideon. "Supposing we take some of the manufacturers—say the shortbread people, one of the smaller firms, and perhaps the two independent whisky distillers. All of these suffer from pilfering, heavy losses in thefts in Great Britain and damage through deterioration due to faulty packing. Tins suffer in the case of the shortbreads, metal fastenings in the case of the whisky. With these, we have a clear-cut but fairly small-scale problem. What would you think if we took up *only* these three cases with the Americans, and see how they react. I'm going to Washington for general business discussion, carrying out my function, or the Faculty's function, of making sure that goods we export measure up to the required import standards. I could mention in passing that we've had trouble with these specific things. I could also mention that by coincidence you are here to discuss the Rite-Time watch mystery with the New York and New Jersey authorities. Happy coincidence. Eh, George?" Allingham's small mouth puckered into a smile. "I could say that I happen to know you know that investigations have been going on into the troubles at the shortbread factory and the distilleries. As you're in the U.S., couldn't we have a round-the-table discussion? If we start like that, we should soon be able to judge the American attitude."

Gideon didn't speak immediately. Allingham stubbed out the cigarette which he had only just lit, and played with the box as Gideon rubbed his chin.

"Not impressed, George?" Allingham murmured.

"I'd like to think about it."

"Nothing much more we can do for the next four days anyhow." When Gideon made no move, except to glance down at a chart showing the total amount of the damage due to sabotage, pilfering in Great Britain, and loss on the high seas or after delivery in New York, he went on: "What's worrying you?"

Gideon gave a little smile.

"You, I suppose. Why do you want to approach this problem so cautiously?"

"I think I'd like to do what you did when you came to see me a month or so ago," said Allingham. "You said you had evidence of trouble in several factories, and we immediately told you that we knew of trouble in a lot more. I would like to find out if we're the only trouble source. I mean, whether goods from France, Germany, Israel, Africa—anywhere in the world—are suffering more than normal damage or loss. In other words, is this just an Anglo-American problem or is it much wider? If it's wider, then I think I would rather find out what the Americans can tell us than tell them all we know in the beginning. The result would influence our tactics, you see. Can't really decide tactics or strategy until we know the size of the problem. If it's exclusive to us, and if it's new to the Americans, then we will have to go about it in one way. If it's common to a number of countries—"

Gideon waved him to silence.

"You win," he said.

"Sure you don't want to sleep on it?"

"No." Gideon hesitated, and then looked at the whisky. "May I have a drink?"

"My dear chap, of course." Allingham poured. "Say when." He began to siphon soda water, pausing expectantly: "You really like to drown it, don't you?"

"Never did like drinking much at midday," said Gideon. "Thanks." He sipped. "Cheers." After a moment he went on: "There are occasions when I seem to spend half my time telling my chaps that before they take any course of action they must see every side of a problem and make sure that what they do today won't rebound on their own heads tomorrow. Most people have a restricted outlook. They don't really believe in a world outside their own. Even my best men have a kind of insular outlook." He drank more deeply. "I thought mine was global."

"So it is," said Allingham.

"When I'm shown the globe." Gideon laughed. "I think I might get a lot more out of this trip than I'd expected, sir."

"Ally."

Gideon said: "Let that come when I'm not thinking about it, will you?"

Allingham chuckled. "All right, George. Now we've had this talk, there shouldn't be much to worry about during the trip. I've some homework to finish on my own problems, and you've got Rite-Time. It might be a good idea if we make these morning sessions a regular thing; then our wives will know they're free of us until half past twelve, say, and we'll be assured of working undisturbed."

Gideon was still laughing as he went into his cabin, where Kate was sitting in her slip, examining a stocking. She looked up, her own face free from anxiety and concern, and her eyes widened.

"It must be very funny to make you laugh like that," she said.

"Funny," Gideon echoed. He went to her and held her head back, and slowly lowered his lips to hers. "I'm learning my job," he said, "and I think I'm going to learn how to enjoy a sea voyage, too. Hungry?"

"Not so very."

"So you won't mind being late for lunch."

"Who are we going to drink with?" inquired Kate. "Justine is going to take Ally to the chief engineer's cabin for cocktails, so it can't be with them."

"We are *not* going to drink," Gideon said. He kissed her. Only when he drew back did it dawn on Kate what he meant.

There were no radio telephone messages, nothing for Gideon in the daily *Ocean Times,* merely a miniature newspaper devoted mostly to sports and Wall Street prices apart from advertisements for goods and places in New York. Gideon, tense until that first morning, began to relax. Orlick kept away from him, the others at the captain's table were easy to get along with, the bars, the deck games, and the swimming pool created their own social circles. Kate was completely at home, never spectacularly but never badly dressed. Her eyes seemed to grow brighter hour by hour. The big public rooms, the turquoise-blue lounge with windows overlooking the ocean were empty most of the time.

So much went on—under Gideon's nose, he realized much later.

Marjorie Webb sipped a Martini almost fearfully, wondering if her husband knew that it was her third.

Orlick sat at a small table in the Observation Bar, where a Filipino played on a scarlet and silver harmonium and waiters threaded their way between the tables. Orlick watched Kitty. By arrangement, they had met an American couple named Brown, whom he had liked at first but who were beginning to annoy him. Brown was a man of medium build with a very handsome face and fine, dark-brown eyes. Far too often his hand closed over Kitty's, and as he watched, Orlick felt a rising resentment. Who the hell did Brown think he was? Business didn't give him the right to maul Kitty about. Brown's wife, brassy-haired Elaine, was pressing her leg against Orlick's as she leaned close to him. Both the women wore low-cut sun dresses. He decided that Kitty's was far too low, he would have to tell her to do something about it.

Justine Allingham came bubbling down to lunch, dropped into the chair which the headwaiter held for her, and leaned across to Kate. As she did so, Ruthven took his seat and Allingham sat on Kate's other side.

"Kate, dear, I want you to use your influence with your husband to have a little competition with Captain Ruthven. He says that he could name at least eleven international criminals on board—*eleven*—and I said that George could certainly double that number. Can you, George?"

"Wouldn't like to say," said Gideon. "I'm off duty. Anyhow, the interesting criminals aren't those you know, but those you don't."

Justine gave an affected little shiver.

"Do you mean that ordinary people looking as if they couldn't possibly commit a crime might be sitting in this very dining room and plotting one?"

Gideon said: "It's a question of how many are plotting, not whether any of them are."

"Oh, you're exaggerating!"

Gideon knew that he wasn't . . . and at her table Marjorie Webb hiccuped, glancing apprehensively at her husband; he gave no sign.

On Friday morning they woke to gray skies, a drizzle, and a swell which made walking difficult. At breakfast only a few tables were occupied. Passengers staggered up to the promenade deck and allowed the stewards to wrap them in blankets. There they lay pale and drawn, pretending to read, feeling every movement of the ship. Only a few, who were hardy sailors, walked up and down the decks ostentatiously. Gideon, slightly queasy but not ill, gripped the promenade-deck rail as he and Kate moved toward the spot where they and the Allinghams had chairs. Justine was already lying down, but her color was good, and her blue eyes bright enough as she waved to them. Gideon went swaying off on his own, and as Kate sat down, Justine remarked:

"I don't know what our husbands get up to in their working sessions, but George looks a new man since he came on board."

"So you've noticed it, too."

"Noticed it—he looks ten years younger," Justine declared. "I nearly said he walks with more of a spring in his step, but that wouldn't be quite true this morning. He works too hard, doesn't he?"

"Much too hard."

"Ally was saying only this morning that he's one of the few really dedicated men—George, I mean. And devoted. He looks at you sometimes as if he—but listen to me!" Justine laughed, and picked up a magazine. "Did you read this . . ."

The sea grew worse during the day, a Force 7 gale sweeping the liner from due north, making her pitch and roll. Safety ropes were everywhere, the decks and public rooms were almost deserted. The wind screamed, spray smashed against the ship's sides, and now and again splashed in where a steward had left a porthole unsecured. No one was surprised that the cinema theater was almost empty that night, and that only one in three of the passengers was to be seen in the dining room.

John Webb, in the bathroom listening to Marjorie gasping and groaning, knew that if he was to carry out his plan, this was the time.

He went into the stateroom. Marjorie was on her back,

whey-green in color, her eyes heavy and lusterless. He poured out a little ice-cold water from a thermos jug, and held out a pill.

"I got this from the doctor," he lied. He had stolen the pill, and several others, a few months before from a doctor's surgery; they were morphine, and one alone would knock her out for some hours. "He says it's certain to help. Sit up and take it."

"I–I can't sit up, Jack. Honestly I can't."

He placed the glass in a recess which made sure it could not fall over, put one arm behind her back and raised her, then forced the tablet between her lips. She gulped weakly. He nipped her nose and held her head back, and thought she was going to be sick, but she recovered. He held the water to her lips and made her swallow a few mouthfuls, and she gulped again, looking at him pathetically.

"I feel awful, absolutely awful."

"You won't feel a thing in a few minutes," he assured her, easing her shoulders back onto the pillows. "I'll come and see you soon."

She watched the door as he went out, feeling too sick to be anything but sorry for herself. She had no idea that he had given her a tablet which should take effect in ten minutes or so, sending her to sleep for several hours. Soon her eyelids began to droop, and she sank lower in the bed, her head lolling.

Twenty minutes later Webb returned.

His heart was beating hard as he locked the door of the cabin and stepped toward her. She was fast asleep, looking an absolute wreck; but he was untouched by compassion. He knew that he must do what he had to do quickly, or his nerve might fail him. He pulled the sheet and blanket back from her. She wore only a flimsy nightdress; he eased her up and took this off, crushing it into a ball.

He leaned across her to the porthole. It was fastened by three loop-head brass bolts, like old-fashioned scale weights, which the steward had secured that evening. Webb took out his penknife, pushed it through the loop of the upper bolt, and began to hoist, careful not to touch the brass with his fingers. It took him a long time; the second bolt was easier, the third as bad as the first, but at last all three were loose, and, wrapping a handkerchief round his fingers, he was able to pull out the porthole cover itself. It was much heavier than he had expected, and for a few minutes he was afraid that he had miscalculated, but gradually it opened. On the lee side there was less wind, and the sea was comparatively calm, although he could hear the rushing water and see the yellow lights reflected on it. He fastened the port cover back, then stood away from the bed and stared down at his wife.

It was now or never.

He picked her up bodily, holding her straight, with her feet toward the porthole. He thrust her through until her legs scraped on the sides, and the calves were flattened. He kept pushing, fearful lest she should prove wider at the hips than he had estimated. Her pale flesh gleamed, unexpectedly beautiful. He found it extraordinarily heavy going, and paused to rest. He was sweating. Marjorie was half out of the porthole, and her hips seemed to be lodged tightly against it. In sudden panic he realized that someone might be leaning over the rail, or looking out of another porthole. He had to get this over, fast, fast, fast. He pushed. She wouldn't budge. Bloody fool, he should have pushed her out head first, her arms stretched *above* her head. It was too late to change. He supported her with one arm and grabbed the dressing-table stool, stood on the bed, and rested her shoulders on the stool, while he worked on the flesh of her thighs, easing it through first on one side, then on the other. God! It was taking an age. His mouth was parched, his lips were dry and taut, sweat streamed off him. He worked on the flaccid flesh for at least five minutes, then suddenly he realized that her hips were through. A roll of the ship actually made her slide several inches farther out. In a frenzy he held her beneath the shoulders and pushed and pushed, until quite suddenly she slid forward. It was almost unbelievable. As she went out, he staggered backward. Reeling, he saw the nimbus of her hair disappearing, then her arms, her elbows, her hands were lost to sight in turn.

He heard nothing except the howling wind.

He felt sick and dizzy, and thought he was going to faint, but after a few moments he recovered enough to remember there was still a lot to do. First, he must get rid of Marjorie's nightdress and dressing gown. Then he must fasten the port, screwing it up tightly, so that no one would suspect it had been opened. He knew exactly what he was going to say: that she had been so seasick she had to get some fresh air, that she had gone to the deck for air several times during the day, that she must have left the cabin during the night, while he had been sleeping.

He started shivering, and could not stop himself.

10:

Last Day at Sea

HOPKINS, THE Gideons' steward, black as ebony, possessed the sunny brightness of a stage Negro. The ceremony of morning tea amused him highly, but it always arrived on the dot of eight-thirty. On Saturday morning, the last day at sea, he put the tray down by Kate's bed, cracked his usual joke about tea being much better than coffee, then put Gideon's shoes down by the side of his bed and, straightening up as if he had been struck, exclaimed:

"Lord forgive me, I forgot."

"What have you forgotten?" asked Gideon lazily.

"The message, sir. The message from the captain's steward.

The captain would esteem it a privilege, sir, if Mr. Gideon would call on him as soon as possible."

Gideon realized that Hopkins hadn't, in fact, forgotten a thing, but was indulging a relish for making the most of every situation. He would not spoil it for him.

"Before breakfast!" Kate exclaimed.

"Yes, ma'am. Us Americans do a lot of business before breakfast—maybe that's why we don't have time for morning tea." He went off chuckling delightedly.

"I suppose that means a message from the Yard," Kate said.

"First one, so we mustn't grumble," Gideon replied philosophically. As he drank tea, shaved and dressed, while Kate stayed in bed, he found himself trying to recall—*trying to recall,* he reminded himself—the urgent cases. Fadiman, of course; and his family. And Lemaitre and the Post Office job. There were a dozen others and for all he knew there might be more news about Rite-Time watches. As he went out of the cabin it suddenly occurred to him that the captain's message might be of an emergency at home, and he hoped that idea had not also occurred to Kate.

He found himself expected all along the line, first one steward then another escorting him from deck to deck, until he walked up the gangway from the sun deck toward the bridge and the captain's quarters. The sea was a bright Mediterranean blue. There was hardly a cloud in the sky, hardly a white horse atop a wave. A few fish skimmed the water and disappeared, and he wished Kate could have seen them.

Ruthven was in his cabin.

"Thank you for coming so promptly, Commander." He was formal, he had always been rather more formal than Gideon had expected of an American; he was a man, apparently, whom it took a long time to know, nearer in manner to Scott-

Marle than to the popular conception of a captain of an ocean liner. He said now: "I've two problems. New York has suggested that I have a word with you about them. I'll be very grateful."

"Anything I can do," said Gideon, overwhelmingly relieved; at least there was no need to worry about the family.

"We seem to have lost a passenger overboard," stated Ruthven, shocking Gideon into full attention. "The wife of one of our English passengers, a Mrs. Webb. Marjorie Webb." Ruthven looked as if he expected Gideon to remember her.

Gideon said: "The name's vaguely familiar. Overboard, you say?"

"The husband says that she was often very seasick and the stewardess confirms this. She kept going to the deck, to get some fresh air—some seasickness sufferers think that is the best relief for them. According to the husband, she left the cabin during the night and didn't come back. When he woke, around half past six, she wasn't there. So he went to look for her, and reported her missing. She hasn't been found. She isn't in the hospital or in any of the public rooms, or in the bathrooms or powder rooms. I have made sure that the whole ship has been searched."

Gideon said: "I'm beginning to remember her—a little, curly-haired thing with a saturnine-looking husband?"

"That is so," agreed Ruthven. "Commander, I shall be seeing Mr. Webb here at half after ten. I would be very appreciative if you would inspect his cabin while he is up here."

"What do you suspect?"

"I would like to be sure there is nothing to suspect," Ruthven said, with a glimmer of a smile.

"I'll gladly look through the cabin," Gideon promised.

"Thank you. I will send a steward to guide you there at

ten-thirty, and I will not release Webb from my cabin until I hear from you."

"I won't take longer than I have to."

"Excellent." Ruthven paused only for a moment before going on: "The other matter also concerns an English passenger, and is something which I would gladly evade."

Gideon waited.

"A Mr. Dirk Orlick attacked a Mr. Inglemann Brown late last night, and Brown—who is an American citizen—has a broken nose and a badly lacerated mouth. I reported this in the normal way to New York, and received a request through Police Headquarters to consult you about it." Ruthven allowed these words to come out flatly, and did not ask any question; but his eyes showed a faint curiosity.

"Orlick," echoed Gideon gruffly. "Does Brown want to prefer a charge?"

"He won't force any issue."

"If you report in detail what happened when you get ashore, could Brown make a charge later?"

"I'm not familiar with the law, but I guess so."

"It might be useful to have a charge like this so that we can hold him any time we want to," Gideon mused. "Was the request from Police Headquarters signed by Nielsen?"

"Yes."

"May I leave the Orlick case like that?" asked Gideon.

"Surely, if that's the way you want it."

"I'd like to send a message to Nielsen, and recommend that he keep an eye on Inglemann Brown in New York," Gideon said.

"I'll be glad to arrange that." Ruthven smiled. "Can I see you around twelve noon for cocktails, Commander? I may have the purser and my first officer with me."

"I'll look forward to it," Gideon said.

He ate the best breakfast he'd had since coming on board. There was no difficulty about making excuses to Allingham, and at half past ten he was taken down to Webb's cabin. Meanwhile he had tried to recall all that he knew about the missing woman: chiefly, that she had been very giggly, doubtless from drink, and that she had been wary of her husband. Wary? Was that the word? Gideon put it out of his mind as he searched the cabin. It carried him back to the days when he had often been the first policeman on the scene of a crime; it was a long time since this experience had come his way. Searching now, he found nothing significant, but when he had finished he stood in the doorway, peering about the cabin, which had not been touched since Webb had reported his wife missing. She could have fallen overboard, or she could have been pushed through a porthole; and this was the most likely porthole. Did murderers ever think like that? He saw the chief steward and the ship's detective looking at him, jealously alert, he suspected, lest he might find something they had missed. He turned to the porthole, which was tightly closed, and the detective, a tall, wiry-looking man with crisp, crinkly gray hair, stepped forward.

"The room steward closed the porthole last night, Mr. Gideon."

"And it's too tight to be opened by finger pressure," the chief steward said. He was a young, very sallow man with deep black eyes.

"The only prints on it were the steward's and Mrs. Webb's," volunteered the detective.

"Has it been opened since the woman was reported missing?" asked Gideon.

"I guess not," said the chief steward.

"Could we have it open?"

Gideon made no comment as he watched the steward use a special tool, rather like a short-handled hammer, to start twisting the holding bolts. They moved with comparatively little trouble. All three men went to the porthole, and studied the smooth sides. Each one seemed to see the obvious at the same time. At the top and the bottom the sides were pocked with rust and with hard salt, dried seawater having left the paintwork crusty and scaly. At each side the surface of hard salt had been rubbed off. Some white paint had flaked too, and something other than paint and rust adhered to it.

Gideon drew back.

The ship's doctor, a burly Irish-American with red hair, was quite positive.

"There is blood and there is skin on that paint, quite enough to indicate that a body was pushed through the porthole." He looked at Gideon as if expecting to be challenged. "And it hasn't been there too long."

"I'm sorry it's a case your courts will have to try," Gideon said to Ruthven later. "If it had been on a British ship Webb could have been sent back for trial at home. Will you talk to Police Headquarters, Captain?"

"I certainly will," Ruthven said, and added grimly: "After that I will talk to Mr. Webb."

Rumors of the missing passenger sped round the ship. Gideon and Kate heard people talking about it. Gideon saw himself being speculatively pointed out, but no one plucked up courage enough to question him outright. He wished it hadn't happened, and that wish had little to do with Mrs. Webb. What little he had seen of Mrs. Webb suggested she had been a brainless little tippler, and he was almost hardened to murder, but it took the edge off the last day, off the Gala Night, even off the discovery that Dirk Orlick was so jealous of his wife that he had savagely attacked Brown.

After the rather forced gaiety of the Gala Dinner and the Last Night Ball, Gideon felt flat when he reached his cabin. Kate looked tired. They did not get to bed until after two o'clock, and packing had to be done before they docked at ten o'clock in the morning. Gideon felt that it was a miserable anticlimax, but that didn't stop him from dropping off to sleep, and sleeping soundly.

Suddenly, in what seemed the middle of the night, there was a banging at the cabin door. Gideon heard it as if from a long way off; heard Kate's quick exclamation:

"What's that?"

Gideon became all at once wide awake. It was nearly daylight, he realized, although the cabin was dark. The knocking at the door continued. He pushed back the bedclothes as Kate sat up and pulled a wrap round her shoulders. He opened the door, in a bad humor, bleary-eyed, dry-mouthed. A tall, handsome, rugged-looking man stood in the passage, grinning at him. He was six feet tall, and solidly built, gray-haired, and scrupulously groomed. His clothes had a characteristically American cut, even his hat, which he held in his hand.

"Hi, George," he said. "Remember me?"

"Kurt Nielsen!" exclaimed Gideon.

"You remember me all right. I came on board with the pilot," Nielsen said, "but I didn't want to wake you too early. George, I hate to say it, but there is a lot of work to do before you can disembark, and my wife wants you and your wife to be home with us for breakfast." He grinned past Gideon. "Don't worry, Mrs. Gideon, I won't invade your privacy right now, but I'm looking forward very much to meeting you." He looked back at Gideon. "How long will you be, George?"

"Half an hour," said Gideon.

"Twenty minutes," said Nielsen, and his eyes laughed. "We hustle in New York."

As he spoke there was a clatter of footsteps along the passage, and before he realized what was about to happen, two men pushed behind Nielsen, each poising cameras; the flashes almost blinded Gideon, coming one after another in quick succession.

Nielsen grinned. "What did I tell you?"

11: Hustle

THERE WAS a curious kind of restrained energy about Nielsen which Gideon remembered from the occasions when they had met in London. It was as if the New York detective believed he could do everything that needed doing in half the time it took others, as if he was unable to hold his thoughts back even if he could restrain his physical movements. Half an hour after he had left the cabin, taking the photographers with him, he was outside it again. Gideon was dressed and ready. Kate had made up lightly and hurriedly and wore a misty-pink housecoat.

"Mrs. Gideon, it's very good to meet you," Nielsen said, and admiration showed in his eyes as he shook hands. "I was serious about your coming to have breakfast with us, if you can hold out for an hour."

"I'm sure I can," Kate said.

"And as it's Sunday morning it's a good time to show you New York without getting caught up in the traffic—do we have traffic problems, George! You don't need to worry about Customs, you'll get the courtesy of the port, I've seen to that. I'll see you, Kate." He took Gideon's arm and led him away—and in the nearest hall there were a dozen newspapermen and more photographers. "I told them you'd spare them five minutes," Nielsen reported, and he gave a curiously one-sided grin. "When they ask you how you like New York, just tell them it's wonderful, and you won't need to say anything more. I'll be around to hold your hand."

Microphones had been placed in a corner of the hall, making this a small-scale press conference, Gideon thought ruefully. The questions came thick and fast, some of them spoken with accents which he found almost incomprehensible.

"Is this your first visit to New York, Commander?" *"Yes."* "First to America?" *"Yes."* "What is the main reason for your visit?" *"Consultations about catching bad men who work both sides of the Atlantic."* Someone laughed, a camera flashed. "Have you come to investigate any special crime, Commander?" *"All crimes are special to me."* There were more laughs, and Nielsen, in a corner opposite Gideon, smiled approvingly. "Do you know anything about the missing passenger?" *"I met her."* "Do you know if it was accident or what?" *"No."* "If it was murder, Commander, would the case be tried in this country or in Great Britain?" *"If you don't know the answer to that, ask Captain Nielsen."* "Is your wife with you, Commander?" *"Yes."* "Is she on vacation?" *"She most certainly is.*" "What hotel will you be staying at, Commander?"

Nielsen called out: "No hotel. They'll be staying with friends at first."

It was all Gideon could do not to show his surprise.

"How do you think crime compares between London and New York, Commander?" *"Both cities seem to do pretty well."* "Do you believe that policemen should be armed?" *"Not English policemen."* "But you do think American policemen should be?" *"I don't think anything about it, I do know that the police in France, Germany, Italy, and a lot of other countries all over the world are armed. There's nothing unusual about armed policemen. In fact it's more unusual for the police not to be armed."* "Did you personally arrest Fadiman, Commander?" *"No."* "Do you believe he killed those women?" *"The jury will decide that."* "How many children do you have, Commander?" *"Six."* "Six!"

"You've had seven minutes and I promised you five," interrupted Nielsen. "O.K., boys, break it up."

"We haven't really started—"

"We'll fix a conference at Centre Street later today or tomorrow," Nielsen promised. "Thank you, everybody. O.K., George." He led the way . . .

They looked into the Webbs' cabin, where Nielsen's men from Homicide were already busy on the familiar routine. "Murder without a body, that's not so hot," a man remarked. There were four of them, and all but one stopped what they were doing to look at Gideon; the other went on taking photographs. There were introductions, smiles, handshakes, before Nielsen led the way to the purser's office, where a small party was assembled, then into a cabin which had been set aside as an office for Nielsen.

"We won't need to be here long," Nielsen declared. "I want to have you free from all questions today, so you can enjoy yourself. I've got some news for you," he went on. "A consignment of fifteen thousand Rite-Time watches disappeared from a truckers' yard at Trenton, New Jersey, two nights ago. In the past week we've had reports of big-scale losses of cigarette lighters, fountain pens, and costume jewelry stolen from a dozen different places."

Gideon frowned.

"What are you thinking?" asked Nielsen.

"Big consignments are stolen every now and again—then there are long periods without any thefts. Right?"

"Right."

Gideon said: "It looks as if there might be a single clearing-house, where the thieves can keep the goods until they are able to ship them overseas, or distribute them. As we get big consignments in England, it looks as if the stuff is held in bulk."

"That's certainly the way it looks," Nielsen agreed.

"Have you put a finger on anyone yet?"

"No, we haven't." Nielsen had a habit of rubbing the thumb and forefinger of his right hand together, as if he were inviting someone to give him something; the movement made a slight rasping noise. "How about Orlick?"

"He must know that. I know he was on board."

"So, if his reason for coming is to get in touch with his associates over here, he may lie low for a few days," Nielsen reasoned. "I can tell you something more about Orlick. He's booked on the *Queen Elizabeth* to return to Southampton—not your trip on her, but the one afterwards, so he won't be in any hurry. What happened to him on board?"

"He ran into trouble because he's jealous of his wife," Gideon said, and passed on all he knew.

Nielsen listened attentively, obviously with some satisfaction. "That could be very helpful."

"I hoped you would think so," Gideon said.

Nielsen looked at him with a curious kind of smile, half affectionate, half jeering.

"How would you play this?"

"I'd do everything I could to make Brown prefer a charge of assault against Orlick. Orlick would have to buy him off, or defend the case. Whichever way he handled it, Orlick would have so much on his mind he might well get careless."

"So I'll have Brown watched," decided Nielsen. "And I'll find out if he can be pushed into making trouble for Orlick." He clapped his hands together, making a loud bang. "George, what else do we have to talk about?"

There were a dozen topics, ranging over the wide field of their mutual interests, including the sabotage. Gideon noticed that on his own home territory, Nielsen appeared to be in absolute command, and he had every detail at his fingertips—names, quantities, dates, everything that could be useful. Liking and respect for the man grew. For the time being the obvious tactics were to allow Nielsen his head, even allowing himself to be pushed in whatever direction Nielsen wanted him to go. It would in all probability be in the right direction.

Just after eight-thirty, there was a tap at the door.

"Who's there?" called Nielsen.

The purser appeared, the expression on his pale, round face inquisitive.

"How are you doing?" he inquired, and before either could answer, he went on: "Captain Ruthven would like you to have coffee with him, if that's all right with you." Obviously it didn't occur to him that it would not be. "We shall be tied up in ten minutes, and half an hour after that you can go ashore, Commander."

There was coffee in Ruthven's stateroom, leave-taking, a brief passport session with the Immigration authorities, a dozen unexpectedly hurried good-bys. Gideon did not see the Allinghams but he knew that Allingham was staying at one of the most exclusive of the new hotels near Central Park. Stewards, officers, passengers were all grouped together in the main hallway, baggage was being unloaded.

"This way," Nielsen said. Hurry, hurry, hurry, he seemed to be saying. "You've got your landing card? . . . Fine." He took Kate's arm. "Don't trip up, ma'am, I want you all in one piece when you meet my wife." They stepped into a huge shed, where a group of uniformed customs officials were standing behind a long desk, dozens of porters were waiting with empty trucks and others were carrying baggage to places allocated beneath the letters of a huge alphabet hanging from steel girders. "In half an hour this place will be bedlam," Nielsen declared. He led the way to the Gideons' seven cases and three small pieces of hand baggage. A customs officer who was obviously of Chinese ancestry came up to them.

He held the Declaration Form which they had filled out on board. Smiling, he stuck a clearance label on each case.

"Kate!" cried Justine Allingham, suddenly emerging from behind a huge pile of luggage. "I hoped we would see you here, isn't it a frightful place? They want us to open *everything*, one of these days I'm sure that Ally himself will burst open, he gets so angry with Customs, but the worst are the East German. My dear, you would never . . ."

They were out of the shed and in a large black car after

fifteen minutes. Overhead was what looked like a huge bridge held up by girders. A line of taxis waited, private cars shone, a few cars rumbled over uneven cobbles, which surprised Gideon as well as Kate. "*Cobbles*," she whispered. Everything here was dark, dingy, littered.

"That's the West Side Highway," Nielsen said. "We're going across town so we won't need to take it now."

A Negro chauffeur closed the door and took the wheel. Gideon felt very warm; much, much warmer than he had felt in London. Sweat was trickling down his face.

"Kurt," he said, "what's this about not going straight to our hotel?"

"What's that?" Kate asked. She was bright-eyed, and flushed with the heat.

"You'll be in your hotel," Nielsen said bluffly. "I didn't want anyone to know which one yet. If I'd told them, you would have newspapermen clamoring after you all day, and you'd get a very bad first impression of New York. Kate, my wife hopes you will be able to visit with her often while you're in New York. We have an apartment near Greenwich Village, and right across the street from us there's your hotel. You'll be nearer Headquarters than you would be uptown. You'll have a pantry, so you can make your own breakfast if you like it that way." Nielsen sat on a seat opposite them in the roomy car. "Now let me tell you where we are and the route we'll take. You're on 50th Street right now, heading east, that's toward England– Don't take any notice if I talk as if you'd never seen a map of New York, that way I won't forget anything. These brownstone houses are about a hundred years old and they're due to come down for a big new project. . . . The streets run east and west, the avenues north and south, and all of them in the downtown area–City center to you–except one or two you'll soon find out about, are one way for traffic. It takes a little time to learn. Right now we're crossing Tenth Avenue."

The Gideons had a bird's-eye glimpse of streets narrower and dirtier than they had expected, and with bumpy road surfaces. Every now and again a glittering modern building, towering very high, made them crane their necks upward. Suddenly they were on Broadway. The streets were almost deserted. There were outsize photographs and posters and mammoth advertising signs, tired-looking street cleaners, some policemen, and a few big fast-moving taxis.

"Times Square," Nielsen announced. "We'll come and look at it again one night in the week. You won't recognize it. This is 42nd Street." Suddenly they pulled up at a corner, Nielsen still talking. "Here is the one place you just have to stop." He opened the door and, bending forward, handed them out. "This is my favorite landmark in New York, 42nd Street and Fifth Avenue . . ."

He kept on, about the New York Public Library, the Empire State Building, the Chrysler Building; but Gideon and Kate hardly heard him as they gazed up and down Fifth Avenue, where the great buildings rose square and spectacular into the blue sky, and only a few taxis and private cars moved along the broad strip of road. Gideon dabbed his forehead.

"The humidity's high today," Nielsen remarked. "I guess we'll go home and cool off." He helped them back into the car, fussing over Gideon as much as he fussed over Kate. "After breakfast we'll take a long drive and you can see everything, but everything."

Soon they were making a turn a long way down Fifth Avenue where the architecture appeared to be rather ordinary. The car pulled up outside a reddish-brown brick building, and as it did so a man came forward.

"I'll look after the car, Captain."

"Thanks, Sam." Nielsen helped Kate out, then led the way down a small, rather gloomy hall, into an elevator only just large enough for the three big people. Nielsen pressed the button marked 14 and they seemed to crawl up. As they stepped out at the fourteenth floor, a door opened and a young woman came forward from an apartment, smiling a welcome. Gideon thought: I wouldn't have expected Nielsen to have a daughter this age. Her hair was fair, touched with gold, and she had light-blue eyes and attractive features set in a long rather narrow face full of expression and character. "Claire," Nielsen said, "I want you to meet Kate and George Gideon—George, I want you to meet my wife."

They were shaking hands.

"Look just as surprised as you want to," Claire Nielsen invited. "Everyone accuses Max of baby snatching, but maybe he's younger than he looks."

"Max?" Gideon echoed, looking surprised at Nielsen. "I thought you were Kurt."

"He's Max in the family," Claire said. She held Kate's hand firmly, scanning her face. "Kate, you and I just have to get along, because Max says that if we don't he'll sue me for divorce." She led the way into a long, cool room with a table set for breakfast; it was not the table nor the room that caught the Gideons' attention, but the fantastic skyline of the southern tip of Manhattan. The sun was still quite low in the east, and shone with startling clarity on the million windows of countless buildings, and on a great bridge sweeping across a shimmering river.

"It's going to be fine," Nielsen said in a rather subdued voice. "They react just the way we hoped they would."

"But it's—it's beautiful," Kate breathed.

"Magnificent," said Gideon.

"Magnificent, yes," agreed Claire. "Most people forget to tell you that New York's one of the most beautiful cities in the world, too." Almost as if in a dream, she went on: "You wait until you see it by night. You have a better view from your hotel rooms—you're ten floors higher."

"How about that drink, honey?" Nielsen reminded her.

Claire busied herself with beers and iced tea, and then showed the Gideons round the homely apartment, taking especial pride in a book-lined room set aside for her husband. The affection between the two was obvious and delightful, and Kate found herself wondering how long they had been married; then with a change of mood, how long it would be before she and George would go to the hotel.

Claire seemed the decisive partner in the home. "Max, you have to take them to their hotel now. It's just across Fifth Avenue," she explained, "not even a block away."

They stood for a few moments longer staring at a great stretch of Manhattan, from the piers in the Hudson where the big ships lay, to the smaller piers near the southern tip where the freighters berthed. The East River looked as if it were made of gold and the southern part of Manhattan Island stretched out before them. As he watched, Gideon thought, I'll never forget this moment; never.

Kate was clutching his arm, and they almost hated to turn away.

In those minutes crime and criminals were wiped out, obliterated in their minds; but in those minutes people who were closely concerned with Rite-Time, with sabotage, and with countless other crimes, were actually within Gideon's range of vision—if only he could have seen through brick and stone.

Among them was Inglemann Brown.

12:

Danger Men

INGLEMANN BROWN was thirty-nine, a medium-built, normally handsome man whose nose was now bandaged and taped, whose lips were swollen and painful, but whose bold brown eyes brooded darkly as he sat back in the taxi with his wife, Elaine. She was tall and rather spare, with long thin legs and arms and a surprisingly thrusting bosom, emphasized by a tight-fitting orange dress. She kept dabbing at the sweat on her forehead. Now and again she glanced at her husband, but she knew that this was not the time to talk to him, sensing that a great deal was passing through his mind that he would not discuss with her. They lived in Greenwich Village, only a quarter of a mile from the Nielsens, in a small luxury apartment building near Washington Square.

As they left the taxi the doorman with a glistening face came forward to open the main door for them—and at the same time, two men traveling in a green Chevrolet passed the entrance to the block. Brown appeared not to notice them, but he knew that the car slowed down a little farther on and stopped, double-parked. Neither of the men got out. Brown stepped into the entrance hall, ignoring Elaine, but she was used to that and it did not worry her. He disappeared, only to reappear more slowly, and peer toward the car. The two men were still there.

"I'll send your baggage up," the doorman said. "Sure glad to have you back, sir. And to have you back, Mis' Brown."

Brown nodded, Elaine smiled, Brown stepped into an elevator and the doors began to close before his wife was safely inside. There had been a time when she had protested at this kind of behavior, but she had lived with him long enough to know that such protests were never worth the trouble. They were whisked up to the eleventh floor. Their penthouse was one floor higher still, and served only by stone steps. Brown went ahead, and when Elaine reached the front door of the penthouse, it was wide open.

Her husband was on the terrace, looking down into the street. The Chevrolet was still there, but now there was only one man in it, and no men were in sight in the street.

The telephone bell rang, startling Elaine, but not surprising Brown.

"Honey," he said, "have the baggage put in the bedroom and don't come in here until I call you." He did not add, "And don't lift the telephone," because he was quite sure she would not; only once had she listened in on a conversation; just once. He lifted the instrument to stop the ringing, waited until the door closed, then sat on the arm of an easy chair.

"Mr. Brown," a man said.

"Speaking."

"Mr. Brown, I'm from the *Daily Post*."

"So."

"I'd like to talk to you, Mr. Brown."

"I've nothing to say to the press."

"I'm coming right up," the man declared and rang off.

Brown put down the receiver, slowly, and stood up. He heard his wife moving about in the bedroom, and the baggage being dumped. He went to the door, not surprised to see her close by, obviously curious, even a little anxious.

"Who was that?"

"A newspaperman. As if we hadn't seen enough of them on the ship."

"What did he want?"

"To ask our impressions of Europe, I guess."

"Ing, don't make a joke of it. What did he want?"

"We'll find out, he's on his way up," Brown told her. "If you stick around you'll hear as much as I do, but leave all the talking to me. *All* of it, honey."

"Ing, will it be about the Orlicks?"

"Nothing else I've done would interest the press."

"You won't—you won't do anything more about that, will you?"

"A guy breaks my nose and pushes my teeth down my throat, so I just forget it because my little wific had a yen for the guy who did it."

"You know that's not true!" Elaine's eyes brightened with anger. "If you sue Orlick, then the whole story will come out. He'll say you kept on molesting his wife, and—" she caught her breath—"and there could be a dozen witnesses!"

"A man isn't molesting a woman by squeezing her hand," Brown said. "If your nose was broken—"

The doorbell rang, across his words, and he gripped

Elaine's arm, and said roughly: "Not a word out of you. Understand? Open the door."

Brown was in the living room when Elaine brought the man in. He was powerfully built, and had a heavy jowl and jaw; there was a curiously lifeless expression in his very dark-blue eyes. It was almost as if a part of him were dead.

"I'm Tony Preston, of the *Post*," the man announced abruptly. "How about this Englishman who beat you up? You going to do anything about it?"

"That's my business," Brown retorted.

"Sure, it is and *I'm* not going to do anything about it. But our readers want to know if you are."

"They'll find out," Brown said sourly.

"Mr. Brown," Preston said, "you're telling me already."

"Ing—" Elaine began, but Brown waved her to silence.

"What am I telling you?" he demanded.

The man who called himself Preston said, without expression: "If you were going to forget what happened, you would say so. How much are you going to try to take Orlick for?"

"I didn't say I was going to claim anything."

"Ten thousand dollars? Twenty thousand?"

Elaine's attention was distracted by baggage being moved outside, but Brown stood staring at the newspaperman who was so poker-faced and whose eyes seemed so dead.

"So it's twenty," he said.

"I'm not after chicken feed," Brown retorted derisively. "There's a hundred grand in this for me if I plan it the right way."

"Ing!"

"So you're after the big money," Preston said flatly. "That's O.K., Mr. Brown, that's what I figured. You'll settle for a hundred thousand."

"Maybe," Brown said.

Elaine's eyes were bright and shining with distress.

"Thanks," said the big man. "I've got all the rest." He did not shake hands, but nodded to Brown and Elaine and turned toward the door. As it closed, Elaine clasped her hands tightly in front of her, stared at her husband, but did not speak.

"I know what I'm doing," he said roughly. "That limey's going to pay for my nose."

The man who had called himself Preston from the *Daily Post* walked along to the green Chevrolet without looking round at the apartment house he had just left. The man in the car started the engine. Neither of them spoke more than odd words as he drove across town to Tenth Avenue, then turned north, passing the piers, the big ships, the *Queen Elizabeth,* warehouses, gas stations, and heavy trucks. At Fiftieth Street, the driver pulled in at a gas station, and as the attendant came up, Preston got out of the car and went to a telephone booth. He put in a dime and dialed a Riverside number. A man answered quickly.

"This is Danny Silvermann."

"Danny," the big man said flatly, "Brown's after the dough in a big way."

After a pause, Danny Silvermann asked: "You sure?"

"I'm sure."

"How big?"

"He'll probably start at a quarter of a million, and be ready to settle for a hundred grand. You know what that will mean."

"Yes," agreed Silvermann softly. "I know. It means Orlick will be big news from now on. It means the confidential magazines will be after him and it means the police will take a close interest. And maybe they're plenty interested already."

"You still think Orlick might sing?"

"He came over here because he was too greedy, and that made him a problem. Now there's a chance that if the police press him hard enough, he'll sing, so that makes him a double problem which would cause us a lot of trouble. We have to make sure he can't do it." Silvermann paused, and when he spoke again his voice was pitched on a lower key. "I didn't want him over here anyway, the Scotland Yard cops have been too interested in the London end already. We've got to put him away. You with me, Mense?"

"I'm with you," said Mense, who had called himself Preston. "There's one possibility we have to consider."

"Name it."

"We could wait until the next shipment is out of New York on the *Hempen.*"

Mense shifted his weight from one foot to the other. "We can't afford to wait," he said flatly. "Orlick knows us, he can sing about us; if the police start talking to him, he might crack soon. If we don't want to close down altogether we've got to put Orlick away. This doesn't have to affect the *Hempen,* we've got the first officer where we want him. We can't wait, Danny."

"I guess not," Danny said, with a sigh. "It's gone too far too fast. O.K., Mense."

"You talk to Orlick," Mense said. "Have him near Joey's at three o'clock. I'll fix the rest."

Danny Silvermann hesitated, before saying more briskly: "I'll talk to him. Don't worry."

13:

Fatal Rendezvous

KITTY ORLICK watched her husband as he stood at the window of the New York Hilton. Between them and the great highway which ran alongside the Hudson River were a myriad houses, all from this point of view seeming dark and squat. The river was dotted with shipping. The high banks of the river on the New Jersey side looked like huge slices of chocolate cake. They could see the S.S. *Fifty States,* a wisp of steam drifting out of its big red funnel.

Kitty did not understand what had happened to Dirk. Even now, she could picture the way he had suddenly launched himself across the dance floor in the Ocean Night Club in the early hours of the morning—only yesterday morning. She had always known that he had disapproved of her low-cut sun dresses, yet she had bought three cocktail gowns which were nearly topless, just for the thrill. She had *had* to wear them on the ship. When Dirk had told her he didn't want her to wear a particular sun dress again, she hadn't given a thought to the strapless cocktail gowns.

She well remembered Inglemann Brown's dancing with her. From the time of their first meeting, he had not been able to keep his hands to himself, but there hadn't been any *harm* in it. Everything would probably have been all right if the band hadn't suddenly started that old-fashioned waltz, and if Inglemann hadn't begun swinging her round so that she was helpless, partly with laughter, partly because of the roll of the ship. She hadn't felt the slightest warning when the strapless dress suddenly acted up to its name and ceased to cover her. Inglemann had been laughing. Suddenly Dirk had been in front of them, smashing his fists into Inglemann's face and stomach. Women had screamed, it had taken three men to drag Dirk off Inglemann. Elaine Brown, who always kept her head, had snatched a wrap from a chair, draped it round Kitty's shoulders and breast, and hustled her out of the room. They had been together in the Orlicks' sun-deck cabin when Orlick had come back, his knuckles bleeding, his face gray-white, his eyes burning.

"Get out," he had said to Elaine.

"Just so long as you understand there will be a steward at the door, and if you so much as lay a hand on Kitty the steward will raise the alarm," Elaine had said.

Even when she had gone, Kitty had expected Dirk to strike her, for his eyes still blazed with fury in a way she had never even glimpsed before. Suddenly, he had leaped at her, and she had raised her hands to defend herself, but all he had done was snatch at the top of the dress with both hands and pull it until it ripped, then tear it across and across and across, flinging the pieces all about the cabin. Violently he had swung round to the small wardrobe where she kept her clothes, pulled out the other two dresses and torn them to shreds. Looming over her, he had muttered in a voice so distorted she could hardly distinguish the words:

"Cover up in future. Understand? Cover up when other men are around."

Since then he had spoken to her only in short, jerky sentences. "Pass this, do that, go there, pack my things." There had been little more than a flow of brusque instructions. She had been so frightened by his outburst of rage that she had obeyed, and obeying had become almost automatic; but she was beginning to feel more herself, and rebellious. Most of all she resented coming straight here from the ship when she had wanted to get a look at New York, the wonder city she couldn't wait to investigate. But Dirk had made her unpack. He had eventually helped a little, and then had led her to this window and stared out.

He was tall and very handsome.

She said, quietly: "Dirk, are you feeling all right?"

He didn't answer.

"Dirk, are you–"

"Yes," he barked. "I'm O.K."

"Dirk–"

"Do you have to keep talking?"

Kitty kept her temper with a great effort.

"Dirk, I didn't know what he was going to do. I'm not interested in any man but you."

He turned to look at her, and she saw the way his lips twisted and quivered, but she did not back away.

"You're interested in any man who can get his hands on you, and you know it."

"I'm *not,* Dirk."

"When I think of the money I've spent on you—"

That was the moment when resentment and exasperation overcame all fears. She stepped toward him, her voice pitched high, her beautiful eyes flashing.

"Don't talk to me like that! I'm worth the money, every penny of it. And I'm your wife, not your servant or your slave. If I want to dance with another man I will, and that's going to be all right with you as well as all right with me!"

His eyes seemed to burn. He raised his hands, the fingers crooked, as if he would bury them in her neck.

"Don't lay a hand on me!" she cried. "Just you do that, and I'll walk out on you, New York or no New York. *Don't lay a hand on me.*" In fact his hands were so close to her that she could almost feel them, could see that they were trembling. Fear was back in her again, but it was different now; an angry fear. "Why do you want to ruin everything?" she demanded, with a break in her voice. "Everything was so wonderful, this was going to be a second honeymoon, and you've spoiled it. That's what you've done, you've absolutely spoiled it."

He stood there, hands outstretched, almost touching her, staring with a changing light in his eyes. She saw his lips quivering, felt her own quivering, too, and knew that tears were brimming in her eyes.

"We ought to be having the most wonderful time, not quarreling. I don't care if I never see Ingy Brown again. *I* can't help it if I've got a figure that makes men want me—why, you ought to be bloody glad I am yours and no one else's, no one at all—Dirk!" she cried. "Dirk!"

But even as he grabbed her she sensed that it was no longer in rage but in flaming desire, and she knew that whatever might happen in the future, this quarrel was over. Suddenly she was wildly, gloriously happy. They were not two people but one again, sharing an ecstasy which outshone everything that had happened between them in the past.

They were lying on his bed, still exhausted, when the telephone bell rang. Kitty was dozing. Dirk was breathing so heavily that he seemed to be asleep. The bell kept on ringing, until at last Kitty stirred herself, and wriggled across him. She lifted the instrument.

"Hallo?"

"Is Mr. Orlick there?" a man asked.

"Well, he–"

"Ask who it is," Dirk whispered. His arm pressed her down against him as she struggled with the telephone.

"Who is that speaking?" the man asked.

"This is Mrs. Orlick."

"Is Dirk Orlick in?"

"Who is that, please?"

There was a pause, before the man said with a laugh in his voice: "What's the right time?"

"Who?"

"What did he say?"

"He wants to know the time. The right time."

"Gimme," said Orlick. He twisted round, their bodies sticky with perspiration, and wrested the instrument from his wife. "Dirk Orlick speaking."

The man sounded delighted. "Hi, Dirk, how are you? It's real good to have you in New York."

"Who is speaking?"

"I'm Danny, you know me. Listen, Dirk," Danny Silvermann

went on before Dirk could speak. "We need to talk soon, and we can't talk over the telephone. Why don't you come and see me right now?"

Orlick thought, If this is the way they want it, I can play it their way.

"Where do I come?" he demanded.

"You got a pencil?"

"Yes." There was a small note pad and pencil on the table between the two beds. "I'm ready."

"O.K., then, Dirk, you write this down. Take a cab to 49th Street and Tenth Avenue . . . You got that? . . . Sure, 49th and Tenth. Get off at the Gulf gas station on the east side of Tenth and 49th Street, then go to 50th and walk half a block."

Orlick, scribbling, broke in sharply: "What's all this mystery about, Danny?"

"Mystery? There's no mystery. I want to show you around the docks, and show you how we operate. Sunday's a good day for that, there aren't so many trucks around."

"How shall I recognize you?" asked Orlick.

Danny said: "I'll be on the dot." He rang off, and because Dirk's wrist was raised awkwardly, Kitty took the instrument and placed it on the cradle. She twisted round, so that she was lying full length on him, face to face, and looked into his gray eyes. She could see that he was very preoccupied, and that what had happened between them so short a time ago was nearly forgotten. She kissed him slowly, fully, pressing harder and harder, stirring only a slight response. She wriggled off the bed.

"Who was that?"

"A business colleague."

"You didn't sound as if you liked him."

"He was showing me how clever he was."

"Why didn't you show him how clever you are?"

"Give me time," Orlick said. He smiled slowly, meaningly. "Just a little time. We're going to take a cab at a quarter to three o'clock, so that gives us an hour and a half. Do you think you can be dressed as soon as that?"

Kitty hesitated. Then her lips curved and there was a wicked gleam in her eyes.

"I don't have any dresses," she said. "They were all damaged in a tornado."

"You can buy yourself a hundred dresses, so long as they have high necks," Dirk growled. He was stirred enough to give her a fierce kiss, then he drew his face away and sprang toward the bathroom.

She thought happily. It's going to be all right. It's going to be wonderful.

And she thought what a beautiful body he had.

Kitty wore a lightweight cotton dress, primose yellow, high at the neck and with short sleeves. It made her look almost demure. It was loose about the bust, too, and if Dirk had ordered it himself, it could not have been more to his taste. It was a quarter to three when they left their room, and they noticed a man coming along a passage as they waited for the elevator, but didn't give him a thought. The car arrived and they stepped inside.

Even before they reached the main floor, the man they had seen was opening the door of their room with a pick-lock. . . .

Knowing nothing of the intruder or the search he made, the Orlicks turned left out of the drive-in of the hotel. They touched hands, but their fingers were too hot and sticky, and slowly fell apart. They walked along, gaping up at the mammoth new buildings of glass and cement and shimmer. The

Sixth Avenue traffic, surging northward as lights turned green, appeared like a moving solid mass across the road; it was hard to believe that it had been so nearly deserted that morning.

"The traffic's very fast," Kitty remarked.

"Stop-and-start stuff, that's all."

"Will you hire a drive-yourself car, Dirk?"

"Don't you think I could drive in this?"

"I know you could." Soon they crossed another street, and Kitty said: "The shops aren't very nice in this part, are they?"

"They're going to be pulled down," Dirk said, as if no secret of New York was hidden from him. "We'll walk as far as Central Park—see those trees straight ahead?—and get a cab."

There was a kind of magic in the air, and as they drew near the park they saw the skyline on either side, half hidden by the heavy foliage of the trees. Their tendency was to dawdle, and they strolled for a few minutes along Central Park South, the luxury of some of the buildings and the quality of the city fascinating both of them.

A taxi, huge and yellow, drew up outside a hotel.

"That's for us," Orlick said.

A moment later they climbed into the refrigerated air of the yellow cab.

"Where to?" the driver inquired.

Orlick said: "Er—Tenth Avenue at 49th Street."

"Tenth at Forty-nine," the driver said.

Soon they were away from the park, the beauty and the crowds, being driven along narrow streets until they came upon another wide avenue with traffic going all one way. On the far side, beneath what looked like a fantastically long bridge, were the piers, and beyond these they could see the water of the Hudson, calm and shimmering. On this side of the road there were warehouses, empty parking lots, gas stations; everything was rough, half derelict, almost sinister. One station selling Gulf was near a corner. They got out, Orlick paid off the driver, and they went to the corner where a sign pointed: W. 50th St.

They turned along this, past blank warehouse walls, huge closed doors, uneven cobbles in the approaches. The dreariness and the emptiness made the street almost eerie.

Orlick concealed his disquiet from Kitty but wished he had never brought her here.

The street was deserted except for a man on the other side. Some old cars were parked at either curb, and one was double-parked halfway along the block. A car passed, and pulled into a parking space; in it were a man and a woman. Yet another car, a sky-blue Chevrolet, was double-parked just beyond this, with a colored man at the wheel.

As the Orlicks drew level, the colored man started the engine.

As the Orlicks neared the corner, the man and woman got out of the car that had just been parked, and stared after them. The lights at the corner were red, permitting the pedestrians to cross, but one thing puzzled Orlick: the car just behind him and Kitty was revving its engine. It snorted, as if the driver was about to make a racing start.

Orlick glanced back as he stepped into the street.

He saw the car hurtling toward him. He saw the wheels, turning his way. He thrust Kitty to one side, and heard her scream. He realized exactly what was about to happen and leaped forward desperately, but he was too late. The sky-blue monster struck him, and he felt the impact and the awful pain. He was flung into the air twenty feet along the sidewalk. As

Kitty Orlick stood in dazed shock, unmoving, tiny red spots appeared on her primrose yellow dress.

Danny Silvermann stood by the window of a motel room on Eighth Avenue, watching the stream of traffic. A dozen green Chevrolets appeared to pass every minute, but he had been watching for a long time before one slowed down, and turned into a parking lot next door. Mense got out of it. He locked the door of the car with great deliberation, then walked from the parking lot toward the motel drive-in. Five minutes later he was at the door of the room, and Silvermann let him in.

Silvermann was a very tall, thin man, with full lips and big bloodshot eyes with drooping lids. His face was vaguely like a starving bloodhound's. When he spoke, it was with a drawl which suggested he was too lazy to form his words or sentences properly.

Bourbon and ice in a bucket stood on a low table. Silvermann poured out two drinks, without adding water. Mense drank his in one gulp. Draining the glass, he held it out for a refill. The two men made a strange contrast, Danny lean, narrow-hipped, immaculate and quick-moving, Mense big, stolid and cumbersome.

He said: "Why the hell did he bring his wife?"

"Why didn't you fix his wife?" Silvermann drawled, but his eyes were angry.

"He was too quick. He pushed her away," Mense said. "Now she's making plenty of trouble. The cops have booked the driver. They haven't booked any of the witnesses yet, but they might if Orlick's wife keeps up the pressure."

"Tell me all about our witnesses, boy."

"I had three—the Bartolls behind the Orlicks and Matson

on the other side of the street. They were all O.K." There was no life in Mense's voice. "They were planted to swear it was an accident, and they swore it. But Orlick's wife is a hellcat, and she could wear the cops down, saying it was murder."

"Think she could know a thing about her husband's business?" Silvermann asked.

"I guess she doesn't. If she did, your Buffalo office would have had a call from the police already," Mense said. "I don't believe Orlick would have talked to her or have put anything on paper about us. I sent Matson to his room at the Hilton before there was any trouble. There was nothing there to tell the cops a thing."

"That's good," Silvermann approved.

"There's one other guy we can't trust. Cordova."

"Cordova, in London." Mense nodded, as if in full agreement.

"Mense," said Silvermann, "we told Darkie what to do in London if there was an emergency. We can trust Darkie. I called him this morning, boy. He won't lose any time. He told me that Orlick and Cordova didn't have anything in the records about us, they were both as careful as we told them to be. When Cordova is out of the way we won't need to worry."

"The English connection was very profitable," Mense said, almost regretfully.

"The day Orlick began to get greedy, that was the day it began to break up," Silvermann said. "He shouldn't have come to New York."

"Maybe he didn't know what would happen to him," Mense remarked without a change of expression.

"I was against him coming, but he wouldn't be put off. It

was his own fault," Silvermann complained. "When he started that trouble with Brown it was curtains—and it's curtains for Cordova, too."

"You sure Darkie will get it over with quick?"

"He'll be quick."

"Then all we've got to worry about is the Orlick dame," Mense said. "It's O.K. if she knows nothing and if she stops making trouble." He paused. "But maybe it's not O.K." He gave the impression that he was trying to think about too many things and finding it laborious; his mind moved slowly when coping with any new or unfamiliar situation. "You want to know something?"

"What's on your mind now?" Silvermann was almost irritable.

"I've just realized it," Mense said. "She saw me sitting in the car."

"She *saw* you?" Silvermann's voice sharpened for once.

"That's right. I remember her looking across at me."

"You shouldn't have been there! My God, she could identify you!"

"I had to make sure the junkie got Orlick," Mense interrupted. His eyes looked big, almost black, brooding. "So it was a mistake but the Orlick dame saw me. Right?"

"So she mustn't be able to point a finger at you," Silvermann said softly. "But we've got to be careful, Mense. If she's telling the police it was murder, and something happens to her—" He broke off.

"Maybe she wouldn't recognize me again," Mense said. "And maybe the cops think she's dreaming it up. We mustn't do anything too soon, that's for sure."

Silvermann said little.

Each man seemed shocked by this new realization, and when Mense left there was disquiet in each of them. Alone, Silvermann lowered himself into a deep club chair, poured himself some whisky on the rocks, sipped, and considered the situation. This job had seemed simple and straightforward, and, like Mense, he had welcomed the opportunity to finish with Orlick; but from the moment they had decided to act quickly there had been mistake after mistake.

Who would have dreamed that the fool would take his wife along?

It wasn't so surprising, Silvermann admitted to himself. In a way, it could have been an advantage. If both the Orlicks had been killed there would have been no trouble at all; but both the Orlicks had not been killed, and the living wife now constituted a dangerous problem, as well as the almost certain probability that the police would investigate Orlick's death as a possible case of murder.

Silvermann did not blink at facts.

He had run the Rite-Time operation on a shoestring for years. There were himself, Mense, and four other men, just enough for the routine of the thefts and shipping, but not enough for an emergency. It was no use telling himself that everything would have been fine if Orlick had stayed on the other side of the Atlantic; nothing would have kept the man away.

He recalled everything he knew about Orlick and Cordova—every detail of a report which Darkie, who worked for the Orlova Watch Company in London, had made. At one time Darkie had operated a small inquiry agency here in New York but after some trouble with a blackmail case, his license had been revoked. He was an uncouth-looking man with great perspicacity and cunning and a surprising knowledge of the frailty of human nature.

Darkie had screened the Orlicks before the business association had started.

Orlick had been an astute fence in watches and jewelry for years, working in a small importing-exporting business in the East End of London. Cordova had been in shipping. Both were known to be ruthless, both had worked their way up, Orlick from a working-class home, Cordova from the slums.

Orlick had been the leader, a good organizer and businessman.

Silvermann could almost see a paragraph in the report.

"Orlick's going steady with a brown-eyed bosomy beauty, Kitty Wallis. She was nothing when he picked her up, but he put her through a model training school, to give her poise and polish. College they called it, he wants his wife to be a real lady! He's stuck on her and maybe he's stuck with her. Looks after the girl's ma, he's free with the buck where the girl's concerned. Always wants to better himself, Orlick does, and he's always looking for the main chance. Cordova's a pimp, but a clever pimp."

The truth, Silvermann admitted, was that he had been desperately anxious to find out if the man Brown intended to cause trouble, and only he or Mense could have done that, and Mense had. He or Mense should have killed the Orlicks themselves, not used a junkie and underlings as witnesses. They had taken success for granted. It had seemed so easy to fix the accident, and all *would* have gone well but for Kitty Orlick. With a sickening feeling he realized that she would have to be killed, that anyone who could identify him or Mense would have to die. The killing of Orlick had started a chain. There was one good thing, he wouldn't need to act himself. Mense would kill human beings as if they were flies; the trouble would be to make sure he didn't strike again without taking every conceivable precaution.

There were Kitty Orlick, Cordova—and there was Marcus Davo, the first mate of the S.S. *Hempen,* who knew Mense well. Three people had to die if Mense and he were to be safe.

In his heart Danny Silvermann knew that he was already on a slippery slope; staging the accident had been a mistake, whether he and Mense were caught for one murder or for four didn't matter. They could not reasonably hope to get away with one; they *might* get away with four.

14:

News from Home

THE CHARMING apartment where the Gideons were to stay had one small window from which several bridges could be seen and another with, unbelievably, a better view than the Nielsens'. There was one bedroom, a tiny but fully equipped kitchen, a sumptuous bathroom; everything was so spick and span that it seemed new. The big living room, with its table and set of dining chairs at one end, was furnished throughout in contemporary Scandinavian style; angular, a little severe, but extremely comfortable.

"You don't have to stay here all the time," Claire Nielsen said. "But I think you might prefer it to a bigger hotel, Kate."

"I'm quite sure I will." There was a glow of contentment in Kate's eyes.

Nielsen said: "It's three o'clock, why don't you take it easy for a couple of hours, and allow George to look through the documents I've got for him?" There was a large yellow envelope on the dining table. "How about meeting again at half past five for cocktails, then we can have dinner some place."

"I'd love that," Kate said. She saw the Nielsens to the door, closed it on Nielsen's "Take it easy now," and saw Gideon pick up the large envelope and step with it toward the window. She joined him. It was useless to suggest that he should leave the working papers until the morning, and it was good to see that the view still fascinated him. All New York did; she could tell that. They had been driven round by Nielsen since ten o'clock, her mind reeling with the names of places, from the Bronx to Brooklyn to Queens, the Triboro Bridge and the Franklin D. Roosevelt Drive—names she had heard of but which had never registered on her mind. As the day had worn on, the traffic had grown heavier, until in the last hour there had been a surging sea of cars hurtling along the broad one-way avenues at alarming speed.

"What are you going to do?" Gideon asked.

"I think I'll look at the newspaper," Kate said, and picked up a mass of newsprint, the Sunday *New York Times*. She gave a helpless little laugh. "It doesn't make sense, does it, there's so much of it, and on such a huge scale—" She broke off, as Gideon grinned at her. "I know, I know, we've said it all before. Why don't you sit in that chair with your feet up, and I'll sit on the bed and look through this."

"Good idea," Gideon agreed.

He was in fact reluctant to open the envelope, which was very heavy. He was slowly coming out of the pleasant and almost lethargic atmosphere of shipboard life, when nothing had really worried or preoccupied him; even yesterday's incidents had not gone very deep. But he had to take the plunge, and so at last he ripped open the cellulose tape which double-sealed the envelope and shook the contents onto the polished table. There were half a dozen airmail letters, some from the Yard, some from the family. There were two flimsy airmail copies of the London *Daily Telegraph*, several reports obviously prepared for him by Nielsen or Nielsen's department. Two of the airmail letters had Lemaitre's copper-plate handwriting, and these brought him back with a bump to Lemaitre's problems and the Great Post Office Robbery. Better get it over. He slit open the first of Lemaitre's letters, when suddenly Kate appeared in the doorway, the newspaper in her hand.

"George!"

She was excited, not alarmed.

"Now what?"

"I can hardly believe—" she began, and padded across to him in her stockinged feet, holding out part of the newspaper. Gideon looked down at it and saw exactly the same pictures that had been in the *SunPic* the previous Sunday, only the headlines were different. Kate was half laughing. "Everybody will know us!"

"Almost everybody," reasoned Gideon, not displeased. "The Lord knows what the picture they took of me this morning will be like. Rather sit in here?"

"No," said Kate. "There wouldn't be room to spread the newspapers out. The advertisements are wonderful, whole pages of them." She went off, still looking at the page of photographs.

Lemaitre's first letter read:

Hurried note to tell you 15,000 *Rite-Times,* 5,000 cigarette lighters, 10,000 sets costume jewelry and 3,500 Fountain Pens (Parqué) discovered in Tejeens Warehouse, London Central Docks. Whole shipment came off *Maruna,* 6,000 ton freighter registered

Liberia, owned by Seven Seas Shipping Company of Canada, chartered by Trans-Ana Line, not sure where she called *en route* but Bills of Lading (etc. to follow) appeared in order from Dar es Salaam but we're checking. How's tricks?

Lem

Gideon's spirits rose; this was exactly what he needed for discussion with Nielsen tomorrow, and suggested there might be the possibility of quick results. It was seldom that he felt more on top of the world. He opened Lemaitre's letter, dated the previous Thursday:

Fadiman hearing went without a hitch all straightforward, committed for trial Old Bailey, probably mid-November, only other development is that the Fadiman daughter has been taken to hospital—hasn't spoken a word since her father's arrest.

Lem

P.S. *G.P.O. N.B.G. so far*

In spite of himself Gideon snorted; at least Lem seemed in high spirits.

It was sad about that child . . .

Miller had sent a full report of the second Fadiman hearing, with some newspaper cuttings. There were a few documents which Gideon should have signed before he left, dealing with outstanding charges; he signed them. That was all the business. The letters were from Penelope and Prudence, lively, chatty, happy. He grunted as he got up and took them in to Kate, planning to take her by surprise. She was lying on one side, fast asleep, the papers spread out, some of them scattered on the floor. He crept back to the armchair and looked through the copies of Thursday's and Friday's *Daily Telegraph.* The Great Post Office Robbery still held the front-page headlines, but reading between the lines he knew that the newspapers as well as Lem felt that there was little hope of immediate progress. Half a million pounds mustn't be allowed to disappear. He sat back, frowning, because he knew only the barest details and there simply wasn't a thing he could do.

By half past five they were ready for the Nielsens, Kate, refreshed and eager for another sortie into New York, whatever the heat and humidity.

At twenty-five to six, Nielsen came to the front door, looking very different from his relaxed manner earlier in the day.

"Kate, I'm sorry," he said, "I'm going to have to take George away for a couple of hours. We'll be back in time for dinner. Claire says will you visit with her or would you rather she came to you?"

Kate looked at Gideon and thought, The pressure's back already, the holiday's over, but there was hardly regret, simply resignation and acceptance. She saw the change in her husband's expression, the hardening of his eyes. Touching his hand, she said:

"I'll go to Claire. Do you need anything, George?"

"No," he said. " 'By, dear." He strode to the lift, the door of which was being held open by a policeman. It was as if he had walked out of her life. As the doors closed behind them, Gideon asked: "What is it?"

"Orlick's dead."

The breath hissed between Gideon's teeth.

"We're going up to the precinct," Nielsen went on. "I only know the bare facts—the 'watch Orlick' request finally got around." He didn't add "too late" but Gideon could imagine the words on his lips.

A police car, with two men waiting by it in a far from casual way, was outside the hotel. Already twenty or thirty people were standing and watching. As the door closed on Nielsen and Gideon, the car's siren started wailing. A sea of blank faces twisted to watch their progress. Once they turned into Sixth Avenue the traffic stopped and most of it pulled to one side to give them a free run. Red lights or green, the driver took no notice. Nor did Nielsen. In short, laconic sentences he told Gideon all he knew, and by the time he had finished the car had turned into 42nd Street and then along to Tenth Avenue. At 50th Street they were slowed down by a flashing light which indicated a police barricade. A few cars were drawn up, and a surprising number of people had gathered about the gloomy street and the marked-off area.

"We don't have to get out," Nielsen said. "It happened at three o'clock. The precinct has taken all the measurements and done everything you'd expect them to do in an auto accident. If I'd known earlier—" Nielsen broke off. Gideon guessed what he was feeling, and knew what he himself would have felt had this happened in London with Nielsen there. "You can see the sand over the blood." Nielsen pointed to brown patches on the street. "There wasn't much of him left. O.K.," he nodded briefly and officially to the police driver and their car started up again. To Gideon, Nielsen went on:

"The driver was a junkie. Swears that Orlick stepped right in front of him. Three eyewitnesses say the same thing. Mrs. Orlick says it didn't happen that way." They were driving past the blank wall of what looked like a theater, judging from the huge posters outside it: *The Little Lemmy Show.* It looked empty, almost derelict. So did the street. They crossed another avenue. Halfway along the next block was a concrete building, bright as a new pin, with police cars lined up, and two or three uniformed men and two plainclothes men standing outside; what was there about so many plainclothes men which made it obvious they were detectives? Gideon wondered. The entrance was small, with bare passages leading from it. Nielsen led the way up a flight of steep steps to a wide landing, then into a big room where two uniformed men by a desk were talking to a tall, shaking, gangling Negro. In a far corner two men and one woman were sitting on a bench, the woman chewing, two of the men smoking.

"I tell you I didn't see that man, I jus' didn't see him," the Negro was saying tonelessly.

Nielsen moved across the room, with its stark walls and yellow-stained wood and its air of bleak newness. A door in the corner opened and a plainclothes detective—unnoticeable, even insignificant in comparison with the height of the Negro—came in. He looked tired and possibly older than he was, what little hair he had being thin and white. He barred their entrance to the room beyond.

"The widow's in there," he said. "Want to talk to me first?"

"Yes," said Nielsen.

They went back across the room and into a small, empty office.

"The junkie's still saying he didn't see Orlick. The two men and the woman are witnesses picked up off the street. They say they were waiting for the lights to change," the nearly bald man reported tersely. "One man was across the street, the couple were behind the Orlicks. There was another car with a driver in the street when it happened, but it went off before we reached the scene."

"Any reason to doubt these three?" asked Nielsen. Before the other could answer, he went on: "Commander Gideon, I want you to meet Lieutenant Sabini, who takes good care of this precinct."

Sabini smiled, and shook hands.

"You get your picture in the paper so often I didn't need to ask who you were! I've had five messages from prowl cars saying you're on the way, Commander. You're that well known already." He went on without a change in tone to a completely different subject. "No, there's no reason to doubt the witnesses if it wasn't for Orlick's wife. She says they're lying."

"How is she?" asked Gideon.

"The doctor says she's in shock, but you wouldn't know it. You'd think she was made of ice. Captain, why don't we have them all in my office together and let them shout at each other? Maybe that way we'd find out the truth."

Nielsen said: "Sure." He looked at Gideon. "George, our ways in New York and your ways in London aren't always the same."

Gideon grinned. "I'll just stand and look on," he promised.

The tall Negro was saying exactly what he had said when Gideon and Nielsen had first stepped into the office. "I tell you I didn't see that man, I just didn't see him." It was like a phonograph which had stuck. The shaking was the same, too, it was almost as if the man's whole body was reacting to some inaudible music. The two policemen took no notice of him. Sabini and Nielsen ignored the two men and the woman and Sabini pushed open the door of his office, and stood aside for the other two to go in. A plump middle-aged woman was at a table. Kitty Orlick was sitting in a corner, a glass of water by her side. She was stiff as if her body had been frozen. Her eyes, so beautiful that even Kate had remarked on them, seemed to have been frozen, too, in a cold brilliance. She looked at the men but didn't speak. Gideon had the disturbing impression that she was twenty years older than she had been on the ship.

On that first day or two she had been so happy.

"Mrs. Orlick, this is Commander Gideon from Scotland Yard, London, England, and Captain Nielsen from Police Headquarters, New York City," Sabini declared. "So do you want any more telling that we're taking this accident seriously?"

Kitty looked at Gideon. When she spoke it was as if she had difficulty in opening her lips, and the words dropped out in icy little syllables.

"It was not an accident. My husband was murdered. Those people are lying."

Nielsen said: "How about saying that to their faces?"

"If you give me the chance, I will."

Sabini seemed to stare at her for a long time, and Gideon thought he read compassion in the man's attitude. Then Sabini simply turned, opened the door, said: "Come in, folks," and held the door open. The middle-aged woman had taken no notice of any of this, but still sat with her back to the room, reading some documents. The two men were just men, with nothing special about them; one was without a jacket and wore a short-sleeved green shirt, the other one wore an ill-fitting biscuit-colored suit. The woman had frizzy black hair and beautifully shaped lips and a cast in one bold brown eye. She wore a sleeveless dress of pale mauve, and the tops of her white arms were huge.

"When are we going to get out of here?" That was the man with the suit, sallow-faced, tired, resentful.

"When we've finished with you," Sabini rasped.

"We just happened to see an auto accident, and we opened our big mouths. Why are you holding us?"

Sabini said: "I know how you feel, but the man who was killed was a guest in our country, so we have to pay a proper respect. Where were you when it happened?"

"We were—"

"Never mind your friend. Tell us about you."

"I was on the north side of West 50th Street, waiting for that car to go by. It had the lights. The guy in the accident stepped straight off the sidewalk onto the road, the driver didn't have a chance to swerve or avoid him in any way."

"That's right," the woman confirmed.

"That's how it happened," the second man declared. "I see it from behind the guy."

"They're lying," Kitty Orlick said coldly. "Those two weren't near the curb. They were further away, behind me. The lights were red, not green. That car shouldn't have come along. It was almost on the pavement."

"She means *sidewalk,*" Sabini whispered.

"My husband looked round and then pushed me out of the way. If he hadn't, I would have been hit too. We would have made sure before crossing because we were nervous of the traffic."

"You see," the first spokesman of the witnesses said. "They were nervous."

"They couldn't see straight," the woman half-sneered.

Kitty Orlick looked at Gideon, and said in a flat, emotionless voice: "They're all lying. You've got to prove that."

"If it can be proved, we'll prove it," Nielsen said. "O.K., I'll see you in a minute." Sabini held the door open again and the witnesses trooped out, defiant and apparently resentful. The door slid to as Nielsen caught Gideon's attention. His nod toward Kitty conveyed an obvious invitation for Gideon to speak to her.

"Mrs. Orlick," Gideon said, "I can't tell you how sorry I am."

"Being sorry won't get my husband back."

"Lying about how he was killed won't either."

For the first time her eyes flashed.

"I've told you the truth—all of it. If you won't believe me, how do you expect these American police to?"

Gideon felt almost convinced that she was telling the truth as she remembered it; no one, hearing such passion, could believe she was lying.

"Why should anyone want to kill your husband?" he demanded.

"I don't know. I only know the evidence is false."

"Why were you in this part of town?" Nielsen asked. "You're a long way from your hotel."

"Dirk had a telephone call from a man called Danny," Kitty explained. "He said he was a business associate."

"What kind of business?"

"I don't know."

"That's hard to believe," Gideon said.

"It's true all the same. He always said a man should keep his work and his wife apart; if more people did that there would be fewer broken marriages."

"Yet he brought you on this business trip to New York," Gideon objected. "And he took you out with him today to meet a business associate."

"I—I didn't want to stay alone on the first day, and he—well, we'd had a quarrel, and—and patched it up."

"What did you quarrel about?"

Kitty didn't answer.

"Why did he attack the man Brown on the ship?" Gideon demanded.

"That's got nothing to do with this!"

"It could have a lot to do with it," said Gideon quietly. "Your husband attacked Brown as if he wanted to kill him. The witnesses in the ship's night club didn't lie and they all said the same thing, that if two men hadn't pulled your husband off Brown, he would have killed him. Did you know Brown, Mrs. Orlick? If you seriously think this was murder, not an accident, do you think it had anything to do with Brown?"

Everything he said and the way he said it was calculated to make Kitty Orlick break down; it might seem cruel, but in the long run it was best. He succeeded, without being sure that he had learned what he really needed to know. The ice in her eyes melted and the ice in her body, too. The tears began to fall, her legs crumpled up, and she started to cry in deep racking sobs. The woman at the table stood up immediately and crossed toward her, officially comforting. Sabini smoothed his sparse hair.

"It's one hell of a problem," he declared. "All she's got is a fancy hotel room with all her husband's clothes around her. My God, what's she going to do?" He looked at Gideon as if demanding an answer from him.

"Any names or addresses in Orlick's pockets?" asked Gideon.

"Come and see for yourself," offered Sabini.

There was an English-type wallet in brown crocodile, twenty crisp new twenty-dollar bills and some smaller bills, Orlick's own business card, English stamps, an American Express Credit Card, a watch, keys, a gold cigarette case and a gold lighter; that was all.

"We'll need to look around his hotel room," Gideon said. "Can we do that before Mrs. Orlick goes back?"

"Right away," said Nielsen. "Hold her for half an hour, Sabini."

"Sure will."

Kitty's sobbing was growing even more heart-rending and Sabini looked at her uneasily.

"What are you going to do with the junkie driver?" he asked.

"Book him," Nielsen said. "That's no problem."

"The witnesses?"

"What do you suggest?"

"I'm a long way from home," Gideon said dryly. "But if I had three witnesses who told an identical story and who had all volunteered to tell what they saw, I would begin to wonder what they were up to. Eyewitnesses of car accidents in England like to make themselves scarce, but here are three who don't. And the driver—may we have the door open for a moment?"

"Why, sure." Sabini opened it, while Nielsen began to smile at Gideon, with a grim kind of humor.

The driver was saying in the same high-pitched voice: "I tell you I jus' didn't see that man, I jus' didn't see him." Before the door was closed he had said it three times.

"Like a phonograph record," Nielsen observed. "As if he was told what to say and keeps on saying it. The others were like records, too. You've got their names and addresses, Lieutenant?"

"Yes."

"Will you have them tailed?"

"Sure."

"It won't be easy to prove they lied, if they lied," Nielsen said. "Let's go."

Twenty minutes later Gideon and Nielsen stepped out of the elevator on the twenty-first floor of the new Hilton Hotel on Sixth Avenue, with the house detective behind them, important with his passkey. He went ahead to open the door, and stood aside for them to enter. Nielsen went first—and stopped so abruptly that Gideon bumped into him.

A glance was enough to show them that the big, sunlit room, in which the air conditioning whispered, had been ransacked.

Ten minutes was enough to make them feel sure there were no business papers here, no documents in any baggage, nothing to tell them whom Orlick had come to see.

Kitty Orlick said, stonily:

"He had a briefcase with all his papers in it. He kept it locked. It's no use asking me who he was coming to see. He didn't tell me. I've told you all I know."

Gideon said: "Max, we must check Orlick's London office, quickly, and I hope you'll soon start checking on the man Brown. I'm going to work on Kitty Orlick, who may or may not be as innocent and ignorant as she seems."

"We can break her down," Nielsen said.

"If she's lying, then she's so tough that breaking her down won't be easy," Gideon argued. "I'd like to try a different way." After a pause, he asked: "Do you think there's a small room at our hotel, on our floor—or one above or below us?"

After a pause, Nielsen began to smile.

"It wouldn't surprise me," he said dryly.

"Then I'll call Kate," Gideon said. "But first I'd like to send a cable to the Yard."

"Sure," Nielsen said. "Right away." He hesitated, and then ventured: "Going to have Cordova watched?"

Gideon said mildly: "Sure."

15:

Police Headquarters

"KATE," GIDEON said next morning, "I can't tell you how sorry I am about this."

"Don't be silly, dear. We couldn't allow the girl to stay on her own, in any case. And you're right. I'm more likely than any American policewoman to find out if she's telling the truth. But"—she turned to face her husband squarely—"I can't be sure I shall find out."

"Nothing beats trying but doing," Gideon said, unusually sententious for him. "If she knows nothing then she needs all the help you can give her—and if she does know anything, she may be in as much danger as her husband was. Whatever you find out will be good for her."

Kate almost laughed. "You've made your point!"

"Good." Gideon became brisk. "Kitty Orlick is one floor below us, two doors from the staircase and five from the elevator. She understands she's been brought here because the police need to seal up the room she shared with her husband. She knows we're staying here." After a pause, he went on: "You won't need to be indoors all the time, though. Nielsen is sending a policewoman round, who'll pose as a nurse. If you learn anything, tell her."

Kate was half laughing at him.

"George, I *am* a policeman's wife. I do know a little bit about what to do."

"Nothing like this ever happened in London." Gideon was glum.

"It will make New York more memorable," Kate said cheerfully. "Don't keep the captain waiting! You're due to meet the Commissioner and some of the other top brass at ten o'clock, and it's half past nine now."

"We aren't far from Centre Street," Gideon reminded her. "Kate—"

"For goodness' sake, George, stop worrying about it!"

She made him feel much brighter, and yet he did worry; it was not only that with Kitty Orlick at the hotel for two or three days, Kate's movements would be restricted; it was the fact that much of the early part of her holiday would be spent with a young woman who was so stricken with grief that it could only have a depressing effect, which might linger for a long time.

Kitty was under sedation, and the doctor had said that she would not wake until the afternoon. Yet Gideon went down one flight of stairs with Kate, and tapped on the door of the girl's room. The nurse opened the door.

Kitty lay on her back on a double bed in the small room, a single sheet drawn up to her neck, one arm over the sheet, the outline of her body very clear. Everything Gideon had heard about the Orlicks pointed to the fact that whatever kind of criminal the husband had been, there was no doubt of his passionate love for his wife.

Kate whispered: "Come *on,* George."

At the elevator, he gave her a peck of a kiss, and went off. Soon he was striding into the street, and a police driver who was talking to the doorman straightened up, and gave a half smile, as if he wasn't quite sure how to handle this Englishman. Nielsen had put car and driver at his disposal for the duration of his stay in New York.

"Good morning, Commander."

"Morning," said Gideon. "Can we get to Centre Street by ten o'clock?"

"You'll be there," the driver assured him. He had a berry-brown face, and it was difficult to be sure whether he was in his early forties or late fifties. His pale gray-blue uniform, RAF blue to British eyes, was immaculate, and although the air was still very sticky by Gideon's standard, he did not look shiny with sweat or in any way tired. Gideon stepped out of a near-Turkish bath atmosphere, into a car as cool as his bedroom. No wonder the driver looked fresh!

He shut Gideon in, slid into his own seat, and started off smoothly. There was no partition, and he spoke without looking round.

"There will be some truck traffic around Centre Street and Broadway, but it won't amount to much. This your first visit to New York, Commander?"

"Yes. I wish I'd come sooner!"

"Never too late, I guess. I hope to go to London before I die. My folks come from London—not my father, you understand, his father and my mother's folk. Name Gentian. Just call me Gent. Come from a place I never can remember properly. Fenn or some such name. There's a lot of water there—broadwater, I think they call it. Must be where the broads come from! You wouldn't happen to know anybody named Gentian from there?"

Gideon kept his smile to himself.

"I should say they came from the Fenn country, probably near the Norfolk Broads."

"Sure, that's it! Same name as the turkeys. Norfolk Broads, that's it. Gentian. It's sure good to have a big shot from Scotland Yard with us, Commander. There was another one here, two or three years ago, man named Rogers or something."

"Rogerson."

"That's the name." All this time the driver had been turning corners round a small square with trees in the middle and a patch of grass, for all the world like a London square. Then he swung onto Broadway, and ahead lay a wide expanse of road, with buses and trucks rolling and rattling, a few taxis and very few private cars. The police car hurtled along, then slowed down at some lights. On the right was another patch of green.

"You see that park? City Hall Park," Call-me-Gent said. "You see that building on the left?" He nodded his head sideways. "That's City Hall, yes, sir, I brought you round this way because I think every visitor should see City Hall. You see the way the road narrows? That's the way to Wall Street, yes, sir, that's where they begin the ticker-tape welcomes for our heroes, last one was that for the astronaut, I guess he'll likely be on the moon next. Gimme Centre Street, you take the moon." The lights changed. "We won't be long now, Mr. Gideon."

The car turned corners two or three times and Gideon lost his sense of direction completely. Suddenly they pulled into a narrow street with some parked trucks and police cars, and a massive granite building on the right. There was no room to draw up in front of the steps, and the driver said:

"This is O.K., Commander. I'll be around when you want me again. Up them steps." Gideon stood and peered up at the old building, realized it was Police Headquarters, and thought, It's like a prison. Then he saw the lions couchant, on pillars at either side of the stone steps, and shook his head with a kind of wonderment. As he did so, a youngish Negro came hurrying down the steps, open-faced, curly-haired, well dressed. He was smiling and gave the impression of physical and mental well-being. Gideon thought: Surely they wouldn't allow the press to start on me like this!

"Good morning, Commander." Gideon was hearing the title much more frequently than at home. "Surprised by the lions? All English people are. They seem to think the British have a corner on lions." There was something very pleasant in this man's manner, and his voice was particularly attractive. "I'm Lieutenant Cassidy. Captain Nielsen asked me to look after you for a while, and to outline the day's plans as far as we know them."

They began to walk together up the steps and into a huge bleak hall. The impression of a prison was strengthened. On either side were barred gates at the entrances to long passages, with two men on duty at each. Gideon was reminded of the newspaper questioner: did he believe in police being armed? Straight ahead were stairs which went up either side of a huge, open-grille type elevator. In front of this was an information booth—something the Yard could do with, he reflected. Everything was old, everything was massive and gloomy. They passed through one of the barred gateways.

"Hi, Joe," Cassidy said to a big guard, who stared intently at Gideon. Gideon half smiled. "We've had to change things around, the Commissioner got a call to City Hall to see the Mayor. At ten-thirty there's a press conference," Cassidy went on. "At eleven-thirty you're due at the River Squad office, where they may have some news about the *Maruna*. At twelve-thirty you will lunch with the Commissioner and two Assistant Commissioners and Captain Nielsen." Cassidy opened a door on the right. "Mr. Lingardo, the Assistant Commissioner in charge of Public Relations, is on vacation, so you can use his office while you're here—there's plenty of room if he should come back, but that won't be until after Labor Day."

"Labor Day?"

"The first Monday in September."

"Thanks," Gideon said. Two weeks stretched out in front of him, and it seemed a long, long time.

"We've got some information that will interest you," Cassidy went on. He led the way through a small office where four men were working, each intent on what he was doing or else determined not to reveal his interest in Gideon. This was a long, narrow room with a desk and a barred window at the far end. The files and furniture were old-fashioned and solid, the chair was modern swivel type and comfortable. On the desk were several typewritten reports, and Gideon's thoughts flashed to his office at the Yard, which was smaller in a cozier, Victorian way. "I can tell you what's in those," Cassidy went on. "One, the driver of the car which killed Orlick has been a junkie for the past eleven years, and like most of them he will do anything when he's desperate for the needle. He's had three prison sentences, all for car stealing when he couldn't get the stuff. It's possible he was hired to run Orlick down. If anyone was hired, he would be just the guy. The witnesses are people of good reputation, they don't even live in the same districts. The woman and one of the men, husband and wife, live out in Flushing, they'd come up to watch the shipping. The other man, a friend, lives around Broadway. He's a bachelor and lives alone. The one thing certain about them is that they don't have much money and they would be right to bribe if you wanted to bribe anyone to give false evidence." Cassidy was watching Gideon as if wondering whether he was taking this in. "Inglemann Brown and his wife stayed one night in their New York apartment, then flew to California."

Gideon exclaimed: "Did they, by George!"

"Mrs. Brown has relatives in Pasadena," Cassidy told him. "Maybe there's nothing remarkable in their getting out of town so quick. We should have a report from Pasadena later in the day, saying they've arrived. In New York their reputation is good."

Gideon said rather glumly: "I thought we might worry Orlick if we pressured Brown, but it looks as if we worried someone else, who didn't want Orlick to be in the news. Have you learned anything else?"

"The doorman said a man who said he was from the *Post* called to see the Browns when they arrived from the ship. He gave a description—a big, heavy man. We've checked, and the *Post* sent no one."

"So who was he?" asked Gideon.

"Unless we can identify him, or the Browns talk, we'll never know," Cassidy said. "Sooner or later the Browns will talk, but we've no reason yet to bring them back from L.A. . . . There's one thing."

"What is it?" Gideon asked.

"The big man was driven off by another man, in a green 1963 Chevrolet."

Gideon frowned in the effort of recollection.

"The car that killed Orlick was a *blue* Chevrolet, wasn't it?" His face cleared. "I've got it! There was a green one parked on 50th Street at the time of the accident—with a big man at the wheel. Mrs. Orlick saw the car as it was driven off, and the witnesses said it was a Chevrolet."

"That's right," Cassidy said. "We're putting out a call for that Chevy. The doorman at Brown's apartment building gave a good description of the man." He handed a sheet of paper to Gideon, and there was an *Identikit* picture of a man with a heavy face, jowl and chin, and dark, brooding eyes.

"That ship Lemaitre told you about—the *Maruna,*" Cassidy said, when Gideon put the picture aside.

"Yes?"

"It called at Savannah, Port Everglades, New Orleans, and two South American ports, with a mixed cargo, then sailed across the South Atlantic to Dakar, went round the Cape and called at Cape Town, Durban, Mozambique, and Dar es Salaam, Port Said, Haifa, and London. If it took those Rite-Times all the way, they cost plenty in freight unless maybe the master was getting a cut."

Gideon sat against the desk.

"We can work on the ship's officers, but it will take some time, and we certainly won't find Orlick's murderer on the *Maruna.* There are two obvious reasons for Orlick's murder, even if there's no certainty that one or the other is the right one. Either he was making a nuisance of himself to the New

York side of the racket or else they were scared he would lead us to them. Any idea at all who they might be?"

"No, sir," said Cassidy. "Not a glimmer of an idea. Would you like to go through these papers until the press conference starts?"

"Where's that to be held?"

"We've got a conference room."

"Right," Gideon said. "And thank you for all you've done."

"Anything I can do for you is a pleasure," Cassidy said, with obvious sincerity. "I heard so much about you from Captain Nielsen I didn't really believe you existed. I have an idea I'm going to know about that before you go! The Commissioner will give you the official welcome and I want you to know that what he says goes for everyone here. We're tickled to death to have you in New York."

He went out, leaving Gideon thoughtful as well as gratified.

For half an hour, with Nielsen on one side of him and Cassidy on the other, Gideon sat in a big bleak hall obviously used for lectures and assemblies, and answered questions fired at him by about twenty newspapermen. The difficulty was to avoid comparing New York with London and not to be drawn into adverse comment. No one pressed him too hard. Prompted by Nielsen, he promised to appear on two television news programs, declined five radio invitations, and felt reasonably well satisfied when it was all over.

"George," Nielsen said, as Gideon was leaving for a visit to the River Squad, "why don't you go into public relations?"

This part of New York seemed to have little to commend it. The streets were drab, dirty and old-fashioned, and a lot of the houses seemed to be falling down. Only a few shop windows and a few cars were new and gleaming. They turned into a narrow street with a bumpy, cobbled surface, but plenty of parking places—which was unusual. At the end of the street there appeared to be a sheer drop into the Hudson. Over the doorway, which was arched in stone rather like that of a church, were the words 06 PRECINCT HOUSE and on the wall was a dilapidated sign reading: RIVER DETECTIVE SQUAD. Cassidy led the way in, past a long bar or rail, behind which a uniformed sergeant sat at a high bench like a judge.

"Hi, Sam," Cassidy said. "Hi, Jim. Meet Commander Gideon."

"Hi, Commander. Glad to know you."

Cassidy led the way up a flight of narrow, badly worn steps with iron railings to the second floor, and then into a room with a hanging sign which read: *River D. Squad*—Lt. Krotzner. He opened the door, and two men looked up from a large flat desk, one man positively huge, the other small and dapper. Before Cassidy could speak, and before Gideon could really see either man clearly because of the brightness from the window shining into his eyes, the dapper man said:

"Glad to have you with us, Commander. We've got news for you." The other man was grinning, and Gideon had a feeling that they were both delighted with themselves and trying to play it down. "The *Maruna* has a sister ship. She's due to berth at Pier 117 tomorrow afternoon. She left here seven months ago, and did the same run as the *Maruna*. Also, she took a shipment of watches and costume jewelry. The *Hempen*. Same owners, Trans-Ana Shipping Company, same kind of freight, same ports of call, uses the same pier in New York and the same longshoremen gangs. How does that sound?"

16:

Cause for Excitement

GIDEON SENSED the excitement in both men, realized that it touched Cassidy, knew that it was partly satisfaction because they had demonstrated that they were on top of their job. It flashed through his mind that the news from Lemaitre, added to this, could bring the end of the Rite-Time affair; it might collapse—or it might blow up in their faces.

"How did you find out?" he asked.

"You have to have some luck," said the very big man. "There was a report of a small freighter in trouble fifty miles off the regular sea lanes, and the Coast Guard Service sent an aircraft out to look for it. She'd been battered during a storm but was making way under her own steam, so there was no need to do anything except note her name. The *Hempen*," he repeated with deep satisfaction.

"Same owners, Trans-Ana, same users, same charter, same ports of call, same pier and same longshoremen," Gideon said, with a glimmer of a smile. "When will she be in?"

"Tomorrow, around three o'clock."

"So we've time," said Gideon.

The dapper little man asked: "For what?"

"Checking some inquiries before the *Hempen* ties up," said Cassidy. "Commander, I would like you to know Lieutenant Krotzner and Sergeant Peek." There was a little ceremony of shaking hands. "Lieutenant, we want to extend all the courtesies to Commander Gideon, and it would be a good idea if they included a visit to the pier where the *Maruna* and *Hempen* tie up, and to the warehouses and the wharves, and maybe the customs office which clears them—just a courtesy visit, you understand."

Peek gave a roar of laughter.

"Sure we understand!"

The dapper Krotzner, who was unexpectedly good-looking in his miniature way, a fact it was easy to overlook because he *was* so small, spoke next.

"When would you like this visit, Mr. Gideon?"

"Tomorrow," Cassidy said.

"No time today?" asked Gideon.

"No, sir."

"What's a good hour for you to start?" Gideon asked Krotzner.

"Will nine o'clock suit you?"

"When do the longshoremen begin work?"

"Eight o'clock."

"Can we make it eight o'clock?" asked Gideon. He saw an

appreciative gleam in Peek's eyes and won a smile from Krotzner.

"Surely," Krotzner said.

"There's one other thing," said Gideon. "It would help if we could find out whether there's any special waterfront interest in the *Hempen,* whether any goods have been held for her—freight which could have gone forward on other ships but was deliberately held back. Would that be possible?"

"Sure," said Krotzner. "We can try."

"We've got eyes and ears all over the waterfront," said Peek. "You'd be surprised how many eyes and ears we have."

"How long before you must go?" asked Krotzner.

"Half an hour," answered Cassidy.

"In that half hour we can show the Commander plenty," said Krotzner. "We can indicate the position of the wharves and warehouses, and we can tell him how we work over here, then when he starts moving in the morning he'll know what the situation is." As if taking it for granted that this would be acceptable, the lieutenant went on: "How about some coffee, Mac? Come into my office, Commander." His office, next door, was small, but there were four chairs round the desk, and on the desk were some graphs and several charts, while maps were pinned to the walls. Peek picked up a telephone and said:

"Coffee for four in the lieutenant's office."

"Sit down," Krotzner said genially. "Mr. Gideon, we don't know how big this thing will be, but however big it is we can cope if we know what we're doing. There are, all together, three police groups working on the waterfront. There are the Harbor Police, who have a fleet of launches and speedboats; they correspond roughly to your Thames Police Division, I imagine. Then there's our precinct, the River Detective Squad, and the regular patrolmen who cover the streets in the district. All three groups are on the lookout for trouble all the time."

"What kind of trouble are they most likely to find?" inquired Gideon.

"Larceny, first, assault, second; a lot of the waterfront men are bad-tempered, and so are the sailors when they come off a long voyage and get held up. There's plenty of smuggling; that is handled by the special Customs Bureau which works closely with us. And there are the labor troubles, which don't rate for criminal statistics yet. But a lot of petty crimes can lead to a strike situation, and we keep our ears open for rumors of situations which could lead to strikes. Too much time is lost on the waterfront, Commander, and a lot more would be if we weren't able to tip off some of the unions when trouble is blowing up." Krotzner was talking precisely and very quickly; obviously the efficient coordination of the departments mattered deeply to him. "I was saying, there are three groups, the Harbor Police who cover the harbor, and they work from here and from other waterfront stations. In this same building there is the precinct house, and the precinct takes care of any crime which originates after a ship is tied up. If it originates on the water, it's for the Harbor Police and for us."

"So you're in each other's pockets," Gideon remarked.

"So we work very closely together," corrected Krotzner. "If we didn't we would soon be in trouble. Here in the River Squad we have thirty-one detectives, one sergeant—Peek—and me. There are times when we could use twice that number. We don't have many personnel changes down here, we get to know everyone and that's good for business."

"Business?"

Peek grinned. "Results," he said. "Where's that coffee?" He

lifted a telephone, and said sharply, "I said four coffees." As he banged the receiver down, Krotzner went on in the same clipped, precise voice:

"We need to know the warehouse men and the longshoremen—you call them dockers. We need to know the dock boss and his assistants, the gang foremen—the gangs are up to twenty strong, remember. We need to know the second mates of the ships, who supervise the stacking and placing when a ship's being loaded. Yes, sir, we need to know them all because they're the guys who will notice if anything is wrong—they're the guys who will tell us if there's any work for us."

Cassidy grinned almost fiercely.

"One big happy family," he said.

"That's right," said Krotzner equably. "There's one other thing you'd soon learn if you worked here, Mr. Gideon. It's taken a pneumatic drill and dynamite to make Headquarters realize that if things go wrong on the waterfront things go wrong in New York. It's the eyes and the ears of New York, and the heart and the lungs, too."

Gideon said: "There have been some big consignments of watches that have been hijacked; and we don't know how."

"Big?" echoed Krotzner. "What's big? One crate of machinery could be twice the size in dimensions of what you call a *big* consignment. You ought to see—" He looked almost appealingly at Cassidy. "You sure there isn't time to take a look at the warehouses now?"

"Not unless you want the Commander to keep the Commissioner waiting."

"I'll tell you," Krotzner said, his eyes lighting up. "You tell the Commissioner that New York's the same as London, it breathes through its waterfront. You tell him you haven't seen a waterfront which matters so much to a city. Give him the big sell." Krotzner was smiling with his lips but not with his eyes; he was joking and yet he was serious. Peek was rubbing his jaw, Cassidy was grinning as if he had heard this kind of outburst before. In the lull that followed, the door opened and a tall thin man came in. He had a Hershey candy box with four waxed cartons of coffee in it, each one lidded. He rolled his eyes as he placed the box on the desk, his mouth twitching. No one took any notice of him. He stood back and looked at Peek, as if for approval, and Peek said:

"O.K., baby doll."

"Yes, sir," the man said. "Yes, sir." He beamed all over his bony face as he backed out.

The coffee was half cold, but no one seemed to care.

"Commander, I've had a report of the discussions you had with Captain Nielsen," Krotzner went on. "Would you be good enough to clarify some of the points you raised?"

"Yes, of course."

"You believe there might be danger to Orlick's partner in England. Does that mean you think there is an English killer there, or do you think he would be an American?"

"If the purpose of the killing is to prevent us from getting a lead to the American side of the crimes, as it could be, then I would expect him to be American," Gideon reasoned. "As soon as the job is done I would expect him to leave England."

"*If* the job is done."

"I can't do more than make a guess," Gideon said equably. "Don't you agree with that one?"

"Oh, sure. I just want to get it clear in my mind. Now this man whom Orlick attacked on the ship. You say they were only casual acquaintances?"

"Everything I know suggests that Mrs. Orlick got drunk, Brown took liberties in public, and Orlick lost his head."

Peek was grinning.

"I guess Mrs. Orlick nearly lost something else," he said.

"One thing," Krotzner went on earnestly. "There is a big time lag between the date the Rite-Time goods are shipped from the factory, and the date they come on the market in the United Kingdom. Where do you think they spend that intervening time?"

"At the docks or on a ship," Gideon answered.

"Sure, that's another good guess," Krotzner said. He made one or two notes, before asking: "You got any questions for me, Commander?"

Gideon asked dozens of questions, but none of them seemed so important as the unspoken ones in his mind. He wanted to know what was happening in London; he wanted to be in two places at once.

Lemaitre pushed open the door of the office and strode to his desk, glancing at Gideon's empty place without consciously wishing Gideon was sitting there or about to come in. It was half past seven, earlier than Lemaitre would usually arrive for work, but the pressures were great and each job seemed to take much more time than he expected; the only way to get everything done was to spend longer hours at his desk. The previous night he had been there until half past eleven; he knew it would probably be the same tonight. He saw a few notes on his desk, but no post had as yet come in. There were not likely to be any early-morning reports from senior detectives, most of whom would not turn up for an hour or more. He saw a Western Union envelope and thought, *George,* and sat down at his desk, picking up the cable. The office was cold. Outside the skies were gray and the Thames was whipped to a miniature frenzy, but he was not thinking about the weather. As he slit the envelope open with a wooden paper knife he wondered what could have been in any of his letters to cause Gideon's cable. All his movements were neat and methodical and well-organized.

He read:

Orlick killed road accident stop question and watch Cordova and everyone at Orlova Watch Company stop please report if any suggestion Cordova anticipated trouble Gideon. Stop. Also advise us of any New York business associates.

"My God!" breathed Lemaitre. "That was murder!"

The remark was exactly what Gideon would have expected from him, that leap to a conclusion which he could not justify but which events might later prove to be right; to Gideon, that was Lemaitre's greatest weakness. Lemaitre read the cable again, snatched up the telephone. When the operator answered he asked: "Is Mr. MacPherson in?" He waited for what seemed a long time before the girl said: "No."

"Keep ringing him. I want to see him the minute he arrives," Lemaitre ordered. Let her give the necessary instructions to the hall duty sergeant or the gate man, he was too busy.

This news jolted his thoughts from his main preoccupation which was fast becoming an anxiety: the Great Post Office Robbery. The simple truth was that the police hadn't a clue worth a row of beans; half a million pounds had been spirited away, and there was no means of telling whether it was still in this country; there had been plenty of time for it to have been taken or sent abroad. He would not have felt so bad if there had been a single clue, if they had found even a few thousand pounds' worth of the old notes which had been on their way to the clearinghouse to be destroyed, but he had drawn an absolute blank.

The other messages were unimportant; tickover notes. Lemaitre unlocked his desk and took out a large, folded sheet of stiff paper which he placed carefully on the desk, so that it took up a big section in the middle. It was a carefully annotated graph and progress chart of everything that had happened in the Post Office Robbery. Everything he had done, everything the divisions had done, every man and woman who had been questioned, was scrupulously entered; it was a perfect illustration of routine methods carried out to perfection.

There was a footstep outside, and the door opened; it wouldn't be opened without a preliminary tap if Gideon were here. Lemaitre prepared to bark at the newcomer, then saw the very man he wanted to see, big and florid MacPherson. The detective superintendent drew back, startled.

"You in already?"

"As if you didn't know."

"I didn't know." MacPherson looked at the chart, which he had seen before, but made no comment. There was a sense of urgency about him. "Lem," he said, "I had a tip from the *Globe.* They say that Orlick was killed in a car accident in New York yesterday. Have you heard anything?"

Lemaitre handed him the cable, and he read it quickly, then said almost reverently:

"Gee-Gee doesn't lose much time, wherever he is."

"Will you see Cordova this morning?"

"Yes," MacPherson said. "I'll be at his office, waiting for him."

Cordova heard the telephone bell and wished it would stop, rolled over in his double bed, and hoped passionately the bell would break. He hurtled a stream of casual obscenities at it, then pushed the bedclothes back. He shivered. It was nearly eight o'clock. He was alone at his flat in Aldgate, only five minutes' walk from the Orlova Company's offices, and often he did not get up until nearly nine. The bell kept ringing. "Bloody thing," he said, and suddenly wondered if it could be Dirk. His eyes brightened and he rushed into the small room where the telephone stood in a wall recess.

"Hallo."

"Can Mr. Cordova take a call from New York, please?"

So it was Dirk!

"Yes, ducks," said Cordova. "Put it through."

"It will be through in about fifteen minutes, sir."

"O.K., O.K., fifteen minutes," said Cordova. He banged the receiver down, stretched and yawned, then went into the bathroom. He was a man who liked small rooms with every convenience at hand, but as he often boasted he liked a king-size bed. He was a widower, and satisfied to leave it that way —he could have all the fun and none of the responsibilities. All that sex life cost was money. A short, dark-haired, olive-faced man with a peach-clear skin, he looked like a Southern European. It was a surprise to people who met him for the first time when he spoke with a marked Cockney accent. He was, in fact, a fifth-generation Londoner. Fastidious in his personal habits, he was still in the bathroom when the telephone bell rang again. He went across to it, stark naked, caught a glimpse of his olive-skinned body in the dressing-table mirror, and approved.

"Hi, Dirk!" he said brightly.

"One moment, please."

"Oh, the hell with you." He thought he was talking and behaving like an American, grinned to himself, smoothed a half-yawn, and then heard a woman say:

"Cordy, is that you?"

"Kit, honey! Is this a surprise! I didn't expect to hear from you."

"Cordy," Kitty Orlick said, "something–something terrible has happened." She sounded as if she was almost in tears. "Dirk–Dirk is–Dirk is . . ."

An awful fear struck Cordova as he listened to her story. Much of it he did not really understand, but the essential things came through, including her distress, the fact that she was staying at a different hotel, the fact that she was alone, the fact that Dirk Orlick had been killed; *murdered,* she said over and over again; murdered.

"But why should anybody want to kill him, why should they?" There was a piteous note in her voice. Cordova did not stop her, he hardly knew what to say, even when she asked: "Cordy, can you come over? I feel so awful on my own."

"But, Kit, the business–"

"Please," Kitty pleaded. "Come for Dirk's sake if not mine. He would want you to look after me, he . . ." She burst into tears.

Cordova said hurriedly: "I'll see what I can do, Kit. Don't worry, I'll see what I can do." He rang off, knowing that she had still more to say, hardly able to think. Dirk *murdered.* He shivered as he went slowly into the bedroom and put on a dressing gown, repeating the one word over and over. "*Murdered.*" He did not really think of Dirk or of Kitty. All feeling was swamped by one–a terrible sense of fear.

17:

Gideon's Badge

THE MOMENT Kitty Orlick put down the receiver after the call to London, the night operator at the hotel called an extension line.

"Did you get that?" he asked the policeman who answered.

"Sure, I got it all. She called this guy Cordova at two o'clock in the morning our time, close on eight o'clock European time. I'm sending a report to Headquarters right now, sweetie."

"Just so long as you weren't asleep," the operator said. "I'll bet that guy won't come to visit Mrs. Orlick. He couldn't get off the line quick enough."

Cordova hadn't started to dress, hadn't made himself tea

or coffee, when the telephone bell rang again. This time he didn't want to answer. He licked his lips and stared at the instrument but it kept on ringing. At last he got up and crossed to it, feeling cold and shivery.

"Hallo?"

"That you, Mr. Cordova?" It was Darkie, the company's London salesman, but a man who was more than just a salesman. He often used threats and force to make retailers buy goods which he and they knew had been stolen. He was really the company's troubleshooter and the contact man of the unlawful side of the business. He had lived in America most of his life, and knew both sides of the Atlantic well. "Mr. Cordova—"

"What is it?" Cordova whispered.

"Mr. Cordova. I've got to see you before you go into the office this morning."

Cordova still had difficulty in speaking.

"Why?"

"Something's cropped up, Mr. Cordova."

"What do you mean, something's cropped up?"

"I'll tell you when I see you," Darkie said. "I got to go out of circulation for a few days. Mr. Cordova, have you got any cash-money?" So it was a shakedown. "Say a hundred quid?"

"What do you want it for?"

Darkie said: "Mr. Cordova, it will be money well spent, I promise you. See you, the usual place."

He rang off.

Cordova put the telephone down slowly. He felt a little better, partly because he had been able to raise his voice at Darkie, but he was still shivering. There had been emergencies like this before, when Darkie had overdone it with some of his customers and had had to go into hiding, and because of these and other crises there had long been a secret meeting place. This was not here or at the office, but in the back room of a café in Whitechapel, ten minutes' walk from the flat and not much farther from the office.

Cordova made and drank instant coffee, dressed quickly, put seventy-five pounds, all in used one-pound notes, in his pocket, tucked another three hundred back in a safe built into the wall behind the shower in the bathroom, and left the building at ten minutes past eight.

The East End looked gray and drab. A cold wind was blowing and he wished he had put on an overcoat. Walking would warm him up. He took a short cut, one which he and Darkie and Dirk knew well. He kept thinking about Dirk's having been murdered, and the fact was beginning to hurt as well as frighten. He turned into a narrow lane with tall, bare walls on either side, the walls of warehouses, and as he did so he saw Darkie move from a doorway recess which led into an empty, derelict warehouse, one used for dry cargoes. It flashed through Cordova's mind that Darkie must be badly scared or he wouldn't have intercepted him like this, he would have waited at the café. It did not occur to him at that moment to be afraid.

"What've you been doing?" he demanded. "Who's after you?"

Darkie moistened his lips and came close to him.

"You'll find out," he said.

It was only then that Cordova realized that there was something badly wrong, but it was too late. He saw Darkie's right hand come out of his pocket, heard the click of a switch-blade, gasped: "Hey!" and backed away, but he could not back far enough. "For gawd's sake—" he began with a spasm of awful, blinding terror.

He hardly felt the knife as it slid in.

Darkie hauled the body into the warehouse, and closed and locked the door; it might be days before anyone found it. He did not hurry, simply made sure that no one was in the passage, stepped outside, and went toward the docks. He called at the café where he often met Cordova furtively, had bacon and eggs and tea, and made an appointment with an acquaintance for a game of billiards that night. Then he sauntered nearer the docks. He was not unknown there because sometimes he cleared shipments for the Orlova Watch Company, and occasionally he came to collect special shipments.

An hour and a quarter after he had killed Orlick's partner, Darkie slipped on board the S.S. *Maruna,* which after several postponements was to sail that day for the eastern seaboard of the United States. He was not the first man to have a free voyage on the *Maruna;* someone else would pay, not he. He was looking forward to going to America again; home was the country for him just then.

At nine-forty-five, MacPherson realized that Cordova might not be coming to the office, and went to his flat. There was no answer when he rang. He forced the front door, and went in, soon finding indications that the bed had been slept in and that the man had left that morning. At half past ten MacPherson thought the situation grave enough to warrant a general alarm for Cordova, but no news came through until the middle of the afternoon, when a divisional detective, on what he called a routine search for stolen goods, found the body.

There was no doubt that the New York Police Department had put out all the flags, being really anxious to show Gideon everything new they were using for the war against crime. He was handed from department to department, shown round with pride. Occasionally he compared a department unfavorably with its counterpart at the Yard, but in most cases it was the other way round. Disquietingly, he learned that they were employing a record system which cut the time of finding a suspect's record by at least three quarters. He also saw developments in infrared and other photography which narrowed down the chances of a forger getting away with his crime to about half what they were in England. What worried him most was the fact that much was strange and unfamiliar, and the methods as well as the systems differed so widely that it was easy to understand why confusion arose on cases which involved both sides of the Atlantic. He was deliberating on this, having reached the big square hall halfway through the morning, when one of the policemen approached him:

"Excuse me, sir. Lieutenant Cassidy is asking for you."

Gideon turned, and saw Cassidy hurrying down the steps. Instantly he realized there was something wrong, for Cassidy's face was stern and unsmiling. He had nothing in his hands, which worked rather like pistons as he walked.

"Commander," he said, "you aren't going to like this any more than we do. Cordova was murdered in London this morning." He ceased speaking abruptly, but gave the impression that he had something further to say.

Gideon felt the sickening impact of the news, and saw at once what it could mean. It really alarmed him.

"That leaves Kitty Orlick," he said, but he wasn't thinking of Kitty, he was thinking of Kate.

"Captain Nielsen's sending prowl cars to the hotel already," Cassidy said. "There will be a special watch kept on the place while the girl is still at the hotel—you don't have to worry yet, Commander."

Gideon said: "You'd be surprised how worried I am already."

"I can understand that, but you certainly don't have to worry about your wife or Mrs. Orlick." Cassidy paused, then switched the subject. "There are some replies to your cable, Commander, the captain thought maybe you would like to check some of Orlick's New York contacts before lunch." Cassidy's smile flashed. "He says not to be late for the lunch."

Almost irritably, Gideon thought: Damn the lunch. He took some slips of paper fom Cassidy, giving them only half of his attention. What had gone wrong in London? Why the hell had they allowed Cordova to be killed? Had they any idea who the killer was? Suddenly he wanted to be at the Yard, to be in the hunt himself, even if only directing it. He was like a fish out of water here, a pampered and feted guest when he wanted *action*.

He read the notes. On each sheet of paper was a name and address, and penciled comments.

"Who penciled the notes on these?" he asked as they walked toward the main doors.

"Captain Nielsen."

Gideon grunted. "Orlick had four main business contacts, each one a hundred per cent reliable according to Mr. Nielsen, two of them unaware that Orlick was coming here, two who haven't yet been interviewed." He paused. "If we put a call in to my office, can I pick it up at one of these places?"

"Surely. I've checked the delay—it's half an hour," Cassidy said.

The first of the two firms Gideon visited was on East 37th Street; it specialized in cheap costume jewelry. The air conditioning was ineffective, and everyone there seemed limp and hot. Gideon felt as if he were in an oven. The firm had a steady business with the Orlova Watch Company, but:

"We had no idea Mr. Orlick was to visit New York," said a tired-looking, overthin man sitting at a spacious desk. "We had a letter from him only ten days ago, and he made no mention of it."

The letter was simply an acknowledgment of a small consignment of cheap rings and watches.

The call to the Yard didn't come through here.

At the second office, smaller, overcrowded, and almost icy cold, with everyone furiously busy, a big, flabby young man with three chins sat at a desk near a window which hadn't been tidied or dusted for months. Telephones rang, typewriters clattered, men and women talked with raised voices.

". . . proud to meet you, Commander Gideon. . . . Yes, sir, we do business with Orlova. . . . Yes, sir, they're a good reliable firm. . . . No, sir, we ship to them, they don't ship to us. . . . Varied, sir, varied—all low priced manufacturers' close-out lines, they're sharp buyers. . . . Sure, sure, you can see their files. Sure—"

He broke off when one of three telephone bells rang. Gideon, sitting uncomfortably on a small chair, was squeezed against the wall. Cassidy was giving him as much room as he could, but was sandwiched between him and the desk.

The chins wobbled, and eyes so buried in pale flesh that they looked small becamc very bright.

"Sure, sure, he's here. . . . A telephone call from Scotland Yard, for Commander Gideon." He handed the instrument over, and then raised his voice to a piercing falsetto: "Quiet everybody! Quiet!"

As Gideon took the telephone an uncanny stillness fell.

"Lem?" He heard crackling. "Lem, is that you? . . . *Lem.*"

"Hi, George!" Lemaitre's voice was suddenly loud and clear.

"How are tricks in the New World, George?"

"Never mind the New World. Have you got anyone for the Cordova job?"

"Only wish we had."

"Any line on anyone?"

"Mac's doing all he can." Lemaitre sounded defensive. "You can rely on us."

Yes, thought Gideon bitterly; he could rely on them to allow the murder of a key man in these crimes. It wasn't any use venting his annoyance on Lemaitre, but he felt very angry as he asked a few more questions, receiving more unhelpful answers. When he rang off he sensed that Lemaitre was as glum as he was himself.

He was watched by everyone in the office as he left.

He was watched by at least a hundred people, mostly men, in a hotel banqueting room which he entered with Nielsen and Cassidy at half past twelve. As he walked to the top table there was a burst of clapping. His mood, sour since he had talked to Lemaitre, began to improve. Suddenly he saw himself as a person doing a vital public relations job. There was more to police work than the simple investigation of a simple crime.

A huge steak overlapped his plate; a baked potato in silver foil swam with butter; a slice of apple pie was enormous. He was kept talking between bites, until the Assistant Commissioner stood up, small, benign, smooth-voiced, quite oblivious of the four microphones in front of him.

". . . we have the privilege of having a visit from Britain's top detective, maybe the world's top detective . . ."

(*"Hear, hear,"* whispered Nielsen.)

". . . and in a few minutes, after I have told you all about this remarkable man, he's going to talk to us . . ."

Everyone clapped as if they could hardly wait.

". . . rose from the ranks, just a London bobby, to the senior executive position in the Criminal Investigation Department . . ."

What was the A.C. saying?

Nielsen nudged Gideon.

". . . before we call on him to speak we want to make a presentation to Commander Gideon. We want to make him an honorary member of the New York Police Force, and so I am going to pin this silver badge onto his jacket. That will give you the courtesy of the Force, Commander, you can do everything with it except make arrests!"

The A.C. was beaming.

Nielsen was banging the table.

The room seemed in uproar.

"Gentlemen," Gideon said, when at last everyone was silent, "I don't think any man could have a prouder moment. Why, I—" He broke off, there was a lump in his throat, he gulped, then threw his head back and almost shouted: "Why, I'm not even nervous of these microphones any more. I don't care if the whole world hears me say this. I am happy and proud to wear this badge. If I couldn't be a member of the Force in London, then this is the Force I would want to belong to . . ."

He didn't really say much, but he knew he had made a lot of friends—for himself, and for the police in London too.

Sitting down to a tumult of applause much greater than he really deserved, he thought suddenly:

"But Kitty Orlick doesn't seem to have a friend in the world."

That was when he knew that he hoped Kate had not discovered Kitty Orlick to be a liar.

18:

Burden of Truth

TWO POLICE cars were in the street outside Gideon's hotel when he reached there late in the afternoon. Two men were in the hallway, obviously plainclothes officers, as well as the doorman, who seemed very subdued. His driver called:

"See you, Commander," as he drove off. Gideon thought mechanically, Just call me Gent. He reached the elevator and stepped inside. He kept telling himself that it was absurd, there was not the slightest reason to worry about Kate, and yet he did worry, and his heart thumped as he stepped out of the elevator and went across to the apartment door. It opened as he reached it, and Kate said:

"Hallo, dear." Smiling at first, she frowned at his expression, then smiled again as his face cleared. "What's the matter?"

"I was afraid you would be out," said Gideon.

"We shopped all the morning and the early part of the afternoon, and then came back—it was too hot to walk any more. The shops are fabulous." He could not remember hearing Kate use that word before except jokingly, when speaking of current pop singers or some enthusiasm of the moment which the younger members of the family were excited about. She closed the door behind him, and glanced toward the kitchen. "Kitty's been with us part of the day, and she's in the pantry now, getting some supper. She says she simply can't sit about doing nothing and would like to make herself useful." They entered the living room, passing the pantry alcove. Kate pushed the living room door to. "She's a really nice girl, George."

"Hmm."

"I can't help feeling that you're too suspicious of her." Kate went on. "I've talked to her quite a lot. She says over and over again she didn't know anything about Orlick's business, he always insisted on keeping his home and business life separate. And she liked it that way."

"She knew his partner well enough to telephone him from New York."

Kate said, almost with reproof:

"You really *are* suspicious about her, aren't you? She says Cordova was a family friend, too—*he* wouldn't talk business to her either."

"Kate," Gideon said, "we're not living in the days of the masterful husband and the meek little wife. That girl's holding something back. Has she been up here much?"

"Only for an hour." Kate repressed some comment, and led the way into the bedroom. Gideon's slippers were by the side of the bed, and across it lay a short-sleeved gray shirt and a pair of lightweight trousers, just as if he were at home.

Gideon sat down and unlaced his shoes.

"George, don't prejudge her."

Gideon looked up with an absent smile, deeply preoccupied. Whatever he did had to be right, and an hour or so of deliberation might make the difference between the right and the wrong decision.

"I don't really suspect the girl herself," he said. "Feel damned sorry for her, in fact. But she must know something, and what she knows might help us to get the murderers."

"If she thought she could do that, she couldn't wait to talk," Kate declared. "The police nurse has been with her much of the day." Kate was thoughtful for a few moments, before going on: "Apparently two detectives and two policewomen were here soon after she woke, to question her."

"I've seen the reports," Gideon said. "She says she never suspected that her husband's business was criminal, in fact she keeps insisting that she doesn't believe it was. As far as she knew, he was in the legitimate fancy goods and watch trade. According to the nurse—one of the senior women detectives in the Homicide Squad, I'm told—she convinced them all of her sincerity in saying that she didn't have any idea what Orlick was up to."

"But obviously she hasn't convinced *you*."

"Kate, let's stop arguing about her," Gideon said. "She's safe enough for the time being, and Nielsen might pick up the killers or we might get a line from the Yard. Nielsen said something about a theater tonight."

"Oh, yes, Claire told me, Tennessee Williams' latest." Kate seemed quite willing to change the subject. "I found out that the Nielsens usually have supper at home before the theater, and if they feel like it go on to a meal afterwards. I persuaded Claire that was what we would like to do, too. We don't have to be ready until half past seven or a quarter to eight—the curtain rises at eight-thirty. I thought that would give you some time to relax in."

"Just right," said Gideon.

"What kind of day have you had?"

"Only half enough hours," Gideon replied. He took a handkerchief out of his pocket, and handed it to Kate—and she nearly dropped the New York Police Department badge. She looked at it from all angles, then placed it carefully on top of the television set.

"They couldn't have done a nicer thing," she said warmly. "I shall treasure that."

"*You* will!" Gideon grinned, then told her about the day's events while they sat in the room overlooking the bridge, the river and the skyscrapers. Although it was still daylight, many of the windows were already lighted, and together they witnessed the birth of fairyland. He had a whisky and soda, Kate a Dubonnet, as he talked and thought and wondered if there *was* really any danger for Kitty Orlick. He was still wondering when the door opened and Kitty came in. He heard her, and twisted round in his chair. She wore a loose-fitting honey-colored blouse and a pair of chocolate-brown pants; she moved lightly and easily, but there were dark shadows under her eyes.

"Good evening," she said.

"Come and have a drink," Gideon invited.

"I'd rather not."

"You'll be very welcome."

She drew nearer, slow step upon step, as if there was something new weighing on her mind. A trick of the light played on her remarkable brown eyes, and they shone. She was obviously ill at ease, and at the same time she spoke very positively, as if she knew exactly what she wanted to say.

"No, I won't have a drink." She stood looking down at him, reminding him of one of his own daughters about to defy him over some edict which he might have uttered without giving it much thought. "*Was* my husband a criminal?" she asked flatly.

Gideon hesitated, but not for long. Kate closed her eyes, as if wishing that she could hide from sight of Kitty's face. Then Gideon said slowly:

"He was suspected of very serious crimes, yes. He had never been charged, and therefore had no record. It is conceivable that when his death is fully investigated we will find that he was not guilty of the crimes. On the other hand, he is known to have associated with lawbreakers in London, and I have every reason to believe that he employed other criminals."

Kitty's expression didn't change.

"But you've never proved he *was* a criminal?"

"No. But I've every reason to think he was."

She stood squarely in front of him.

"Well, I didn't have any reason."

"You never had a suspicion?"

"Not—not really."

"That means you had some inkling," Gideon said sharply.

She said hesitantly: "I thought it was a kind of business he—he didn't want me to know about, that he was a bit ashamed of—well, sensitive about, anyhow."

"What kind of legal business would a man be ashamed of?"

Kitty's eyes flashed, and she clenched her hands as she answered thickly:

"Contraceptives, if you want to know. I thought he dealt in them and didn't want to tell me. *I* didn't care, but he used to treat me as if I was a child, he—" She broke off, choking, and turned away to hide her tears.

Gideon caught Kate's eyes, and saw her expression. She leaned forward, and whispered:

"Satisfied?"

"Could be." Gideon kept his voice low.

"Of course she didn't know what he did!"

"She could still know something to help us."

"If she does, she'll tell you."

"*If* she knows she knows," Gideon objected softly. "She *must* know something."

"Hush." Kate moved away as Kitty turned round. Her eyes were glistening, but she had herself under strict control and her voice was much steadier and clearer.

"It's obvious what you think. It's obvious that if my husband was killed in such a way after being lured to that place, then you are probably right. Looking back, I can recall a lot of peculiar things. Telephone calls late at night, for instance, and his always refusing to confide in me about work. He even got angry if I tried to make him tell me anything! Oh, I can see you're probably right, but that doesn't mean I didn't love him, and it doesn't mean anyone had a right to *kill* him. You've got to find his murderer."

"You can be absolutely sure that no one wants to find him more than the New York police and I do," Gideon said dryly.

"Then why don't you believe me?" she cried. "I *know* those witnesses lied. Dirk was run down deliberately." After a tense pause she went on in a different tone: "Did you come to New York to investigate crimes which—which you think my husband committed?"

Gideon answered gravely. "That was one of the reasons for my coming."

"So in a way *you* may be responsible for his death. If his —if these other people learned you were after him, they might be afraid he would lead you to them, mightn't they?" When Gideon didn't answer, she went on in a harsher, accusing voice: "In a way it could be your fault that he's dead."

After another long pause, Gideon said: "If that's how you want to look at it, yes. I think it would be the wrong way." But another great burden began to weigh down on him, because of the anguish in the girl's eyes. He was aware of Kate looking at him, and realized that he must tell them about Cordova. He was not often at a loss for words, but he was now, for he knew that the right ones were all he had with which to help Kitty Orlick.

Kate's lips moved as if she wanted to speak, or was praying.

"Yes, I may have sparked it off," Gideon said with an effort, "but I don't think I did." It would be too cruel to say that he thought the attack on Brown, and Brown's threat of action for damages, could equally have been a cause. With luck, Kitty need never know that. "I've a feeling your husband's New York associates were worried, in any case. Something like this was probably inevitable."

Kitty began to frown; she looked pathetically beautiful.

"Something like this what? This—*accident?*" She almost sneered.

"I don't think it was an accident, I agree with you there," Gideon said, and then decided that he must now give her the other shattering blow; certainly it must not be left to anyone else. "Kitty, I hate to say it but I've some more bad news for you. You must believe that I am sorry. Cordova was murdered in London, early this morning. There is a nation-wide hunt for his killer."

Kitty backed away, her hands rising in front of her breast. For a long time she stood absolutely motionless.

Then she whispered, "Oh, my God," and repeated: "Oh, my God. Cordy. Oh, my God." She began to tremble, as she had trembled when Gideon had talked to her at the precinct house. Kate jumped up and helped her to a chair, otherwise she would have fallen. She covered her face with her hands and began to cry, and Gideon watched for a few moments, before getting up.

"She had to know," he said, and to himself he muttered: "What a hell of a job this is." Soon he went on glumly: "I'll have a shower." He went into the bedroom, despondent not only because of the girl but because it was obviously possible that the American criminals *had* killed the two Englishmen to make sure they couldn't talk. If they had, there was another obvious possibility: that the American side of the business would be closed down, to obviate other risks. An even greater burden of responsibility would then be his, for such an eventuality would be partly attributable to him. He could have had both Orlick and Cordova questioned and charged in London, but he had preferred to wait until he could trace the American end. He pictured Scott-Marle judging the wisdom of the line he had taken.

He was under the shower when the telephone bell rang. It rang repeatedly. In exasperation he shouted: "Kate!" but the ringing persisted. He wrapped a towel round himself and stepped out of the bathroom. The telephone was in the bedroom, near the door. He could see into the living room where Kate was kneeling in front of Kitty, holding the girl's hands; he doubted if either of them had heard the bell. He picked up the receiver.

"Gideon."

"Ally here."

"Who—*oh*. Ally. Oh, hallo."

"Did I catch you in the bath or something?" inquired Lord Allingham brightly.

Gideon was surprised into a laugh, and a laugh was just what he needed just then.

"You did exactly that!"

"You really mean it," Allingham chuckled. "Well, I'm sorry, but I won't keep you out of it for long. George, I've been in touch with our commercial attaché in Washington and with a number of other interested people. Are we onto something! Only British goods are affected by the sabotage. And a hell of a lot of recent consignments, from harmonicas to bicycles, and motorcars to whisky, have been damaged here. See what that means?"

"Not yet. But I've just seen something that might help."

"What is it?"

"Can anyone possibly make a profit out of this?" demanded Gideon. "It isn't the odd single firm of distillers—it's most distilling companies; it's not one make of British car, but practically every make. Unless there's a profit in it, only a lunatic would do it on such a scale."

"Go on," Allingham said softly.

"And to organize it on this scale it would have to be a damned wealthy lunatic," Gideon declared. "I've been thinking along the lines of industrial and commercial sabotage, aimed at spoiling the market for one producer so that another can take over, but the damage is too widespread. We want someone on the lunatic fringe at home, someone who's anti-American in the extreme—what the hell have I been wasting time for?"

"You won't ever waste time," Allingham said.

"I won't waste any more on this job, anyhow," Gideon declared gruffly. "I'll talk to London about this new angle."

"Fine. How are you finding the cooperation from the New York police?"

"Couldn't be better."

"What a welcome thing to hear," said Allingham. "George, I hoped we could have a meal together in New York but I'm flying to Washington first thing in the morning, and Justine is coming with me. We'll be there for two weeks, staying at the Shoreham. I may have to come back to New York for odd days, and I'll keep in touch. You'll let me know if you get any news at all on this sabotage angle, won't you?"

"Of course."

"Give our love to Kate," Allingham said.

Gideon rang off, and went back to the bathroom, dabbing himself because he had learned that to towel vigorously here was to bring on a heavy sweat. He put on his special lightweight suit but didn't knot his tie, hesitated, and went into the living room. As he neared the door he heard Kitty speaking in a hurried, high-pitched voice. He felt almost certain that she was talking freely, without suspicion or restraint. Bless Kate! He stood by the door.

". . . and that's all that happened, everything. I had too much to drink. I wasn't *drunk* but I was a bit tipsy, and I wore this dress. Oh, I know what you would think about it, you'd say the same thing my mother would have said if she hadn't died. 'You're a brazen hussy,' she'd have said, and there'd have been a hell of a row, but—well, I *wanted* topless dresses, and this was as near as I could go. There's such a lot of smug hypocrisy, why the hell should a girl give in to it? I just *wanted* to have the dresses, I didn't really mean to wear them, except for Dirk. Not really. But I'd had about four dry

Martinis before dinner, and gin always makes me sort of—well, reckless. Dirk was still in the bar, so I changed into one of the dresses. Dirk didn't really know what it was like. I—I camouflaged it a bit, but I suppose I showed plenty at dinner, but so do a lot of women; that didn't worry me and I don't think it worried Dirk. It was the dancing that made the real trouble. I think Ingy knew what would happen, there aren't any flies on Ingy Brown. I kept seeing him squint down at me during dinner, and then on the dance floor he started swinging me round and round—and everything came loose. Before I knew what was happening Dirk was absolutely flying at Ingy. I thought he would have killed him. And when he got to the cabin he tore the dresses up. He just tore them up as if they were rags, over a hundred pounds' worth. He ripped them across and across, and I thought he was going to start on me."

She broke off, and even Gideon was arrested, for the telling of this story held a certain poignancy.

More slowly, Kitty went on: "It was horrible after that. He just hardly said a word to me. When we got to the hotel, it was just as bad, until—until something happened. I—I suppose he loved me as much as I loved him. We couldn't stay angry with each other, thank God, thank God, thank God. I know you don't talk about these things, I never have to anybody, but everything—everything went right. I went to bed with him, the very last time, the very last time. Oh, God. It was so—so wonderful. It was absolutely wonderful." She sounded as if she were going to cry. "I'll never forget it, that last time was the best we'd ever had. I can't help it if he was a crook. I just can't help it, he was such a wonderful *man*. And he was the kindest man I've ever known. Until that awful night on the ship he was never anything but kind and gentle. I think that was why it was a shock. I didn't realize he was so jealous. If I'd dreamed he would be as upset as all that I wouldn't have bought those bloody dresses, but in a way I'm glad now. I'm glad because otherwise we wouldn't have had that last wonderful, wonderful time together."

There was a long pause; Kitty was making little gasping sounds, as if having difficulty in breathing.

"And then—then there was the telephone call. I put on that yellow dress. It's primrose color. Dirk always liked yellow, it was his favorite color. Now—it's all spotted with his blood, with Dirk's blood . . ." Her voice trailed away.

Should he go in? Should he start to ask questions?

Kate was saying: "Oh, my dear. I know how you feel, I really do." And softly: "Did you say your mother was dead?"

"Yes, she died two years ago, cancer, that was terrible, too. And Dirk was so good to her. He wouldn't let her go in the public ward at the hospital, he put her in the private ward. He was so kind to her, and—and she was my only relative. It's funny, isn't it? My dad died years ago, he was a steeplejack, he used to boast he would live to be a hundred, and then one day he slipped. Just slipped. I didn't think my mother would ever get over it, you see we—we'd lost my brother, my only brother, he had leukemia. He was only six. It's just as if there's a curse on my family, an absolute *curse*."

After a pause, when those restrained sobbing sounds came again, Kate said:

"Kitty, I want to do everything—everything—I can do to help. You must stay here for as long as you like, and treat this as your home while we're here." As Kitty didn't reply, Kate went on: "This man who telephoned, Kitty. Did you speak to him?"

"I answered the telephone. Oh, God, God, *God,* if only I hadn't. If only I'd pretended to be asleep."

"But you really can't remember what he sounded like?" Kate asked, and Gideon thought, She reminded me she was a policeman's wife.

"I don't really—I'm not used to American voices," Kitty said, almost desperately. "He spoke with a kind of drawl. I've heard people speak like it on the television, but I couldn't possibly imitate it."

"Would you recognize it again?"

"Oh, yes, I think I certainly would."

"Ah!" exclaimed Gideon, *sotto voce.*

"My husband's often said that a lot of criminals have been caught because someone remembered how they spoke," Kate remarked.

Kitty didn't answer, but the violence of her grief seemed to lessen. Soon after Gideon went in she seemed anxious to leave as if suddenly self-conscious about having stayed so long; probably she was embarrassed because she had talked so frankly.

A detective, outside the Gideons' door, escorted her down to her room.

Almost before the door had closed on her, Gideon was at the telephone. Kate glanced at him as she checked what Kitty had put out for the simple supper of cold ham and salad, very soft bread, and strawberries.

Kate could just hear her husband's voice. "Max, there's a line we haven't followed up properly. . . . The voice over the telephone. . . . Yes, the man who told Orlick to go to Tenth Avenue. . . . I tell you we haven't. Kitty Orlick heard the man speak but can't give us any idea what he sounded like because she can't use or catch American intonations. . . . Good Lord, I know they're regional. . . . What we need is someone who can mimic most of the accents, someone to talk to Mrs. Orlick. . . . Ah, I thought it would. . . . Yes, it will give the girl something to occupy her mind, too. . . . Tonight, I'd say. . . . Fine! . . . One other thing, I want to send a cable to the Yard about the sabotage job. . . . No, on second thoughts don't worry, I'll telephone them in the morning. . . . Yes, nearly ready."

When he put down the telephone Gideon was smiling. He ate too quickly, and when his plate was empty cast a hungry glance about the table, but didn't ask for more.

"George," Kate said.

"Yes, dear."

"Do you realize I've never seen you *working* before?"

"Nonsense—I'm often like this at home."

"You're not, you know. . . . Feeling easier in your mind?" Kate asked.

"I suppose so. Feel we're *trying* something, anyhow."

Even when Kate suggested calling to see how Kitty was, on their way out, Gideon agreed cheerfully. He was glad they looked in, for Lieutenant Cassidy and a "nurse" were there, talking animatedly to her. She seemed more cheerful than she had been all day.

"Now perhaps you'll stop worrying about her," Gideon said to Kate.

Five minutes before the curtain rose they were in the gilt and plush theater, small and crammed but comfortable, almost cold because of the air conditioning. Claire Nielsen was next to Gideon, Kate next to her, Nielsen next to Kate. As the curtain rose it occurred to Gideon that he was now sure that Kitty had been telling the truth. If she knew anything more to help the investigation, she was unaware of it.

But he had an uneasy feeling that there were a lot of difficulties ahead, over both this case and the sabotage affair.

19:

Bait?

Kitty sat on a high chair in her apartment, "Nurse" Detective Jessica Matthews on another chair, Cassidy leaned against the pantry sink. Coffee was bubbling in a stainless steel percolator. Cassidy cracked mild jokes as they waited for the coffee, a tray with cups and cream and sugar already prepared.

Kitty told them what she had already told the Gideons. It was less difficult now; not easy, but markedly less difficult. Every time she related the story the vividness faded a little, as if Dirk were drawing farther and farther away.

Cassidy said almost casually:

"This man on the telephone, Mrs. Orlick. How do you say he talked?"

"In a kind of drawl," Kitty answered. She tried to imitate the voice she had heard, but then broke off, actually smiling. "Not like that really, but something like it."

Cassidy interrupted: "Did the man speak like this, honey?" His voice had changed, there was a singsong note in it, and at the same time a more English-sounding vowel.

"Just tell us, honey chile, if that's how this man talked to you," Jessica asked, in the same kind of voice.

Kitty said almost unbelievingly: "That's *exactly* how he spoke!"

"So we know this much about the man," said Cassidy. There was nothing in his voice to indicate the satisfaction he felt, for it might prove only a tantalizing tidbit of useless information. "The man on the telephone was a Southerner, or he pretended to be."

"Would he pretend," asked Jessica, "if he didn't think either of the people he talked to would live to describe his voice?"

"Sure he would pretend," said Cassidy. "And he had to talk to the hotel operator first. That operator would be quicker than most to identify his voice. He would have faked it, all right."

"There was something else you said," said Kitty thoughtfully.

"What was it?"

"You said that he didn't think Dirk or me would live to say what he sounded like."

Cassidy said quietly: "That's right, honey. I did say that."

"You mean—you think they meant to kill *both* of us?"

"I wouldn't like to bet against it."

After a long pause Kitty said: "You really think they wanted to kill *me*?" When Cassidy didn't answer, she went on:

"They may still want to kill me. Is that right?"

Jessica said: "We'll take care of you, honey."

"They might," admitted Cassidy.

"Just because I heard the man's voice?"

"Not only because you heard the voice," Cassidy answered. "Because of what you might have learned about them from your husband."

"But he didn't tell me anything about them! I keep telling you, *I* didn't know his business was criminal!"

"I believe you, but how can this man be sure?" demanded Cassidy. "Your husband might have let a name slip, maybe, or given you some other clue you would pass on to the police. No one can be sure you know nothing—whether you know any of the gang in London, for instance, or whether Cordova ever talked to you about the business. You could know plenty."

"Do you seriously think I'm in any danger?" Kitty asked very quietly.

"If you were to ask Mr. Gideon that, he would say sure you are," replied Cassidy. For a few seconds the only sound in the kitchen was the bubbling of the coffee, for both detectives were looking intently at Kitty Orlick. A new and strange kind of dignity seemed to sit upon her, and it put a proud light in her eyes that they had not seen before.

"Then I can help find them," she said. "If they make an attempt to kill *me,* that will give you a chance to catch them."

"Now that's a crazy idea!" exclaimed Cassidy.

"And you think she was serious?" Gideon demanded, at half past seven next morning.

"Sure, she meant it," said Cassidy.

"So she wants to avenge Orlick that badly," remarked Nielsen. "Do you intend to give her the chance, George?"

Gideon brooded as he regarded the New York policeman.

They were in Nielsen's office. Cassidy had put in his report by the time the Gideons and the Nielsens had returned to the hotel the previous night, and the men had set up this meeting; after it, Gideon was to go to the River Squad's precinct house to hear more about the S.S. *Hempen*.

"Make up your mind," Nielsen urged.

"We've got to use Kitty Orlick one way or another," Gideon said at last. He was heavyhearted, but convinced he was right. "She gave us the lead to that voice, and she might have other things hidden away in her mind." He tapped a thick fold of paper, the report on Kitty's statement about the actual murder. "If we can set her mind working, instead of brooding, we might get somewhere."

"You should read it," Nielsen said. "It's in the latest report."

"That report won't reach Mr. Gideon until later," Cassidy put in hastily.

"Have you found the car?" Gideon asked.

"It was in a parking lot on the East Side. We've worked it over and found some prints but they don't belong to anyone we've had through our hands before. There were some blood spots on the fender and windshield, and the doorman at the Browns' apartment house identified a big scratch on the door panel."

"Has Kitty seen it?"

"We only found it late yesterday, there hasn't been time."

"Get her up," urged Gideon, glancing at Cassidy. "Can we postpone that meeting at the River Squad for an hour?"

"Sure. It will make no difference."

"Then let's call Kitty right away."

"First we want to set this thing up properly," said Nielsen. "I'll need some time. Lieutenant . . ."

There was a change in Kitty; hopefulness was in her manner, instead of hopelessness. How young and resilient she was, thought Gideon. She listened intently as they sat in the big car, Gideon doing most of the talking.

"There was one man in the car you saw," Gideon said. "We want his description. That's all that matters."

"I've told you, I hardly noticed him!"

"Concentrate on the moment when you saw him," Gideon urged. "Try to picture the scene as it was just before the crime."

He was fully aware of the awful effort he was asking her to make, but in this new mood it did not seem to worry her.

They pulled up by a nearly empty parking lot on First Avenue. Traffic was hurtling by on a sequence of stop-lights set at green. It was already hot, the sun was high, there was a steamy look about the river visible along a side street.

The green Chevrolet had been moved out of the lot to the street itself, and was double-parked. One man (at Nielsen's instructions) was sitting in the front. Across the street was a man on his own. As they walked past the green car, the door of another car opened, just ahead, and a man and a woman got out.

Kitty caught her breath . . .

She realized exactly what had been done; these men had reconstructed the situation as it had been immediately before the crime. Instead of Dirk by her side, there was Gideon, massive and fatherly; the two New York detectives were some way behind.

Kitty stood absolutely still, her eyes feverishly bright. As Gideon gripped her arm, she could feel the warmth of his hand. Everything—*everything*—came back to her; the whole scene was slowly unfolding like a macabre nightmare.

An engine roared deafeningly, just behind her.

"No!" she screamed. "No!"

She screwed up her eyes, to shut out the awful vision of the hurtling vehicle, Dirk shoving her to one side, the way she had staggered, the thud, the blood. She stood absolutely still when it was all over, glad of Gideon's nearness, of his hand. Other cars turned into the street, the parking lot attendant watched from his little box.

Gideon said calmly: "Kitty, that man in the green car—what was he like?"

Kitty said: "He was a big man—like the one in it now. He had very dark eyes, and a heavy face and chin. I did see him—he was looking round at me. I did see him!"

Nielsen came up.

"Take a look at this," he urged, and held one of the *Identikit* pictures in front of her. Kitty stared at it, then at Nielsen.

"That's what he looked like!"

"That's the man who called himself Preston when he talked to Brown," Nielsen said with deep satisfaction. "Now, if those witnesses were lying, they might know this guy. I'll get busy on them."

"One other thing," Gideon said quickly.

"Anything you say, George."

"You could find out if this man's known at the docks, where our trouble starts."

"*You* fix that," Nielsen said. "You're going to the right place."

"Does this mean you think you'll find him?" Kitty asked tensely.

"Sooner or later, we will."

"And sooner or later you'll be the one to help again," Gideon told Kitty. "I don't object to you offering yourself as bait, but do it our way. Is that clear?"

"Yes," said Kitty. "Just so long as I'm helping."

The police car driven by Gentian was rattling along Lafayette Street at a quarter past nine that same morning; Cassidy was sitting with Gideon in the back of the car. The success of the effort to stimulate Kitty's memory, and the newness of the surroundings, had worn off for Gideon. There were wonders to behold but the urgency of business preoccupied him here just as much as it did in London.

As they turned into the now familiar street, Gideon felt that he couldn't wait to get to the docks and the warehouses for a firsthand knowledge of the situation.

He knew London docks as did few men who had not worked in them all their lives. He knew that dock and harbor men were of a different breed from others; that the roughness and the harshness of much of their work, and the fact that they were dealing all the time with ships which sailed the seven oceans, affected their attitudes. They lived and worked and drank and played their lives out on or near the docks, with the tang of salt water, the scent of the spices, and the stink of rotting cargoes and of oil forever in their nostrils. They rubbed shoulders with the rest of the world, with people of all nationalities, the white, the yellow and the black, the free and the captive. They picked up a rough-and-ready knowledge of far-off places and they learned some of the customs and much of the vice that was born and thrived in those places.

They were hardheaded, practical men, mostly of great physical strength, with a history of social victimization, and an ingrained sense of it even today. In one nation it would be victimization by the unions or gangsters, in others victimization by the employers; wherever and whatever it was, there was a sense of frustration. At times Gideon thought that it was partly because the men in the ships they loaded and unloaded were always restless and because of the lands they heard about but never saw, the exotic and the erotic things they heard about, calculated to stir a desire which could never be gratified.

Whatever the reasons, disaffection could spread more swiftly among dockworkers than among most other groups, and it could cause more damage in a few days than in some industries in weeks. So perhaps the men had acquired a sense of their own power.

Given these circumstances and conditions and the types of men and the history of abuse and violence, obviously the seeds of corruption were ever present. And corruption was the greatest enemy of the police.

20:

Old Crate

KROTZNER WAS saying with characteristic intensity:

"Sure we have troubles, plenty of troubles. Sure there's corruption. Sure there's organized and habitual larceny—pilfering you say—all along the line. We know it. You know it. But there isn't so much as there used to be, and it's getting less. We have our problems, we have plenty of lawbreakers, more than our share maybe. Did anyone ever start counting the numbers of longshoremen who do their job the way we all want it done? Longshoremen and cops—if you listen to the big mouths, they never do anything right."

"Why don't you show us what they are doing right?" asked Cassidy.

"Such as whether they can identify this man," Gideon said, handing a copy of the *Identikit* picture of the man from the green Chevrolet.

Cassidy put in: "We're sending over plenty more of those pictures. You want to give every patrolman on the river and every customs official one, and try to put a finger on this guy."

"Will do," said Krotzner. He was staring at the picture. "Excuse me." He went out for five minutes, and came back to report that the pictures had arrived and distribution had been arranged. When Gideon went downstairs again half an hour later he saw one pinned to a notice board under a headline: "*Can You Name This Man?*" Krotzner, Peek, Gideon and Cassidy crowded into a big police car.

"First we look at the pier, then we look at the warehouses and the sheds, O.K.?" Krotzner said. "The *Hempen* is seventy miles out, she should be tied up around three-thirty. We'll be told if there's any delay. . . . We haven't learned of anyone in the longshoremen gangs showing a special interest in her or in the *Maruna,* but they may have some news the other side. . . . The New Jersey officials will be right glad to see you, Commander. I've got some pictures for them, too." The lieutenant kept on talking, until the car turned off the ordinary streets and into a cutting, shadowed by a high wall on each side. "Entrance to the Holland Tunnel," Krotzner said. "There was a time when I thought we had the longest underwater tunnels in the world, then I was told you have a longer one in Birkenhead, England, the Mersey Tunnel." They were going downhill and the car seemed to move very fast. Soon they were passing under a series of girders and gray underpasses, until abruptly they were in the tunnel itself, with the rows of lights on either side giving a ghostly kind of gloom, the stink of exhaust fumes, the curiously harsh tire noise, the booming roar of trucks ahead and behind them. No one spoke until daylight glowed at the far end, and then they found themselves slowing down as a line of cars and trucks waited to pay the toll.

"What's this?" asked Gideon.

"The toll booths," Krotzner said. "Don't you have tolls in England?"

"Very few," Gideon said. "There's talk of having more for more motorways." He felt the brightness of the sun on him, although it was very cool in the car. There was a mass of trucks—he had never seen more together, not even on London's A1 and A4—and they created a constant boom of sound. Most of the trucks were much larger than those in England, and the chrome shone like silver in the sun. There were a few minutes of skillful maneuvering as the police car slid through them and then turned into a huge yard where there seemed to be hundreds of the leviathans, dozens of truck bodies, and as many truck motors, standing waiting.

Gideon stepping out of the car almost trod on Cassidy's heels, so taken aback was he by the scene in front of him. They were on a slight rise in the land, and he could see across the Hudson to New York City. No sight had ever affected him as much. The shimmering blue water was dotted with ships, with the S.S. *Fifty States* sailing toward the tip of Manhattan, smooth and graceful as a toy in an enormous decorated bath. A faint haze grayed the far bank of the river, softening the outline of the piers and the loading and the customs sheds. Beyond these stood the tall buildings. The spire of the Empire State Building, so slenderly graceful, set the others off to greater magnificence. There was a huddle of tall buildings in the middle of the island and another at the southern tip, the Wall Street end.

Cassidy, beside Gideon, looked at his set face and said:

"Some people see it a thousand times and never see it. You won't forget it all your life, Commander. And you'll want to come back again and again."

Krotzner said: "Sure, it's something to see." He moved closer to Gideon. "How about London, Commander? How does it compare? All my life I wanted to see London."

"Come and see it," Gideon said gruffly. "But don't try to compare it. It would be like comparing a desert with a mountain, they're so different." Reluctantly he looked away, back at the huge yard.

"This is the lineup for the trucks coming from the northeastern states," Krotzner explained. The car slowed down, and two men in plain clothes came forward from a stationary car. "Here are the New Jersey officers." There was a flurry of introductions, smiles, inquisitive glances at Gideon, and as the group stood together Gideon realized that Peek was the biggest man among them, and that he himself came an easy second. The sun burned, yet he did not feel the heat so much as he had felt it in New York.

One of the New Jersey men took up where Krotzner left off. The story was simple and straightforward. Hundreds of trucks a day from the main manufacturing centers in the northeast brought their loads down here, where they were parked in the waiting line. Some of them might wait for two or three days before being unloaded direct to the ships or barges. Often the motors were disconnected and the vans themselves were left. "There are three vans to one motor," the New Jersey man said. He was very, very lean, very brown, very precise. "All the trucks bring goods for export, so the driver has a copy of the shipping documents, including the bills of lading. These are tied up with the dock boss, who is in charge of the checkers—"

"Tally clerks to you," Krotzner said to Gideon.

"Thanks."

"Now there's a truck in from Rite-Time's Buffalo plant," the New Jersey man continued. "It's going to unload in a couple of hours, I guess. We can take a look around."

"Take a look at these first," Krotzner said. He took a dozen copies of the *Identikit* picture out of his pocket and handed them to the New Jersey man, who glanced down and said laconically:

"This guy could be one of three or four I often see around."

"We'll want to see each one," Krotzner said.

"Sure, but they may not all be on duty today." The New Jersey man called a younger officer, explained, and went on: "Two of the possibles are checkers, so don't let anyone see those pictures except police or customs officers."

"Right."

"Spread them around fast," the New Jersey man ordered.

Gideon kept wondering whether he seriously meant that there were three or four men who might fit the picture. In the next half hour he himself saw two men who resembled it. If four or five or six "suspects" were found, Kitty could be brought to see them; her recollection now seemed clear enough for her to identify the man on sight.

He could hardly wait for results, yet so much here was fascinating. The huge warehouses, the ships alongside, the Hi-Lo hoists, the constant seething movement of men, trucks, hoists, goods and machines, the heat, the sweat, the stink, the harshness, the almost naïve obscenity, the shouting, bellowing and whistling, even occasionally the singing of lewd ballads. Everyone seemed to be putting his back into his work.

"Here's the Rite-Time load," the New Jersey man said.

A motor was hitched onto one of the vans which had been parked at the side, and was maneuvered alongside a ship which already looked too low in the water to take more cargo. Gideon saw the Hi-Los, realized there was a great deal more automation here than in the London docks, sensed the curious glances of the people staring at him. He saw a big, heavy man in a blue shirt carrying a sheaf of documents. The man had a barrellike torso, a big jaw and heavy jowl, and his neck seemed stiff; when he looked about him he swiveled his nearly-black eyes, as if he had difficulty in turning his head.

Gideon gripped Krotzner's arm.

"See the man in the blue shirt?"

"He could be our man," Krotzner agreed softly. "He could certainly be."

"He's a receiving clerk, named Mense," the New Jersey man volunteered. "He's giving the longshoremen's gang their dockets."

The man in the blue shirt handed the documents to a smaller man, and went off, glancing covertly toward Gideon, who pretended not to see him. The second of the New Jersey policemen moved away casually.

"So we could be getting close," Cassidy said.

"There are others who would fit that picture," Krotzner declared. "Commander, I was saying . . ."

The Rite-Time truck was opened at the back, and crate after crate came out, some to be put on one side, some to be hoisted on the Hi-Los and then onto cranes which swung them overboard. Men on deck, men on the dockside, men in the deep cavernous holds were making little signs to each other, like tick-tack men on an English race course, to make sure that the crates were placed in the best position for all stages of loading.

One of them was marked: *S.S. Hempen—Dakar*. Huge black numbers were stenciled across it. The New Jersey man seemed to be interested in everything but that particular crate, and moved along, taking the party with him. He whispered:

"That's going on a barge across to Pier 121—that right, Krotz?"

"That's right," Krotzner said. "The barge is alongside the pier now, partly loaded. We could open the crate here or we could wait until it gets across the river." He glanced at Gideon tentatively asking what he thought, but Gideon made no comment; this was their job. Without full knowledge of the background he would probably suggest the wrong thing, anyhow.

Peek was staring at the crate.

"That one's been around a long time," he said. "You remember the trouble we had with Hurricane Vera last September?"

"Who could forget?" asked Cassidy.

"She hustled up the Hudson River and caused the nearest we've had to a tidal wave in twenty years," said Peek. "Most of these warehouses were flooded to a depth of four to five feet. Remember the oil?"

Gideon could sense the tension in the others caused by these remarks, but they meant nothing to him. He could see that the yellowish white wood of the crate was in two shades; that about a foot from the top was pale, that below it had a slightly darker tinge. Cassidy moved toward it and studied the line of the dark tinge.

"Sure we remember the oil," Krotzner said. "In one of the warehouses there were ten thousand gallons of crude oil. Some of the drums were smashed, and plenty of oil leaked out. It rose to the top of the water, and made a mark—and it stained a lot of crates which were waiting to be shipped. Some of them were damaged and the goods spoiled." Now all of the men were looking at Gideon, and he caught some of their excitement.

"You mean that that crate's been here since the hurricane,

and it's only now being loaded?" he hazarded. "Is that what you're driving at?"

"That's what we're saying," declared the New Jersey lieutenant. "The significant fact being that it's been hidden—covered up, maybe—and for a long time, then put with the consignment taken off this truck. The quicker we look inside the crate the better."

Krotzner said: "You don't agree, Commander, do you?"

Gideon rubbed his chin.

"Let me read your thoughts," went on Cassidy, with that quick and infectious grin. "You think that if the crate is taken to the pier and then loaded onto the *Hempen* you could find out exactly where it is going and whether the stevedoring company and the Trans-Ana Shipping Company are in this racket together."

"Right?" Krotzner demanded.

"I'm wondering what would happen if the barge ran into trouble and the cargo went overboard," Gideon said thoughtfully. "Then we wouldn't have much evidence of any kind."

The New Jersey man said: "If we open it here, we can't lose it."

Krotzner said: "If we wait until it's loaded on board we'll get all the angles, like Cassidy says."

"Your vote," Cassidy said to Peek.

"Wait until it's on the *Hempen*," replied Peek promptly.

"I'm for opening it here," argued Cassidy. "We don't have to do it ourselves, we can get Customs to become curious and take a look—they're always poking around somewhere." Cassidy glanced at Gideon. "You've got the casting vote, Commander."

"Ring Captain Nielsen and get his advice," Gideon suggested.

"There's a Solomon for you," boomed Peek.

"Have the crate watched, have the barge watched, don't let it go out of sight, make sure the crate isn't pushed overboard, and wait until it's on board the *Hempen*," Nielsen said to Cassidy. "Is Commander Gideon there?"

"Standing right by me." Cassidy handed the telephone to Gideon, and shifted back in the little customs office which had windows all round. They seemed to be surrounded by a sea of trucks, cranes, men, crates and sacks, barrels and boxes.

"Gideon," said Gideon, and he felt uneasy for no reason at all.

"George," said Nielsen, "I want you to know that Kitty Orlick had a call from a man who says he's an old friend of her husband. This friend says he read about the accident and sure is sorry and he would like to meet the widow and demonstrate how sorry he is. He wants her to meet him at Grand Central Station, at the Information Desk. Kate—"

Gideon caught his breath; where did Kate come into this?

"Kate advised her to arrange to meet this guy at eight o'clock tonight," said Nielsen. "I think Kate intends to go with her."

Very slowly Gideon said: "I'll go straight back. Anything else new?"

"Those three witnesses to the accident," Nielsen said. "They're scared, George—too scared to talk. Given time we could break them down, but that won't help Kitty Orlick. The first thing you have to worry about is your wife. Her heart's too big."

Danny Silvermann was in his office close to the big chemical works at the city limits of Buffalo, looking out onto the trucks standing in the big parking lot. A few men stood about idly; two mechanics worked busily on a diesel engine that was giving trouble.

His telephone bell rang.

"Danny," Mense said, "they're onto that crate in New Jersey."

Silvermann caught his breath.

"There were two New York cops and the limey," Mense went on. "There's no doubt about it."

Silvermann said slowly: "So what do we do?" Before Mense could answer, he went on: "The girl goes quick, right?"

"The girl goes quick. I've fixed that."

"How about—" Silvermann almost choked. "How about the *Hempen*? She's got a big consignment for us."

"We can't handle it," said Mense flatly.

"We've got to handle it."

"We can't," Mense insisted. "Not if the pier's being watched. Listen, Darkie handled the *Maruna* and the *Hempen*, only Davo the first officer knows us. So we've got time."

"Time for what?"

"Time to fix him. Time to get out of the New Jersey business, and concentrate on this end. We wanted out in any case. We get it quicker than we expected, that's all."

"We can't get out while that girl's around."

"So I've fixed it. So where's the worry?" Mense demanded.

Marcus Davo, the first officer on the *Hempen*, was in his early thirties, a man of little imagination but always on top of his job. He had been at sea since leaving high school. He had problems—money problems. He did not have a wife in every port, but he had three "wives" in overseas ports, as well as a legal one who lived in upstate New York. He was at heart a generous man, and his natural goodness as well as his weathered good looks and quick, easy laughter were at the core of his problem. He did not like having a pretty girl in tears. He could not resist wooing and winning and bedding them, and at times he almost laughed, ruefully, at his quite remarkable fecundity. He spawned children, and he felt and accepted financial responsibility for seven outside his lawful family of three.

That was why he had made the deal with Mense.

That was why he was hoping there would soon be another deal, because he needed the money badly. He had borrowed against his salary to pay out at the various African and European ports, and he was in desperate need of two thousand dollars to take home the day after tomorrow, when the cargo would be discharged and he would have his between-voyages leave.

Two thousand dollars . . .

Given that two thousand, he could make his wife happy, everyone would be happy.

While Marcus Davo was ruminating on his chances of getting more money from Mense, Mense was considering how best to kill him, and Gideon was wondering how to deal with Kate, whom he had never known in such a mood before.

21:

Old Friend

"KATE," GIDEON said, "there's no sense in it. She doesn't mean anything to you. She can't. There's no reason at all for you to become involved."

"There's a good reason," Kate argued.

"I've yet to hear it."

"I should have to live with myself afterwards if I didn't help, and if anything happened to her."

They stood together in the bedroom of the apartment, knowing that Kitty was in the living room. Gideon tried to keep his voice low, but sound traveled freely here. Kate felt so deeply about it that she was talking more loudly than usual, and he wished she wouldn't. It wasn't a quarrel; it couldn't become a quarrel, Gideon told himself, and yet there was tension between them.

"Kate—"

"I'm going with her," Kate declared.

"Kate," Gideon protested, "there's a good reason why you shouldn't, one which you haven't thought of."

"What is it?"

"If anything happened to you, and I'd allowed you to go, I would have to live with myself, too."

He saw from the softening of Kate's expression that this made sense to her, and he hoped that it conveyed some of the depth of his feeling and of his fear. As he watched her, another thing impinged sharply on his mind. He felt so anxious for her because he and Nielsen seriously believed there would be an attempt to kill Kitty.

"You've taken a lot of chances for people you've hardly known," Kate said. "You've even put yourself in danger to make sure a criminal didn't get hurt, before now. Just because you're in New York it doesn't alter your responsibility, dear, and you know it. If the New York police are as good as you say they are, they'll make sure that nothing happens to either of us."

Very slowly, very deliberately, Gideon replied: "No one can prevent an attack. All the police in New York couldn't prevent a shooting if an unidentified assailant was determined to carry it out. They might be able to stop the man's getting away, but that's all. The moment you step outside of this building with Orlick's widow, you'll be in danger. There could be a man sitting at a window at this very minute, with a gun ready to shoot her."

Kate considered, and then asked quietly:

"George, do you think she might lead us to the murderer?"

"It's possible."

"And you're prepared to use her as a bait?"

"So as to catch the man who might otherwise kill her, yes."

"George," said Kate, "I think you ought to stop Kitty from going. I don't think you ought to let her take such a risk. But if she goes, *I'm* going with her."

Now Gideon knew what Kate was up to—trying to compel him to prevent Kitty from meeting the stranger. Kate knew perfectly well she could not actually help the girl here in New York, offering to go was little more than a gesture—but her insistence put great pressure on him.

A moment of strange tension followed. In it a miracle in time occurred. Gideon's mind slipped back to a night many years before, when Kate had been at their home, with their seventh child close to death. Out in the vastness of London a killer had been at large—a killer whom Gideon had had to find. He could leave Kate and do his job, or he could postpone his job for a few hours. And she had wanted him to stay so desperately.

He had walked out on her.

For a time it seemed almost as if it would end their marriage, for the child died before Gideon returned, his task performed. It had been a long, long time before they recovered from the loss, and from the rift which it had created between them. As he looked at her now, Gideon wondered if the same thought was in her mind, the same hurtful recollection.

The unusual tautness of her lips, the curious hardness in her eyes, reminded him of that night so long ago. She did not speak.

He said, with an effort: "You must do what you've got to do, Kate. I hate the thought of it, but you must do what you think right. So must I."

Gideon was frightened for his wife and disturbed by other things, and yet he did not think he had ever known such peace as he knew in the half hour that followed. It was his and Kate's. They said little and they did nothing, just sat together and watched the ever-fascinating changes of the brightening light and the moving traffic, the purpling sky and the stars which grew sharper and still sharper as the heavens darkened. At last Kate stirred, stood up, leaned over him and kissed his forehead, and said in rather a shaky voice:

"I mustn't be late."

She went out, and he sat frowning, still not quite sure what he should do, not even sure whether he should make another attempt to persuade her to stay.

Then Kate came hurrying back, her voice high-pitched, her face flushed with alarm.

"Kitty's not here!" she cried. "She must have heard us talking."

Kitty Orlick had stood at the bedroom door and heard the Gideons arguing; almost quarreling. She had been intrigued by Gideon's tone when he had come in, and then realizing that they were discussing her, she had listened. As they talked, as the tension between them increased, she felt like crying out: "Stop, stop, stop!" but something kept her silent. Numbness gripped her whole body. She could not see either of them and yet could imagine their faces.

Then slowly, speaking almost as if it hurt him, Gideon had said: "You must do what you've got to do, Kate. I hate the thought of it, but you must do what you think right. So must I."

Had they come out of the bedroom at that moment they would have seen Kitty, for she stood there incapable of movement. Gradually sensation returned to her legs. She turned and stumbled down to her room, flung herself on the bed and buried her face in her hands. She fought against hot tears, gritting her teeth, screwing up her eyes, kicking up and down on the mattress, fiercely, savagely, until the paroxysm exhausted itself. At last she became calm and with one of those flashes of insight which often came to her she knew exactly what she must do. She washed her face, made up quickly, and went out. With the prospect of physical action, grief and emotion dried up. When she reached the street she was, to a casual observer, her normal self; few would have noticed that she walked quickly and stiffly.

She knew exactly where she had to go.

She knew also that the police were following her.

As she turned into Fifth Avenue, clutching her handbag, she stepped into the street against the lights, and a car horn blared. It made her leap back onto the curb, and the sound went through her as if a jagged knife had been buried in her breast. It revived so poignantly the image of what had happened to Dirk that she caught her breath.

For a hideous moment she thought, What have I to live for? Then, fighting down self-pity, she returned courageously to her resolution to lead the police to Dirk's killer.

She waited for the lights to change, but did not hurry across. As she reached the far side an empty taxi crawled by. She waved, it stopped, and she got in.

"Grand Central Station, please," she said.

The driver grunted, and moved off into the traffic. The terrible scene she had lived through, the frightful moment of her husband's death, was so vividly before her, that she had to choke back her tears. She made herself remember what the "old friend" of Dirk's had said: she should meet him at the Information Desk at Grand Central Station—she couldn't miss it.

It seemed so long before the taxi stopped that she began to wonder if she would be late; but at last the driver drew up outside a corner entrance, with a big clock above the doors.

"How much?" she asked.

"One-thirty-five."

She fumbled for a dollar and some coins, and he seemed satisfied.

A number of people stood about as she left the cab, some of them policemen, some of them just men who liked to look at a pretty girl; one of these might be an "old friend" of Dirk's. She recognized no one. The street was crowded, but the pedestrians moved unhurriedly. Tall new-looking buildings were on either side. She had good time, after all. It was a quarter to eight, she had to meet the man at eight o'clock. The doors were heavy to push, as she followed half a dozen people into a long passage. It wasn't very bright, rather like any big station approach. There were lights farther on, shops, shoeshine boys, a lot of ordinary-looking people. She kept following the crowd, until she stepped into the biggest hall she had ever seen, so huge, so fantastically high-ceilinged that for a moment she could only gape. Near one end was a motorcar, glistening red, going slowly round on a swivel base; dozens of people stood around it. There was a kiosk in the center of the hall, there were ticket offices and crowds—but there were no trains and no platforms. She peered up at some huge photographs, then looked about her again, and saw a big, circular Information Desk. Two or three men and several women stood near it. Was the "friend" among them?

Her heart began to beat very fast.

22:

Capture

A FEW MINUTES later, when she felt steadier, a man came hurrying toward Kitty. He carried a small black briefcase and wore a small-brimmed hat; all in all, he was very neatly dressed. There was something vaguely familiar about him, but his brisk approach did nothing to make her suspect he was the man she was to meet. It was when he stopped abruptly at her side, that she was startled, and her heart began to thump.

"Kitty Orlick?" he asked in a soft voice.

She turned round. "Why, yes!"

"I'm very glad you've come," the man said warmly. "I can't tell you how much I wanted to meet you." He took her arm, and led the way towards the entrance through which she had just come. She noticed two heavily built men, one of whom she had seen outside the Gideons' hotel several times.

Suddenly she heard the man by her side catch his breath. At the same moment, he pushed her to one side, turned, and raced away in the direction from which he had come. On the instant, men leaped forward toward him, the crowd of people seemed to sway to one side, a woman cried out as she was pushed and sent headlong. The big man whom Kitty recognized was near the runaway—and he snatched out a gun.

"Don't *shoot!*" someone roared.

Panic showed on the faces of a dozen people who scattered in all directions. The calm of the huge hall was broken, people cried out, screamed and ran. To Kitty, the confusion was worse because there seemed so many tunnels, gateways, and passages. Then a big man came to her side, and she recognized Cassidy.

"You O.K.?" he asked.

"Yes."

"Next time you feel like being a heroine, let us know in advance," Cassidy said tartly.

Another man came hurrying up.

"Looks like he got away," this man said gloomily. "If you'd let me shoot the guy—"

"One stray bullet in a crowd like this—you're crazy, man," Cassidy said. He turned to Kitty again. "I'm going to send you back to your hotel in a police car. Don't you move out again without telling the guard where you're going. Understand?"

"All right," Kitty said in a subdued voice. "I promise."

An hour later there was a knock at the door of the Gideons' apartment, and Kate went to open it. Gideon was at the telephone, listening to Nielsen, who was obviously restraining his anger.

". . . he got away but one of our men recognized him. . . . He was one of the witnesses to the accident, dressed up like a business executive so that he didn't look the same man, but there's no doubt about his identity. Sooner or later we'll pick him up, and we'll work on the other two witnesses again, maybe this will make them unbutton."

"Where's Kitty?" asked Gideon.

"On her way back to the hotel. Why did she go off on her own?"

Gideon heard Kate's voice, followed by Kitty's.

"She wanted to make sure Kate didn't go with her and run into trouble."

"That Kitty Orlick's quite a girl," Nielsen said, as if mollified. "Still want to use her as bait?"

"It could be the right thing to do," Gideon said stubbornly.

"You don't give in easily," Nielsen said. "George, I want to talk to you about the *Hempen*, and some of the men at the docks. Will you be at my office at ten o'clock?"

"Of course."

"There's some mail in for you here. I meant to hand it over when you arrived back from the harbor but you didn't come," said Nielsen. "I'll give it to you tomorrow. George, why don't you and Kate visit with Claire?"

"Don't worry about us," Gideon said. "We're fine. I'll see you at ten in the morning." He turned round as Kate came into the room with Kitty, and he noticed how frail—almost fragile—the girl looked, as if this last shock had robbed her of both her youth and her vitality. Kate had an arm round her shoulders as Kitty looked across at Gideon without expression.

Gideon poured a whisky and soda, and took it across to her. She sipped, moistened her lips, sipped again, and then handed it back. Her voice croaked when she said, "Thank you." Tears, long held back, suddenly spilled over. "Thank you for everything," she said. "I'll never be able to thank you, never." She looked at Gideon, her lips trembling. "Thank you for—thank you for saying your wife could come with me." She was fighting against breaking down. Suddenly she jumped up. "Can I *do* something? Is there anything I can *do*?"

"I was going to cook bacon and eggs," Kate said.

"So long as I can do something!" Kitty cried.

It was nearly two o'clock in the morning in London, and most of that great city was asleep. But Mrs. Fadiman was awake. It took her a long time to fall asleep these days, because she was haunted by a fear she would not share with anyone, the fear that Cedric *had* committed those awful crimes. She was alone. She would not go up and stay in Birmingham with David, and she had no one but the Todhunters to stay with nearby, and they already had Leslie. In any case, she didn't want company; alone, she could talk to herself without the fear of being overheard. The only thing that she wished, now, was that her daughter was better, but Elsa lay in the hospital not saying a word; Mrs. Fadiman had spent half an hour there that evening, just watching her child, until the nurse had persuaded her to go home.

Mrs. Fadiman pushed the bedclothes back and got out of bed, a shapeless figure in a pink flannelette nightdress. She put on a bulky dressing gown and a pair of flimsy slippers, a present from Leslie on her last birthday, and went down to the kitchen.

"I'm all right so long as I'm doing something," she said to herself, and she put on the kettle to make tea.

The tea itself was kept in a tin caddy, decorated with Indian scenes, which Cedric had brought home from a second-hand shop many years ago. She knew that it had a trick lid; that was why he had bought it. If one hoisted the lid in a certain way, a spring would be released, and metal cutouts of an Indian scene would appear. Leslie had broken the cut-outs years ago, and she had almost forgotten how the lid worked. Yet in some dim corner of her mind memory stirred. She twisted in one direction and another, the inside of the lid sprang open, and two or three tiny white tablets fell out. There were still others inside.

She stared at them.

"Oh, no," she said in a choking voice. "Oh, dear God, no!"

The kettle came furiously to the boiling point.

She began to cry.

Suddenly she snatched up two of the tablets and tossed them into her mouth, then put the milk jug to her lips and washed the tablets down. She turned off the kettle, and left the kitchen, quite sure of what she had done.

She knew now that Cedric was guilty; and felt there was nothing left to live for.

The pain came in thirty minutes.

She thought, even in this agony, of the other women and what her husband had done to them; even in the first relaxed moment, she was still determined to die.

Darkie was asleep in a small cabin next to the captain's quarters of the *Maruna*. He was sleeping the sleep that is supposed to be reserved for the just.

Chloe Lemaitre was awake, lying in a bed next to Lem, who was breathing very heavily. When he had come to bed, twenty minutes before, she had pretended to be asleep because she hoped he would drop off quickly. He wasn't getting enough sleep; the Post Office case was too much for him. He had not arrived home until ten o'clock, and then he had sat poring over his graphs and his notes until she had gone to bed, at twelve or so. And when he woke, the first thing he would start talking about was the case.

Suddenly he startled her.

"You awake, Chloe?"

"Yes," she said.

"Bloody good job I've got you," he said. She half expected him to cross to her bed, but he didn't. Street lamp-light shimmered on his eyes as he looked at her. "You want to know something, duckie?" He hesitated but it was not simply for her to answer. "Well, I'll tell you. They've got clean away. They've beat me—the bastards. We won't get 'em now. Or if we do it won't be because of anything I've done. The hell of it is I don't know what I did wrong. I can't help feeling that if old George had been here he would have spotted something."

"Oh, you and your blasted George! I wish he'd stay in New York and never come back."

"Well, I don't," said Lemaitre. "I'll tell you another thing I'm bloody sure of. If George had been here he would have told Mac to be at Cordova's flat, not to wait until he got to the office. I could cry, I tell you I could cry. The moment I heard what had happened I knew what I ought to have done."

"I thought MacPherson was in charge of that," Chloe said.

"So what? I'm in charge of Mac." There was a pause, which lasted for so long that she began to wonder whether he had dropped off, but she should have known better. At last he pushed the clothes back and nipped across to her bed, and she shifted over for him. He was thin and bony, and she was soft and cuddly; but cuddling obviously wasn't in his mind. "Let me tell you something," he said. "I'm not going to take the deputy commander's job. Even if they ask me, which they bloody well won't. I'm not going to take it. It would mean another thousand quid a year but you'll have to manage on what I get, duckie. It's not for me. I haven't got what it takes. That's the truth of it. Old George—he's one in a million. I'm twice as good when he's around, because I know he'll tell me what to do next and where I've slipped up. Good old Gee-Gee. Wonder how he's getting on. Probably got the Rite-Time case sewed up. Wouldn't I like to see him when he's with the New York coppers. You want to know something—he'll be sorry. That's the truth. He'll be bloody sorry that I won't get the job, but he knows I'm not right for it. Never said so, in fact he did his best to put me right, and I told him where to get off. How crazy can you get?"

There was another silence.

In a faraway voice, he said: "You'll have to get a job, that's what you'll have to do."

"Lem, don't be daft," Chloe said. "You earn all the money we need. Don't be silly."

"It won't worry you if I don't get promotion?"

Get promotion, Chloe echoed silently; by morning he would probably have persuaded himself that the job was his for the asking but that he was going to talk himself out of it; that would be the best possible frame of mind for him.

"Worry," she said. "*I* don't want you to take the blasted job. This last few days has told me all I want to know about it. Up at six, in the office before seven, home at ten, up half the night doing what you didn't have time for at the office—

what do you think I am? A paid housekeeper? I want a husband, and don't forget it. I want to spend some time day *and* night with him. Strewth, I wouldn't change places with Kate Gideon for all the commanders and deputy commanders at the Yard, and *that's* a fact."

Lemaitre, his heart lighter than it had been for a long time, suddenly slid his arm round her and hugged her so tightly that she gasped.

Sir Reginald Scott-Marle was asleep.

The Allinghams were asleep.

Even John Webb was asleep in the police cell in New York. The Gideons slept.

Kitty Orlick, tonight in sedation, was sleeping soundly and deeply.

The only one of the police whom Gideon had met who lay awake was Lieutenant Krotzner. He had heard of the attack on Mrs. Orlick and had spent much of the night thinking about the Rite-Time case.

He blamed himself for the fact that he hadn't found that old crate of goods before. He should have. He knew that someone had deliberately and carefully hidden it, but he had been in charge of the investigations into Rite-Time and no one else was to blame. This was so clear to him that it seemed to make everything else clear, and one thing was even more apparent than the others. If he wished to re-establish himself in his own eyes, then *he* had to break this case wide open. He, Lieutenant Abel Krotzner, who knew the docks and the waterfront better than any other policeman. It was a matter of pride. He was essentially a proud man—proud of his efficiency, proud of his record, proud of the River Squad, proud of the waterfront, proud of New York, proud of America. The fact that he was a humorless individual who seldom saw the funny side of any situation added immeasurably to its essentiality. If Nielsen or Cassidy or even Gideon solved the case, then he would never really recover from a sense of failure. It did not occur to him that no one else would blame him; he felt that if he let himself down it would automatically let the River Squad down, and so to some degree it would let the United States down.

He had more clues, now, and he saw the whole affair stretched over nearly a year—every single thing he knew about it was crystal clear in his mind.

He lay on his bachelor's bed near the precinct house, envisaging all the individuals whom he had seen. If he could only work the problem out so that he could give Nielsen and Gideon the answers tomorrow, he would feel great. The greatest.

Mense was calculating the risks of dealing with Marcus Davo himself, or through someone else. It should be easy to get a crane driver or a hoist operator to cause a fatal accident, but it had to be over quickly. Much depended on whether the police moved before or after the *Hempen* berthed. Mense thought they would probably let it berth and unload and wait to see what happened to the crate they had discovered. Providing they did that, he would have plenty of time for the next move.

If the police moved in as soon as the ship tied up, then he would have to act fast—and act himself.

For Kitty Orlick and Davo *had* to be killed. The girl had escaped once, but he would get her. It did not occur to him to question the need, nor the morality of it. He had no feeling for other people, in the sense of compunction or remorse;

what had to be done for self-preservation had to be.

The strange thing was that, although it should have been glaringly obvious to him that he no longer had a chance of getting away even with the murder he had already committed, that did not occur to him. The only question in his mind was not whether he should or should not kill again but the method of that killing.

23:

The Triumph

"THERE'S THE *Hempen*," said Nielsen.

He was standing with Gideon in an observatory tower on the top of a tall building in the Wall Street area, looking down on the piers in the Hudson River. The river was busy with the trafficking of barges, ferries, freighters, among which the *Queen Mary* and the *France* reared majestically in their nearly adjacent piers, ready to sail during the following day. Gideon could see the top of the precinct house as he gazed through field glasses at the S.S. *Hempen*.

"Looks a rough old crate," Gideon said.

"It's rough and it's ancient," Nielsen agreed. "And tough, too—those old Liberty ships certainly stand up to heavy seas."

Gideon noticed that the hull was badly in need of scraping and painting, but the ship looked serviceable. Both holds were open, cranes and booms were working, and he saw a barge alongside; it might be the one with the Rite-Time on board. He knew that the Harbor Police were watching closely, that once the signal was given there would be a surge of police toward the ship just as there had been a surge on the assailant at Grand Central Station. Men, antlike, were bustling about the decks, there was continual movement.

"You seen all you want to?" Nielsen asked. He was brusque.

"Yes, thanks."

"I want to tell you," Nielsen said, as they turned away, "that we've questioned the other two witnesses again, and checked on the one who was at Grand Central and the picture's much clearer. This one lives in the same apartment house as a man who fits the *Identikit* picture, a man named Mense. He's a checker who stands in for the receiving clerk sometimes. The other two now admit that they lied about Orlick's death, and they all say they were paid to go along by Mense."

"So we're much closer," Gideon said. They stepped into an elevator, and Nielsen glanced up with a ghost of a smile. "Have you arrested Mense?"

"Not yet. Krotzner is doing a lot of work on him; we'll have the whole story when we get to Krotz." Nielsen paused. "The other man and the woman say that Mense paid them a hundred bucks apiece to be near the accident, and to lie. They say they don't know whether the junkie driver lied, but I'm sure he did. He is a delivery boy for a grocery market." The elevator doors slid open. Peek loomed close to them, one thumb hooked in his belt, looking very slightly cretinous; Gideon hadn't noticed that before.

"Trouble?" asked Nielsen.

"Not that I know of," answered Peek, "but the lieutenant says he's got something in his office you would like to see."

"What I would like to see is that checker, Mense," Nielsen said. "I'm told he's been talking to the first officer of the *Hempen*, a man named Davo. The first officer would be a good man to work through over a cargo fix, wouldn't he?"

"What I want is two thousand dollars," Marcus Davo said. He was half smiling, half frowning, not liking Mense, and uneasy about the fixed expression in the heavy man's eyes.

"For what?" Mense asked heavily.

"In advance, for the next job."

After a long pause, Mense said: "O.K. There's a crate marked 'XZ4153 DAR' waiting to come aboard. Get it stowed away, and put it on your ships stores list and I'll pay you the two grand."

Davo's eyes lit up.

"Where is it?" he asked.

"What time can you come ashore?"

"In about one hour."

"Wait for me by the crane working the No. 3 hold," Mense said.

He left the *Hempen* five minutes later, now confident of the best way to handle the first officer. He knew the operator who was working the crane, knew exactly how an "accident" could be arranged at short notice.

That would leave only the Orlick woman.

Nielsen led Gideon to his own car; Gentian was off duty this morning, and Peek's Ford was double-parked. They pulled up outside the precinct house five minutes later, and Gideon thought he glimpsed Krotzner's face at the window. When they went upstairs, Krotzner stood up from his desk, coat off, shirt spotless, tie precisely knotted, everything about him neat and tidy. Except for papers, there was nothing on the desk that Gideon could see. Nielsen's glance swept every corner, and gave the impression that he could easily lose his temper. The moment they sat down, the door opened wider and the messenger brought in coffee in a carton placing it on the table exactly as he had before, and stood back, looking at Peek.

"That's fine, baby doll," Peek said. "You got it right on time."

Cassidy appeared a moment later and took the only spare seat. Gideon caught a glimpse of the two men together, thought: Which of these is a typical New Yorker?, and looked at Krotzner, who seemed to be very sure of himself.

"What's so good to see?" asked Nielsen.

"This," said Krotzner. He reminded Gideon vividly of Lemaitre when Lemaitre was eager to justify himself. He unfolded a chart, and that was like Lemaitre too, but this wasn't a graph as such, it was more like a family tree. Krotzner had six copies, and pushed one across the desk to each man. "Captain Nielsen," he said, "I've been giving this case a lot of high-powered concentration. I've been checking all the men involved. I came to the conclusion that this was a racket worked by very few men. When I knew Mense was involved, that confirmed what I already believed to be true. Mense, the checker working in the trucking shed, was the guy in the green Chevrolet. He used to own one, but said he traded it for the black Plymouth he's running now. His prints are on the Chevrolet, so we've got him cold—but he's not the big fella, there must be someone else. I'm sure it's not a large outfit. They had to use the same people for different jobs, even though it meant taking a hell of a risk. The man at Grand Central was a false witness of the accident, remember. There certainly aren't many in this racket. Does that make sense?"

Nielsen said: "Some."

"Very good sense," Gideon found himself saying. He hoped it wouldn't sound smug, but Krotzner looked gratified.

"We know, *one,* that whole cases of these goods disappear. . . . *Two,* they disappear at the trucking shed. . . . *Three,* there must be a place they can be hidden until the heat's off. . . . *Four,* this could only be done if there was an arrangement between the driver of the truck, the receiving clerk, and Mense. Sometimes he stands in for the receiving clerk. . . . *Five,* I checked and found that the same trucking company does all the Rite-Time work and they've used some drivers for ten years. . . ."

"Which trucking company?"

"A small one with a depot in Buffalo, where Rite-Times are manufactured, and one in Jersey City."

Krotzner hesitated, and Gideon sensed there was something he was reluctant to say.

"Doesn't this company have a name?" Nielsen demanded.

"It certainly has a name. It is the Silvermann Trucking Company. The owner is a man named Daniel Silvermann. I talked to Silvermann and he's originally from the South."

"Danny! The man who talked to Orlick!" Gideon exclaimed.

"I guess so." Krotzner was almost smug. "*Six,* the haul had to be held for a suitable ship with a master who would co-operate. It would be easy enough to put a big crate—two—or three crates maybe, onto the *Maruna* or the *Hempen* with genuine bills of lading and other documents showing delivery for Dakar, say, or maybe Dar es Salaam or some other African port. . . . *Seven,* it wouldn't cost much to persuade the official at the African port not to worry about a consignment they didn't receive; it would be very different if they had to forget a consignment in excess—but this would be shortage, and what port officer cares about a shortage? And the African consignee wouldn't know anything about it, because there wouldn't *be* a consignee."

Krotzner paused, looked round, giving the impression that he wanted to ask "Does that make sense?" but instead he picked up his coffee, took off the lid, and drank. He banged down the paper cup.

"*Eight,* such a consignment could easily stay in the hold. . . . *Nine,* forged bills of lading and other documents would now be sent to the Orlova Watch Company in Aldgate, London, S.E. They have a lot of shipments. They've got the matching documents with those on the ship. So they're legal when they reach England. *Ten,* they're trucked from London docks to the Orlova warehouse, arriving there six, maybe nine, months after the theft. What could be safer? There is plenty of profit, they get away with a whole consignment, they see how big the business can become, so Orlick comes to make arrangements for extending the business. . . . *Eleven,* it's his bad luck he's traveling on the same ship as Commander Gideon. It's bad luck Inglemann Brown pets his wife and makes him mad, bad luck that Brown wanted to sue him for damages. Because Silvermann and Mense couldn't take the risk of publicity for their British agent. They had two good reasons. This Orlick can turn into a crazy guy, see what trouble he causes if someone lays a finger on his wife. Also he will be under pressure if Brown sues him. The only way to make sure he can't cause trouble is in his box. You with me?"

No one argued.

"I've been working all night on this," Krotzner continued, and his glassy eyes confirmed how little sleep he'd had. "The Silvermann Trucking Company has a contract with Rite-Time, so they don't have any trouble finding out when a crate can be sneaked away and hidden until it's convenient to ship." Krotzner was so carried away by his own story that he had stopped numbering the points. "That crate of Rite-Times which was marked by the oil, that worried me. Yes, sir, that worried me plenty. It made it seem as if I'd missed something which was right under my nose, but I didn't want to believe that was so. So I started thinking some more. If that crate hadn't been in the trucking shed, then where had it been? Where could you hide it? And the answer came up," went on Krotzner with deep satisfaction. "The answer was simple, Commander. It could be put back *in* the truck. It's been delivered, it's been signed for by the receiving clerk at the docks, so no one finds out it's missing for weeks, maybe months. It can go back into the truck and be put in a safe place until the time comes to ship it aboard a freighter. This morning I got busy," went on Krotzner. "Yes, sir, Captain Nielsen. I got busy proving the following: On the day of Hurricane Vera, Mense was acting receiving clerk. On the day before Hurricane Vera one of the Silvermann Trucking Company's trucks was in line with a load of Rite-Times, but no trucks moved in and out for two days because of the flooding. It's all there." He tapped the "tree." "Everything's there for you to see and check, Captain, including the reason we took so long finding out the truth. We were looking for evidence of theft from the yard after the load reached the truck lineup. We didn't reckon on the case being delivered *and taken away* on the same truck. Once we started to think around that, the rest fell into place."

Krotzner leaned back, his arms stretched out and his hands flat on his desk, and looked hopefully from Nielsen to Gideon. Gideon wondered how Nielsen would react, then saw him smile faintly.

"How would you have worked that out in London, England, Commander?"

Gideon said: "I would have sent for Lieutenant Krotzner."

Krotzner's eyelids dropped to hide his pleasure, Peek slapped Gideon on the back, then looked as if he doubted whether he should have, Cassidy clasped his hands together, pushing back his chair. He waited for Nielsen to speak, but when Nielsen sat silent, he said:

"The question remains, do we go aboard the *Hempen* and pick up that crate and question the captain and the first and second officers, or do we—"

"We can't wait any longer!" Krotzner cried.

Nielsen was sharp-voiced. "Go and talk to the *Hempen* officers, Lieutenant Krotzner, and hold any of them if you think we can justify it. In particular, work on the first officer, Marcus Davo. Cass, call Buffalo and have Silvermann brought in and questioned. We'll need an extradition order but they can hold him until that comes through."

Even as he gave the instructions, men began to move.

Gideon listened and watched and marveled, and yet realized that if he were at the Yard in a similar situation he would act in much the same way. He felt an affinity with Nielsen which he had experienced with few men in his life. He even believed Nielsen felt toward men like Krotzner much as he felt toward Lemaitre—a kind of paternal responsibility, and satisfaction and pleasure in any success such a man achieved.

Nielsen *wanted* Krotzner to feel the glow of success.

It did not occur to Krotzner, as he approached the *Hempen,* that he might be in physical danger. He had only one detective with him, so as not to arouse alarm, and he believed he could make the first officer talk if he had anything on his conscience.

The ship was being worked, a crane was hoisting a huge wire rope net with barrels of molasses which was now hovering about twenty feet above his head. A man was walking down the gangway, wearing an officer's cap, a lithe, alert, youngish man who was obviously looking for someone. That made Krotzner glance round, and Krotzner saw Mense standing near some stacks of shiny black barrels. The officer reached the side, and out of the corner of his eye saw Mense make a hand signal to the crane driver; the unmistakable: *Let her go* signal.

Krotzner glanced up suddenly to the barrels swinging above his head. Fear flooded through him, and he lunged forward at the *Hempen's* officer, flinging him with such force that they hurtled together toward the gangway. As they fell and rolled over, the barrels came crashing down, and one brushed Krotzner's leg. The booming metallic thunder of the barrels echoing in his ears, Krotzner scrambled up and sprinted towards Mense, who, backing farther and farther into the shadow, had finally turned and begun to run.

Krotzner pulled his gun, and fired once. Mense staggered, went on, staggered again and fell.

Nielsen rubbed his thumb and forefinger together in the way with which Gideon was now familiar.

"So that one's over," he said. "Mense is in hospital, but he's not badly hurt. The first officer of the *Hempen* has made a full statement about fixing the ship's papers and carrying cargo he knew to be stolen. He's also implicated some of the crew of the S.S. *Maruna,* which just sailed out of London. There's no need to worry about Kitty Orlick any more."

Gideon said: "For one young woman, she has had a lot of bad luck."

"Until she met the Gideons," Nielsen said dryly "Well,

George, you've a week before the Conference in Washington, and you shouldn't have much to do in that week except look around and enjoy yourselves. You don't want Kitty Orlick with you."

"If I know that young woman, she'll have some ideas of her own," Gideon remarked. "How much time will you and Claire have to spare?'

"Most evenings and the weekend," Nielsen replied. "But I must get back to the office now. Reports will be in by the time I get there, and I don't want to miss a thing. You want to come with me?"

Gideon thought: I would ask him exactly the same thing if he was in London, and I would hope that he would say no. So he pursed his lips, apparently considering the invitation, shook his head as if reluctantly, and said: "I won't, thanks. I'll go and see Kate. Unless you think I can be useful."

"You'll always be useful," Nielsen said, and his eyes crinkled. "Right now I imagine you will be most useful opening your mail." He handed Gideon a large envelope. "If you see Claire, will you tell her I will be home around five-thirty?"

"I'll be glad to," Gideon promised.

A young police driver, stiff and unbending in conventional officialdom, took him back to the apartment. Gideon opened the letters from London. It was already obvious that Lemaitre wasn't having any luck, a problem he would have to face as soon as he got back. He knew now that he was quite sure it would be wrong to let Lemaitre have the deputy commander's job. Once away from the man, and subject to no sentimental or emotional influences, he realized that it simply wasn't right for him. How would Lem take it? He could worry about that later. There was another report about Fadiman, and a single paragraph, written by Miller, held his attention:

Mrs. Fadiman was found dead of strychnine poisoning by her son early this morning. The poison was found in a trick lid of an old tea caddy. Mrs. Fadiman's fingerprints on inside and outside of trick cover. Mrs. Fadiman appears to have discovered it.

Gideon felt a sudden weight of depression because of what the woman must have suffered, and to some degree that offset the satisfaction of knowing that the Fadiman case was nearly over.

He didn't open the letters from Penelope and young Malcolm, Kate could have the excitement of doing that. He got out of the car, and the driver moved off again almost before he started toward the apartment. The doorman came hurrying. Gideon reflected on how quickly the different scene and the different conditions became familiar—even to the yellow taxi waiting outside, and the tops of the distant skyscrapers. He opened the door of the apartment, and only silence met him. He closed the door, and called:

"Anyone at home?"

Kitty Orlick appeared, and for a fantastic moment he thought that she was his oldest daughter. The notion faded as soon as it was born.

"Hallo, Kitty."

"Mrs. Gideon and Mrs. Nielsen have gone shopping," Kitty said. "I asked if there was anything I could do, and there was some ironing. They'll be back for lunch, they said will you wait for them?" She was searching Gideon's face for news.

"Yes," he said. "I've finished work for a few days."

Her eyes lit up.

"Finished?"

"We know who the men are," Gideon told her. "It's all over bar the shouting, and you've nothing new to worry about." He saw relief take possession of her, the tension lessening second by second. He nodded toward a chair. "Sit down, Kitty. Take it easy."

She sat down. She wore the honey-colored blouse and the dark-brown stretch pants, her hair was held back with a band of velvet. She looked fresh and very attractive, and he hoped that soon happiness would come to her again.

"And it's all over because of you," she said.

"As a matter of fact, it was a lieutenant named—"

"No," Kitty interrupted. "It was you. Mr. Gideon. . . ." She hesitated for a few moments, but he did not speak. "Mr. Gideon, do you think there will be any difficulty about me staying in America for a while?"

"None at all," he answered. "I'm sure of that."

"I think that's what I would like to do," said Kitty. "I don't think I want to go back home, not yet anyhow. I've no one there—you see—no one left. I wouldn't be able to help with the business, even if it goes on, I just don't care about it. I've enough money if I'm careful, until I get some work. Do you think Captain Nielsen would help me to get a work permit?"

"I'm sure he would," said Gideon. "But, Kitty—"

"I want to go over to the other hotel and get packed and settle my bill, and leave most of the luggage in store. I hope I don't sound ungrateful, but I don't want to see Mrs. Gideon again yet. She'll try to make me change my mind, try to make me stay here for a few days anyhow. I don't want to—I don't want to feel that I'm under your feet."

"Kitty, you won't be—"

"Yes, I will," she interrupted firmly. "And the longer I have you and Mrs. Gideon to lean on the harder it will be to stand alone. After all, I've got to start some time. What—what I would like, if it's all right with you, is to send you a postcard now and again. And–and perhaps see you again when I'm back in England."

Gideon said slowly: "There's one thing I know my wife wouldn't forgive you for."

She looked anxious. "What?"

"If you didn't put your address on every postcard."

Kitty's face lit up.

"Oh, I will! And–and I wish I could say thank you, I really wish I could I–"

Suddenly, she was close to him, crying again, her body convulsed. He patted the hair gently, and stood very still and solid, saying nothing. Soon she stopped crying, moved back, and wiped her eyes with her fingers.

"Please let me go," she said. "Please." She turned and hurried out.

Gideon went to the window and looked down in the street. Kate would be vexed, of course, and would say that he ought not to have let the child go, but courage had to be allowed to make its own way.

Alone now, he couldn't resist temptation; he opened the family letters, read them, and felt happiness creeping over him. At last he stood up, and moved across to the television set, where the New York Police Department badge lay bright on a folded black scarf. He picked it up, looking at it with contentment, with deep pride.

His telephone bell rang, and he put the badge down and answered the call, still preoccupied. After a moment the operator said:

"There's a call for Mr. Gideon from Washington. . . . Can Mr. Gideon take the call, please?"

This would be Allingham.

"Yes, Gideon speaking."

"Just one moment, sir."

It was in fact half a minute before Allingham came on the line.

"George."

"What are you after now?" demanded Gideon.

"You," said Allingham. "I'd like you to come and assess the situation in the light of all that's turned up here. There isn't any doubt in my mind, this sabotage is intended to injure Anglo-American trade. It could do it in a big way, not only by the damaged goods but by creating a loss of confidence and lack of trust. It's important, George."

"That's one reason why I'm in America," Gideon reminded him.

"That's why I want you in Washington, too."

"Don't rush me," Gideon said. "I've been thinking. Have you ever tried to find out if there's any damage done in England to American goods?'

After a long pause, Allingham said: "No."

"Why don't you ask your London people to check?" asked Gideon. "Then when I get to Washington we'll have all the facts." As he spoke, the deep familiar excitement he knew so well gripped him again. "One rich fanatic or a group of fanatics could be doing it. . . ."

He could hardly wait to get his teeth into this next major job.

Format by Ronald Farber
Set in Linotype Caledonia
Composed by York Composition Co., Inc.
Printed by York Composition Co., Inc.
Bound by The Haddon Craftsmen
HARPER & ROW, PUBLISHERS, INCORPORATED